SAMANTHA SHREVES

Journey of the Heart: Wrecked and Washed

Independent Work Statement

This book is an independent work and is not affiliated with, sponsored by, or endorsed by any organization, ministry, or institution.

First edition

ISBN: 979-8-9996160-3-6

This book was professionally typeset on Reedsy.
Find out more at reedsy.com

Dedication

To the broken, the healing, and the brave—
this story was written with you in mind.

To my brothers and sisters in Christ—
who walk the narrow road with trembling feet and unwavering hope.
Keep going. Keep rising.

To everyone who has ever fallen
but still chose to get back up—
may you never forget: grace still calls your name.

"When you pass through the water, I will be with you, and the river will not overwhelm you. When you walk through fire, you will not be scorched, and the flame will not harm you."

— Your First Love

Contents

Maps

Dorm Ariel view, Men Derish/Men D'resh Angle

Dorm aeria view, Tsad Angle

Content Disclaimer

Journey of the Heart: Wrecked and Washed is a work of fiction that explores deep emotional themes, including faith, identity, trauma, relationships, and personal growth. While the content is not explicit, it does contain mature subject matter that may be sensitive for some readers.

Reader discretion is advised.

This story is intended for thoughtful young people and adult audiences who are comfortable engaging with complex topics in a respectful and reflective context.

Chapter 1: The Path Awaits

Mita stood at the edge of her dorm building, looking up at the grand structure with both excitement and trepidation. It was real now—university life. The step she had been dreaming about for years was now right before her. No more high school rules, no more watching the clock tick by, waiting for freedom to arrive.

But what kind of freedom was it really?

She shifted her suitcase, feeling the weight of her past, her upbringing and her own expectations, tugging at her as she looked at the crowd of students rushing around her. She could almost taste the excitement in the air. The campus, full of students rushing to their dorms or socializing between buildings, was a far cry from the quiet life she'd known at home. It was alive—alive with possibilities, choices, and freedom, or at least the illusion of it.

She tightened her grip on the handle of her suitcase, a little unsure whether she was ready for all of it. As she continued to make her way to her dorm building, or what she hoped was her dorm building, her gaze wandered over to a bulletin board, plastered with colorful flyers for party events, group meetups and student socials. Her heart skipped a beat at what these different gatherings could mean for her. *So this is what is university like*, she thought.

"Excuse me!" a voice pulled her from her thoughts. Mira turned to see a tall girl with a big smile and a clipboard in hand, dressed in a denim jumper that was so vintage and nostalgic all at once, her hair dark brown had a bit of red hue to it in the sun, was done up into a ponytail.

"Hi, I'm Jasmine," the girl said, holding out her hand. "You look a little lost. First year?"

Mita laughed at how obvious she had been without even knowing, and took her hand. "Guilty as charged," she said. "The whole 'freshman' vibe is kind of obvious, isn't it?"

Jasmine chuckled. "It's all good. It's my second year, and I still get that 'freshman' feeling sometimes," she said, releasing Mita's hand, to look her up and down in a way Mita wasn't sure if Jasmine was sizing her up or just taking in her outfit, but since she couldn't tell, Mita wasn't comfortable under her gaze . "Are you looking for something specific?" Jasmine asked after a breath

"Well, I'm trying to figure out where I'm supposed to be," Mita said. "I'm just… getting the lay of the land, I guess."

"And I guess, I'm just in time," Jasmine said. "First things first, don't miss the Freshman Welcome Event coming up. It's huge. The entire first-year class meets up for games, free food, and a chance to meet people from different departments in the institution, to expose you to different clubs to find your interests. The perfect place to make friends, or at least pretend like you know what's going on." She winked. "They say it's the best way to get your foot in the door, especially if you're trying to avoid being a total hermit."

"Ah, the magic of free food. I'm sold," Mita said, grinning. "Do I need to RSVP or…?"

"Nah, just show up. It's on Friday evening. You'll hear about it all week. Trust me. You won't be able to escape it." Jasmine turned to the bulletin board, hanging a flyer about said event before turning back to Mita. "It's gonna be held by the Student Council in the Quad. They're handing out free T-shirts for the event. You don't wanna be the person who missed out on that."

Mita raised an eyebrow. "T-shirts, huh? Who knew college would be so high stakes."

2

Jasmine laughed, turning to walk away. "You'll see. Have fun, freshman!" she called as she walked away, disappearing into the crowd.

As Mita scanned the bulletin board for any more useful info, a loud, upbeat voice made her freeze due to the sudden outburst.

"Hey, hey, hey!" A group of sophomores and juniors came bounding toward her like they were on a mission. They were laughing and talking, clearly buzzing with energy. One of them, a guy with a messy mop of curly hair and a wide grin, approached her holding a neon flyer.

"New blood?" he asked with a wink, handing her the flyer.

"You gotta come to our party tonight. Freshman-only event. Great way to meet people, have a blast, you know, the usual."

Mita took the flyer, her gaze flickering over the colorful words, *"Freshman Bash—***Tonight!*** Free drinks, music, free-spirited fun!"* She looked up at him, raising an eyebrow. "I didn't realize university was an all-you-can-eat buffet for temptation."

The guy laughed. "It's all about balance, right? You don't have to go wild, but, hey, you're here to have fun. Don't let anyone here tell you that you're supposed to be all serious. That's for people who've forgotten how to live. Don't be that person, trust me."

"Right," Mita said sarcastically, tucking the flyer in her pocket. "Thanks for the tip. I'll be sure to keep that in mind."

"You're welcome! Don't say I didn't warn you," the guy said, throwing a casual salute. "We'll be in the dorm shared common building. Don't be a stranger."

Mita rolled her eyes as they walked off, muttering to herself, "If I don't know any better, this campus is like a bad reality show waiting to happen."

She gave one last glance at the bulletin board, trying to locate any information on where to find her room. Finding nothing, she let out a small groan. *Okay, Mita, don't panic. You've got this.* She turned and walked towards the doors of the building, her suitcase clicking against the floor with each step.

Pushing through the rotating doors of the dorm building, to say the dorm was bustling was an understatement, with students moving in, unpacking, and setting up their new homes. Everywhere she looked, she saw older students—sophomores and juniors—calling out to the freshmen with varying degrees of enthusiasm. Some offered pizza slices, others gave unsolicited advice, and a few handed out party invites with the casualness of handing out flyers for a high school prom.

Mita shook her head, amused but slightly overwhelmed. *Do I just walk through this maze until I find Room 246?*

Before she could figure out her next move, a girl who looked like she walked off a GQ magazine cover, her chestnut coloured hair with blonde highlights bounced up to her, holding out a flyer with a grin. "Hey, you're a freshman, right? We're having a party in the lounge later, it's gonna be tons of fun, music with snacks. You should totally swing by."

Mita took the flyer, eyeing the girl suspiciously. "So, is this the part where you tell me to be wild and free?"

The girl laughed, clearly unphased by Mita's sarcasm. "It's not about that! It's about experiencing university life to the fullest. You know, connecting with people, making memories, all that jazz."

Mita held up her hand, tired of hearing the same thing all over again. "I get it. I'll think about it. I'm sure I'll be *real* busy with my... study schedule." She waved the flyer in front her chest mockingly.

The girl smirked. "Well, don't be a stranger. Everyone's invited, so if you do decide to change your mind, we'll be there."

With that, the girl disappeared into the crowd, and Mita continued on her track upstairs, where the noise from the common area was muffled but still made it feel like a high school reunion was happening down there. After she climbed the stairs, walking down the corridor of doors led to rooms on each side, she took her time to take in the interior. The corridor was bigger than expected, allowing four, maybe even five people to walk alongside each other. She counted the numbers on the doors as she walked the length of the corridor until she finally came in front of her door, mentally preparing herself for whatever awaited her on the other side of Room 246.

When she finally found the courage to type in the code the school had given her at orientation, she opened the door to enter a medium-sized living room area. Stepping in, she closed the door behind her, hauling in her heavy suitcase and her bag secured atop it. She looked around the space, taking in everything and noting every detail. It was then she saw the entrance to an equally sized kitchen on the right. *"This place is bigger than I thought. We even have our own living room and kitchen. At least I don't have to go downstairs and share one with everyone else,"* she thought, looking around the space.

She walked further down the passage leading away from the living room to find two doors on opposite sides, but not directly in front of each other. *That was convenient,* she thought. She heard movement in the room on the left side.

She took a deep breath and knocked twice, her heart. beating just a little faster.

"Come in!" a soft voice called from inside.

Mita turned the knob and stepped in.

The room was small but cozy, already adorned with pastel-colored bedding, a few plants on the windowsill, and some motivational quotes pinned on the walls. Sitting on the bed was a girl with short, messy hair, wearing a soft pink and purple sweater and leggings. She sat atop her bed, books sprawled out before her , seeming as if she was sorting them to put them up, but looked up with a smile when Mita entered.

"Hey!" the girl said warmly. "You must be Mita. I saw your name on the dorm chart. I'm Amerei! It's so nice to meet you!"

Mita raised an eyebrow, not knowing there was even a chart and feeling like she had the short hand as she already knew her name, but Mita didn't know hers, but couldn't help the small smile that tugged at her lips. "Hey, Amerei. Thanks for not being a party animal... yet."

Amerei giggled, setting her book down. "Oh, no worries. I'm more of a *quiet party* kind of girl. You know, the type who has tea parties with themselves and reads a book in a corner." She laughed lightly. "But I'm really excited to room with you!"

Mita let out a chuckle, glancing around the room. "Tea parties? I can see why we'd get along."

Amerei shrugged, her smile shy but warm. "Yeah. I mean, I'm not great at… big groups or wild parties. I'd rather have a quiet night in, but if you want to go out, I'll totally give you space."

"You got it," Mita said, still looking around the room at the decor. "I can already tell this is going to be… interesting."

"Oh, definitely!" Amerei said, her voice a mix of excitement and nervousness. "But I'm really glad you're here. And I don't know, maybe we'll figure out this whole 'college' thing together."

Mita gave her a sly grin. "Yeah, well, you better buckle up. I've got this thing figured out *—sort of.*"

Amerei laughed softly, her eyes sparkling with a quiet excitement. "I think we're going to be just fine."

And just like that, Mita realized that she might not have all the answers, but this was exactly where she was meant to be.

And as her journey began, she knew one thing for sure, it was going to be anything but ordinary.

Mita sat on her bed in her room, feeling both strangely comforting and eerily unfamiliar. The white walls, the soft beige curtains, the small desk still empty, waiting to be cluttered with textbooks and half-unpacked items—all of it felt temporary. She was still adjusting, *still figuring out where the heck everything went, not only in the soulless room but also in life.*

But as she sat there, staring at the phone in her hand, it wasn't how to start unpacking that consumed her thoughts. No, it was the message on the screen.

A text from Joshua.

"Hey, Mita! Did you get settled in? You're probably surrounded by tons of people by now, huh? You might think this is cringe, but remember, you don't have to change who you are just because everyone else is doing it. College is famous for doing just that. Stay true to yourself. And hey, remember, don't let the environment influence you—be the influence! Stay strong. I'm rooting for you. Always."

Mita read the message a few times, her thumb hovering over the keyboard, unsure how to reply or if she should. *Stay true to yourself. Be the influence.* These were words she'd heard before, words she wanted to believe. Joshua was, logically, her childhood friend, but growing up with him, he was more like her older brother for years back home, he and Ruach. I mean, they were actual siblings to each other, and she was kind of the little sister they never had, always there, always encouraging her, even when she ignored them all the way up to high school and had some friends who weren't the best and did things that weren't the best. They'd bonded over their shared faith in God, well, *her* journey to faith. Joshua and Ruach had always been solid, certain in their beliefs, while Mita... well, she was still figuring things out. It wasn't that she didn't believe, because she did. But sometimes, it felt more like something she *hoped* for, something she was *trying* to live up to.

She knew Joshua was right. She had been raised to honor her faith, and there was a deep part of her heart that knew that faith was the foundation of who she was. But here, at university, everything was new. And everyone around her seemed so... *different.* Her future classmates, whoever they were, her peers, they were all so confident in their choices, living their lives as if the world was their playground, and Mita couldn't help but feel like an outsider looking in.

It wasn't just the message that was tugging at her. It was the invitation she had received earlier that afternoon, the one flyer that sat beside her phone.

"You're invited! Freshman Bash—Tonight! Music, drinks, dancing, and all the fun you can handle! See you there!"

She'd stared at the invitation for what felt like forever, as if trying to will herself to make a decision. The party was tempting, no doubt. It was everything the world had promised. A chance to let loose, to meet new people, to step into a new world of possibilities. Everyone at orientation had been talking about it—about the friendships, the stories, the connections made.

But as Mita's fingers hovered over the phone's screen, she felt the weight of Joshua's words pressing on her heart. *Stay true to yourself.* What did that even look like here? Was she supposed to walk into that party, surrounded by people who would be drinking and dancing and doing everything her family had warned her about? Was she supposed to let the crowd of strangers decide who she was, or was she supposed to hold onto something deeper?

Her phone buzzed again, snapping her from her thoughts. Another text from Joshua.

"Don't forget: you're the light, Mita. The world is a little dark sometimes, but you can make a difference in it. You don't have to fit in to belong. Be bold."

Mita bit her lip. *Be bold.* That was the hardest part. Being bold when everything inside her screamed to blend in. She was new to all of this, new to the idea that faith could change the way she approached life. Back home, in her small neighborhood, faith was something she'd always *believed* in, but never *lived out* publicly. At least, not in the way Joshua did. Joshua didn't care who saw him pray or talk about his beliefs; it was just part of who he was. Mita, though… she wasn't sure if she was ready for that kind of boldness. *What if they didn't understand? What if they thought I was weird?*

The text messages from Joshua were slowly starting to sink in, but doubt still lingered. *What if I go to the party and just… try it? Just once. Just to see what it's like?*

She stood up and walked over to the window, looking out at the bustling campus below. It was almost sunset. Students were gathering in groups, laughing, chatting, and already heading toward the event. She could hear the music drifting through the air, the bass thumping, the crowd's excitement palpable. The *freshman buzz* was real.

Mita's stomach twisted. She wanted to be a part of that. She didn't want to be the one sitting in her room, scrolling through her phone, while everyone else made memories. *Maybe I could just go for a little bit,* she thought. *I could hang out, meet some people, and leave if it feels like too much. Besides, who knows? Maybe I'll find some new friends.*

But as soon as she thought that, a voice inside her whispered the reminder again: *Stay true to yourself.* And suddenly, it wasn't so easy to dismiss.

"Ugh," Mita groaned, dropping her head into her hands. "Why is this so hard?"

The door to the room creaked open. Amerei, her soft-spoken roommate, peeked her head in, her wide eyes filled with curiosity. "Are you okay?"

Mita gave a tight smile, trying to pull herself together. "Yeah, I'm good. Just thinking about this party tonight. I don't know what to do."

Amerei stepped into the room fully, her arms crossed over her chest. "Oh, I see. The party dilemma. It's hard, isn't it?"

"You have no idea," Mita said with a sigh, dropping back onto her bed. "I want to go. I want to fit in and make friends, but... I don't know if it's worth it. I mean, it's just a party, right? But what if I go and it's not my scene? Or worse, what if I end up doing something I'll regret?"

Amerei hesitated, as if weighing her words. "I don't know... I'm not really the party type. But... I think if you go, you should just be yourself. You can make new friends without compromising who you are."

Mita let out a laugh. "Yeah, okay. You're saying that, but you're not the one with all the peer pressure hanging over your head."

Amerei smiled softly, her eyes bright with understanding. "I get it, Mita. It's hard. But you don't have to do anything you don't want to. You're not going to lose friends if you don't go to a party. True friends will come, and when they do, they will respect you for standing your ground."

Mita nodded, though her mind was still swirling with doubt. *But what if I don't make friends? What if I'm left out?*

Amerei sat down on her bed, looking thoughtful. "You know, I used to think that being around people who don't share your values was okay. But then I realized... I didn't want to compromise myself just to feel accepted. Being authentic to who you are, no matter how uncomfortable it feels, is way more important in the long run."

Mita looked at her, feeling a flicker of hope rise in her chest. "That's... actually good advice. Thanks, Amerei."

Amerei smiled shyly, her voice quieter now. "You're welcome. And hey, if you do decide to go to that party, just remember, you don't have to lose yourself in the crowd. You can still be you, even when everyone else is doing something different."

Mita stared at the phone in her hand once again, then glanced at the party invite beside, but this time, it didn't seem quite as alluring. The pressure to fit in was still there, but now there was something else too: the weight of the choice. *What kind of person do I want to be?*

The answer was still unclear, but one thing was for sure: she wasn't going to let anyone else decide that for her.

She took a deep breath, typed a quick response to Joshua: *"Thanks. I think I needed to hear that. I'm figuring it out."*

Mita looked over at Amerei and smiled. "Maybe I'll stay in tonight. I don't need to fit in to feel like I belong."

Amerei beamed. "I think that's a great idea. And hey, if you change your mind… you know where I'll be……still in my room"

Mita chuckled, feeling a new sense of peace wash over her. For the first time in a long while, she felt a little bit more grounded. The world was wide open, yes, but she didn't have to let it swallow her whole. Not yet. Maybe not ever.

Tonight, she was going to make her own path.

Chapter 2: New Beginnings

The classroom buzzed with the chatter of first-year students settling into their seats. Mita adjusted in hers, casting a glance around the room, absorbing the faces that would soon become a part of her new world. She wasn't quite sure how to feel about this whole college thing yet, but it was only the second week since she moved in and the first day of classes, and she was doing her best to be open-minded. She pulled her notebook out of her bag and tried to focus on the front of the room, where the professor was now standing, organizing his notes for what would undoubtedly be her first real taste of college-level math.

The room was a mix of anticipation and the usual first-day awkwardness. Mita could hear the shuffle of papers, the tapping of pens, and the murmurs of voices discussing their various backgrounds and expectations. Everyone seemed to know someone already, whether they were roommates or had run into each other at the student center or at the numerous parties that had taken place since she moved in. Mita felt like the odd one out, but she was used to that feeling by now. New environments. New faces. It was all part of the deal.

The professor, a middle-aged man with salt-and-pepper hair, adjusted his glasses and cleared his throat.

"Alright, everyone," he began in a voice that sounded like he'd been lecturing for years, "Welcome to college math. I'm Professor Lawson, and

I'll be guiding you through this semester. We'll be covering everything from algebra to calculus, so if any of that sounds like a foreign language to you, don't panic. We'll take it step by step."

Mita blinked. *Algebra to calculus?* That was going to be a ride.

"Before we dive in, I'd like to get to know you all a bit better. I know, I know, it's the first day, and the last thing you probably want to do is stand up and talk about yourselves," he chuckled, "but bear with me. Just give your name, what you're studying, and one word that best describes you."

Mita's stomach fluttered nervously. *Why does it feel like everyone's watching me?* She resisted the urge to tug at her sleeves or hide behind her hair. Instead, she focused on the task at hand: the introductions.

The first student to stand up was a tall guy with shaggy brown hair. His red turtleneck was already speaking volumes before he had uttered a word. He matched with cream-colored slacks, and the seam in his pants was so crisp, it looked as if it was his first time wearing them. He had a quiet confidence about him, as though he already knew what he was doing.

"I'm Ethan," he said, his voice firm and calm. "I'm studying business, and I'd describe myself as… grounded."

Grounded, huh? Mita thought. *He looks like he's been to the ground and back, like he knows how to stand firm when life tries to knock him down.* She smirked to herself, imagining Ethan as the type to calmly walk through chaos without flinching. There was something compelling about him, though.

Next was a girl with platinum blonde hair who looked like she belonged in an ad for luxury skincare. Andromeda. Her name sounded like it came from some ancient myth. She stood up slowly, almost like she was performing.

"Andromeda," she announced, voice crisp and deliberate, "I'm studying medicine. I'd describe myself as… above it all."

Mita raised an eyebrow. *Well, that was certainly bold, if a bit over the top, it was two words more than the professor instructed us to. She's probably the type to order a latte and talk about yoga in the same sentence.*

"Andromeda," Mita muttered under her breath with a dry smile, "Above it all… Right. Someone definitely got the memo on the whole 'self-importance' vibe."

The next person was Reed, and Mita instantly picked up on his energy. He had an easy smile and an even easier laugh, the kind of guy who never seemed to let anything phase him. He stood up and gave a relaxed wave to the class.

"I'm Reed, studying environmental science," he said casually, leaning against the desk as if the world was a beach and he was just there to enjoy it. "I'd say I'm... free-spirited."

Of course, he is, Mita thought with a small chuckle. *He's like the human version of a hammock—easygoing and comfortable, like he can make any situation chill.* She couldn't help but admire the way Reed seemed to just... *be himself.* She envied that.

Then there was Cassian. He was the kind of guy who didn't even need to speak to communicate. He had that distant look in his eyes, as though the world didn't quite interest him. He slouched in his chair before standing and muttering his introduction.

"Cassian. Undecided. I don't know. Whatever." He sat down immediately, not bothering to add more.

Mita couldn't help but feel a strange sympathy for him. *He looks like he's carrying some heavy weight around in that mind of his.* She didn't know why, but she could tell there was more to Cassian than the aloof attitude he was putting on. He wasn't the kind of guy you could figure out easily.

Finally, Odessa stood up. Her presence immediately filled the room, and not just because of her stunning outfit—tailored blazer, high-waisted pants, heels that looked like they belonged on a runway. She had this magnetic aura, the kind that turned heads as soon as she entered a room. Her posture screamed confidence, and the way she spoke was slow, deliberate, like she was savoring each word.

"Odessa," she said, her voice smooth and almost... seductive, "I'm studying communications. I'd describe myself as... unapologetically confident."

Mita resisted the urge to roll her eyes. *Unapologetically confident?* Of course, she is. *What is this, an audition for the next fashion magazine cover?*

When it was finally Mita's turn, she stood up, adjusted her shirt nervously, and gave the class a quick wave. Her heart was pounding, but she kept her face neutral, willing herself to seem calm and collected, even if she was anything but.

"I'm Mita," she said, flashing a small, confident grin. "I'm studying digital marketing. And I'd describe myself as… *'underestimated but always right.'*"

She waited for the awkward silence to hit, but instead, she got a couple of awkward chuckles from the class. She could feel her face flush but quickly recovered. "You know, I like to say I'm always right… even when I'm wrong. It keeps things interesting."

The class seemed to warm up a little after that, chuckling along. Mita sat down, secretly relieved that she hadn't completely embarrassed herself. *Note to self: Sarcasm is your friend. Now, just try to use it wisely.*

The professor nodded appreciatively, then gestured toward the door.

"Alright, thank you all for sharing. I think we'll get along just fine this semester. Now, before we dive into the course content, I'd like to introduce you to someone who will be working with us this semester. He's a senior, and he'll be assisting with some of the lectures and exercises."

The door opened, and a guy walked in, and suddenly, the room felt a little less like a classroom and a little more like a runway. He was tall—maybe around six foot two, with tousled dark hair that looked like it had just been ruffled by the wind. His eyes, from where she sat, seemed to be dazzling green, and he had that kind of confidence that didn't scream for attention but demanded it anyway. His jawline could've cut glass.

"Everyone, meet Merrick Hughes," Professor Lawson said with a smile. "He's been helping out with this class for a while now, and we're lucky to have him."

Mita blinked. *Oh.* She'd seen good-looking guys before, but this? This was like someone had taken the idea of "tall, dark, and handsome" and made it into a reality.

Merrick gave a small, polite nod, his smile subtle but present. "Hey, everyone. Looking forward to working with you all. Feel free to ask questions or come by my haunts if you need any help with the material," he said, his voice smooth but casual.

Mita noticed that Reed's eyes flickered over to Merrick, his expression

14

shifting slightly. He was either impressed or interested, Mita couldn't decide which. Odessa, too, seemed to study Merrick for a moment longer than necessary, her gaze lingering before she looked away, a small smile playing at her lips.

And then there was Cassian, who didn't seem to care about Merrick at all, but the way he slouched in his chair suggested a cool indifference.

Mita found herself watching Merrick too, though she quickly looked away, telling herself it was ridiculous to get distracted by some guy who was just doing his job. But something about him stuck in her mind. *Why do I have a feeling this semester is going to be more... complicated than I thought?*

She shook her head, forcing herself to focus. *Stay focused, Mita. You came here to learn.* But she couldn't help the small, rebellious thought that slid into her mind: *And maybe to learn a little bit about the people around you.*

Chapter 3: A Day of Surprises

Mita's day was a blur of new faces and information. After the math class introduction, she found herself walking to the next building with her head swimming from all the new concepts. She was a little overwhelmed, but in the best possible way. College felt like this enormous sea of opportunities, and she was trying to swim without sinking.

Her second class was academic writing, where she found herself sitting next to a familiar face, Reed. He leaned over with a grin as they opened their laptops.

"So," Reed started, tapping the screen of his MacBook, "I guess we're stuck in this class together too."

Mita gave him a dry smile. "Great."

Reed chuckled. "I can already tell we're going to get along just fine. Just don't ask me to do all the work for any projects we work on together or something."

Mita raised an eyebrow. "Wouldn't dream of it."

The rest of the class was a blur, with a few practical exercises on audience targeting and hooking readers. Mita's head was still spinning, but she found herself oddly comforted by Reed's easygoing presence. He was... different, not like the others. He didn't seem to be trying too hard to fit in, and she appreciated that.

Next class, it was still me and this Reed kid, but this time, Odessa the confident appeared at the door to the classroom, her gaze scanning the room like she was choosing which seat would provide the most "clout." When she spotted Reed, or I assume because her face lit up a little, and she sauntered over, taking the seat beside him.

"Didn't know you were in this class, Reed," she said, flipping her hair over her shoulder as she sat down.

Reed shrugged, his usual laid-back demeanor unchanged. "It's a prerequisite, Odessa. Gotta make it through somehow."

Mita watched the exchange but didn't add anything. Odessa was… well, Odessa. Impressive, in a way that felt like she was trying to prove something. But Mita wasn't in the mood to judge. She'd made her decision to keep things low-key for now.

The next class, psychology, turned out to be a whole different beast. Mita walked in, feeling like an imposter with her half-caffeinated brain, and immediately spotted Andromeda from math class sitting front and center. She was already hunched over her notebook, scribbling notes in perfect, legible handwriting. A little too perfect for Mita's taste. But she said she wasn't going to judge; she made a different call.

"Another class with you, huh?" Mita murmured, sliding into the seat next to her.

Andromeda glanced over but didn't say anything for a beat. Then, with a cool smile, she responded, "I guess we're stuck with each other."

Mita couldn't help but smirk. "That's one way to put it."

Andromeda turned her attention back to the professor, who was now explaining how to construct a thesis. The tension between them was subtle but definitely there. *Great,* Mita thought, *another person I have to navigate.* But it was fine. It wasn't like they *had* to be best friends.

The rest of the class passed in a blur of dry lectures and academic jargon. At the end, Mita slowly packed her bag, allowing students to leave, so she could leave in peace to escape the clutches of lecture hall monotony for the day. As she did, she saw Odessa, Andromeda, and Reed gathered by the door.

"And then we meet up at the student council event later?" Odessa asked, already looking like she had a hundred things to do.

Reed smiled lazily. "I'm game. You know I'll be there."

"I'm not sure yet," Andromeda responded, casually administering eye drops in front of them to both her eyes without a care in the world. "I'll decide later."

Mita hesitated in the background, but before she could make a move to leave,

Odessa made eye contact with her. "Mita, was it? You coming to the freshman mixer thing?" Mita was taken aback by their acknowledgment of her and the suddenness of the question, "Umm, yeah, I think so. I heard there would be free food, so I thought I would swing by." Mita said looking at their varying expressions "Great so we will see you there" Andromeda said finalizing something Mita hadn't even agreed on but this could be what she needed wasn't she saying she wanted friends, not to be a suck-up or that person who begs for companionship, but no friends throughout college seemed depressing and lonely, so this could be a win. Then a girl with short hair in a pink sweater and tights ran through her mind. "Actually, I was thinking of going with my roommate, Amerei, so she would come along too. Does that work for you guys?" Mita said. She knew it would be good exposure for both her and Amerei, and to have the same friend group would make friends more manageable. "Yeah, sure, that's cool; the more the merrier. We'll see you there," Reed said. "Great," she said, and with a nod, she took that as a dismissal because there was nothing more left for me to say. They seemed to already know each other long before math class. She didn't, so staying back there would be futile, as she didn't know them, and at the mixer, she would see them again, and that would be a better opportunity, and it would be less likely to be an awkward situation since she was practically invited and not forcing her presence.

As she left the classroom, heading toward the exit of the building, wherever that is, she saw someone signaling to her. It took a second to figure out who it was since they were at a huge distance ahead. It was Jasmine, one of the girls she met on her first day, who spotted her in the hallway

"Hey!" Jasmine waved her over, beaming like she had just spotted a long-lost friend.

The guy next to her—one Mita didn't know but had seen around campus—grinned, his tousled hair giving him that effortless cool vibe, and he was good-looking too.

"Hey, I didn't see you at any of the freshman parties," Jasmine said, leaning in as if they were besties already. "We were hoping you'd show up to the student council event and the party later. You know, freshman bonding, all that good stuff."

Mita glanced between them, feeling the pressure of her decision.

"Yeah, I… had a lot of stuff to get done, with unpacking and preparing for class and all," Mita said with a smile that didn't quite reach her eyes. "You know, college stuff." She shrugged, making it sound casual.

Jasmine raised an eyebrow, clearly unconvinced, but she smiled anyway. "No worries. We just wanted to remind you about today's event too. We hope to see you there! It's the annual freshman mixer—it's going to be huge. You can meet a ton of people. Free food, music, all that jazz."

The guy next to Jasmine gave her an amused look. "And if the food's bad, at least the company's good, right?" He gave Mita a friendly wink. "You can't go wrong either way."

Mita couldn't help but laugh. "Yeah, well… I do like free food. How can I say no to that?"

Jasmine's eyes brightened. "Exactly! So, are you coming? You should totally bring your roommate too! The more, the merrier."

"Yeah, I was planning on going with some classmates," Mita said, "and bringing my roommate, Amerei. She's not a party person, but I can drag her along."

"Oh, please do!" Jasmine grinned. "The more, the better. It's in the quad tonight, right after dinner. Don't miss it!"

The guy nodded, flashing a quick smile, one that held the quiet promise of not trying too hard to impress. It felt… genuine enough, I guess.

"Alright," Mita said, "I'll show up. But I'm not making any promises. If the food is terrible, I'm out." Like she was already planning on showing up in the first place.

"Deal!" Jasmine laughed, giving her a quick hug. "See you later, Mita!"

As she watched them walk off, Mita turned back to her dorm, contemplating the evening event later. She still wasn't entirely sure if she should go, even with her new friends but the pull of meeting new people and breaking out of her shell was enough to convince her.

When she got back to her dorm room, she found Amerei sitting cross-legged on the floor, organizing her bookshelf again, in her room with the door open. Mita gave a casual knock on the door frame.

"Hey, so… There's this event tonight—the freshman mixer. You in?"

Amerei looked up from her books, her glasses perched on the tip of her nose. She was dressed in a cozy sweater and leggings, her usual understated style. "I don't know… parties aren't really my thing."

Mita grinned. "Same, but it's not really a party per-say. But it'll be a good chance to meet people, you know?"

Amerei hesitated for a second, then shrugged. "I guess I could go for a bit. But if it's really loud and obnoxious, I'm out."

"Fair enough," Mita agreed. "But hey, we'll at least get some free food out of it."

Amerei smiled faintly. "You make a good point. Alright, I'm in. But don't expect me to dance or anything."

"Don't worry," Mita said, winking. "I don't think anyone is expecting that from us."

After getting ready, Mita and Amerei walked to the event together, both dressed in their own personal style, Mita in a fitted graphic tee, skinny jeans, and her favorite pair of sneakers, while Amerei wore a modest floral dress with a cardigan over it, her hair neatly tied back into a cute updo of half up, half down to accommodate the short length of her hair. Despite their different styles, both sharing a quiet confidence.

Tonight, they would step into this new world together,

Chapter 4: The Freshman Mixer

After leaving the art department booth, Mita and Amerei weaved their way through the crowd, eventually spotting Reed and Odessa standing near a booth dedicated to the campus environmental group. Reed was casually leaning against a pillar, looking relaxed, while Odessa was browsing through pamphlets about sustainability initiatives, her fingers delicately tracing over the pages. Andromeda stood a little apart from the group, surveying everything with a cool, almost regal detachment.

Mita nudged Amerei. "That's them. Reed, Odessa, and Andromeda."

Amerei gave a small nod, and Mita led her over to the group.

"Hey, guys!" Mita greeted, a smile on her face. "This is my roommate, Amerei."

Odessa looked up first, her expression friendly yet calculating. She gave Amerei a once-over, her eyes gleaming with interest. "Hey, nice to meet you," she said smoothly, offering her hand. "I'm Odessa."

Reed followed Odessa's lead, grinning as he made eye contact with Amerei. "I think we've already met, though, right?" he said with a slight chuckle, as if he was remembering their previous interaction that Mita knew nothing about. "Good to see you again."

Amerei smiled shyly, clearly unsure but trying her best. "Yeah. Nice to meet you guys, too."

"Amerei's pretty quiet, but once you get to know her, she's got this killer sense of humor," Mita teased. "You'll love her."

"Thank you?" Amerei replied dryly, a glimmer of sarcasm in her tone, though her lips twitched into a half-smile.

Andromeda, still a little aloof, gave Amerei a small nod. "Welcome to the chaos," she said in her usual enigmatic tone. "Just don't let it swallow you whole."

Before anyone could respond, Mita's attention was caught by a familiar voice,

"Mita!" Jasmine's voice rang out from behind her, and Mita turned, surprised to see her.

"Jasmine," Mita grinned, stepping forward to return the hug Jasmine was already leaning in for.

Jasmine, wearing a fitted black dress and a leather jacket, raised an eyebrow. " I really didn't think you'd miss this."

Just as Mita opened her mouth to respond to that confusing statement, a tall, striking figure stepped forward beside Jasmine, his presence immediately noticeable; he was totally different from the guy this afternoon.

Mita blinked. *Who is this?*

"Guys, this is Rune," Jasmine introduced with a knowing smile, gesturing to the guy standing next to her. "He's a senior, majoring in Music and Entertainment."

Rune stood with casual confidence, his dark, slightly fluffy hair perfectly tousled in that effortlessly cool way that only certain people could pull off. His hair was layered just right, sharp at the ends but soft enough to look natural, and his chiseled jawline was framed perfectly by the strands. He wore a fitted black t-shirt that highlighted his lean build, paired with dark jeans and boots that made him look like he belonged on a music video set.

Mita couldn't help but notice how he carried himself; there was a mystery to him that was hard to ignore. His aura was magnetic, his energy quiet but compelling, drawing her in without trying. When his eyes locked with hers, she felt an inexplicable pull, as if the conversation would be far more interesting than it appeared.

Rune smirked slightly, his eyes scanning her for a moment too long. "So,

Mita," he said, his voice low and smooth, with a hint of sarcasm. "I see you made it, I wasn't sure you'd be the type for big events like this."

Mita raised an eyebrow, *Who the heck is this guy?"* slightly thrown off by the boldness of his comment. "And what type would that be, exactly?" she replied, her voice a touch more teasing than she intended.

"I don't know," Rune said, leaning in a little closer as if he was letting her in on some private joke. "I just thought you might be the type who likes to avoid crowds. Stay in, you know?"

"Oh, I *love* crowds," Mita shot back, her tone dripping with playful sarcasm. "They're my favorite. Nothing better than getting lost in a sea of people, right?"

Rune grinned, clearly amused. "Good to know." His eyes shifted from her face to her outfit, giving her a once-over in a way that made her feel strangely seen. "You're rocking that look, by the way."

Mita fought the impulse to blush. *What am I doing, getting caught up in some 1900s flirtation?* she thought to herself, unsure of how to handle flirtations overall, though she matched his gaze with a smirk of her own. "I know," she replied a second too late.

"Ah, but I think I'm getting the picture," Rune said, his smile widening. "So, what brings you to the event? Just the usual freshman curiosity or… are you actually looking for something?"

She tilted her head, trying to gauge where this conversation was headed. *Am I flirting with him? Is he flirt with me? Is he a stalker? Mit*a wasn't sure, but she had a sudden surge of boldness creeping up on her. "I'm here to explore. Meet new people, see what's out there. You know… find the hidden gems."

The heck am I even saying, hidden gems

Rune's eyes sparkled with intrigue. "Well, lucky for you, you just found one."

There it was again. Those dumb pick-up lines that are supposedly working. Mita wasn't sure if he was teasing, flirting, or just being his usual charismatic self, but she liked it. She liked how easy it was to talk to him. She liked the way he made her feel like she was part of some exclusive club, even if she barely knew him.

Jasmine, noticing their back-and-forth, threw her hands up in mock surrender. "Okay, okay, let's not make this a whole *thing*," she teased, nudging Rune with her elbow. "You two are *dangerous* together, aren't you?"

"Dangerous, huh?" Rune raised an eyebrow, glancing at Mita with a wry smile. "I like that."

Before Mita could respond, Rune shifted the conversation. "Anyway, if you want to know what's next, stick around. There's a surprise event coming later tonight. Something you won't want to miss." He paused for a moment, his expression unreadable. "Trust me, it's going to be... unforgettable."

Mita couldn't help but feel a twinge of curiosity. "A surprise event?"

"Oh, yeah," Rune replied, his tone low and almost conspiratorial. "But I won't spoil it for you. You'll see when it happens."

As the conversation shifted toward the upcoming event, Mita found herself reluctantly drawn into the crowd, and she felt a sense of anticipation creeping in. Even Reed and Odessa, who had been quietly observing the exchange, started to murmur between themselves.

"Do you think it's some kind of performance?" Odessa asked Reed, her brow furrowed. "What kind of surprise would that be?"

Reed shrugged, but there was a flicker of excitement in his eyes. "I don't know, but I've got a feeling it's going to be something worth sticking around for."

"Yeah, me too," Odessa added, her gaze lingering on Rune for a moment before shifting back to the stage, where the first acts of the night were starting to get ready.

Mita, meanwhile, couldn't shake the feeling that Rune was a puzzle she'd like to figure out. His words were cryptic, but there was an underlying sense of mystery that was irresistible.

As the night wore on and the students from the music department took to the stage, Mita found herself caught up in the performance, but her thoughts kept drifting back to the "surprise event" Rune had hinted at. What could it be?

With that question swirling in her mind, Mita felt the night take on a different energy, a sense of anticipation that hummed through the crowd like electricity in the air

Chapter 5: The Hunt Begins

The night had been electric. Music from the student bands, a few impromptu dance-offs, and general mingling created a vibrant atmosphere, yet the energy in the air seemed to shift as the clock ticked toward the surprise event Rune had mentioned earlier.

Mita found herself caught between curiosity and a bit of apprehension. The students had been talking about it all night, but none of them knew exactly what to expect. It was clear now that Rune's cryptic words about the "surprise event" were more than just playful teasing. The thrill was tangible, hanging thick in the air like the electric hum before a storm.

The lights flickered.

Mita paused, glancing around the darkened room with a slight frown. The hum of excitement from the crowd turned to murmurings and confused chatter as the lights flickered again, then *went out* entirely.

"Uh… what's going on?" Amerei whispered nervously, grabbing Mita's arm in the sudden darkness.

Mita's heart skipped. A murmur rippled through the crowd, and a few nervous chuckles followed.

"I don't know," Mita said, trying to remain calm. "Maybe it's part of the event?"

Before anyone could respond, the lights flickered back on, but the area had changed, sort of. The atmosphere had shifted. A sense of mystery hung in the air like fog, and the murmuring from the crowd grew louder. Something big was about to happen.

"Welcome, freshmen and upperclassmen!" The voice on the speaker rang out into the night air, playful and confident. "You've been having a good time, but it's time for the real fun to begin. You've all heard of icebreaker activities, right? Well, tonight's icebreaker will be unlike any other."

A chorus of excited whispers filled the room as the lights dimmed slightly. Mita felt an anxious thrill bubbling up inside her.

"You're about to participate in a *treasure hunt,* a campus-wide challenge designed to test your wits, your teamwork, and your ability to think outside the box. But beware... this is no ordinary scavenger hunt. You will face riddles, puzzles, and challenges that will take you all over campus. But remember, there's a prize at the end, and only those who work well together will reach it first."

The crowd went silent. It was a bizarre shift from the carefree energy of the event just moments before. Mita exchanged glances with her friends. Odessa had a skeptical look on her face, Reed was grinning, and Amerei seemed uncertain, though she had a little spark of excitement in her eyes.

"Form groups of three; each group will get their first clue shortly. The clock is ticking, and the hunt begins... now!"

A student in a black, featureless mask appeared at the front of the stage. The masked figure stepped forward, holding a large basket filled with black envelopes. Mita's heart raced as she watched it pass from hand to hand, eventually landing in Reed's possession.

"Alright, here we go," Reed muttered, tearing open the envelope. He pulled out a small folded paper and read aloud:

"The place where history and knowledge meet, where you'll find a place to sit and think. Seek out the room that's older than time."

Mita blinked. "The library?" she suggested.

Reed nodded, his eyes gleaming with excitement. "That's got to be it. Let's move."

Without another word, they began moving toward the doors, joining the throng of other students who were already headed in the same direction.

27

As they walked through the crowd, Mita noticed some familiar faces. Among the students who were racing to solve the clues, she spotted **Zyran**, a guy she'd never seen before but who was with Amerei's and Andromeda's group.

Zyran was tall with a kind of wiry build, wearing a hoodie and sneakers. He looked somewhat aloof, like he was too cool to care, but still somehow in the thick of it all. There was an almost exaggerated slouch in his posture, making him appear like he didn't belong, but in a way that made him stand out.

Mita raised an eyebrow. *"Weird."*

Zyran caught her eye, and there was an awkward silence before he turned to catch up to his group.

As they reached the library, the group stopped, taking in the tall, ancient building. There was something imposing about it. "Okay, now we really need to figure out where the next clue is hidden," Mita said, glancing at Reed and Odessa.

Meanwhile, Mita noticed **Ethan**, the serious guy from math class, standing off to the side near the building entrance with a group of other students. His stern expression and posture remained unchanged as he surveyed the group. Behind him, **Cassian** lingered, looking as though he were lost in thought. Mita couldn't shake the feeling that Cassian had an odd presence about him—like he wasn't really present, yet somehow aware of everything at once. It was as if his mind was disconnected from reality in the strangest way.

"Looks like we're not the only ones who got the clue," Reed remarked, pointing out the two guys.

Mita nodded. "Yeah, seems like everyone's getting in on the action."

"Let's get moving, then," Odessa said, brushing her hair out of her face. "We're not here for sightseeing."

As they stepped into the dimly lit library, the chill air of the ancient building greeted them. The musty scent of old books and the flickering light made the whole situation feel like a mystery waiting to unfold.

They wandered down narrow aisles between the tall shelves when Reed suddenly stopped in front of a massive wooden door. "It's gotta be in here," he said, eyes narrowed as he turned the handle.

Before they could step inside, though, **Zyran** and **Amerei's group** appeared, blocking the entrance.

Zyran smirked, hands in his pockets. "Looks like we got the same ideas. Good luck. This place isn't as simple as it looks."

"Whatever," Mita shot back, feeling the competitive pulse surge inside her. "We'll see who gets there first."

The challenge was on. The treasure hunt might be about to truly test everyone's abilities and maybe even alliances, but Mita was starting to feel the weight of it in her competitiveness, and there was a rush in it.

Chapter 6: The Treasure Hunt — Clues, Competition, and Chaos

Remaining at a standstill in the library that felt like it had just been pulled straight out of a mystery novel—creaky wooden floors, rows upon rows of bookshelves packed with forgotten knowledge, and the eerie hum of old lights flickering overhead. Mita couldn't help but feel like she was walking into the belly of the beast. The treasure hunt had just begun, and already it felt like everything around her was designed to test more than just her intellect.

So as it turned out, that door wasn't the answer, and everyone was confused.

"Alright, no more stalling," Reed said, his voice low, sounding a bit annoyed but still excited.

"Do you think they really thought this out?" Odessa asked, her eyes darting around as she glanced at the dusty books that lined the walls. "I mean, it's like they *want* us to get lost in here."

"Maybe that's the point," Mita mused, feeling a strange thrill in her chest as her brain clicked into gear. She loved a good challenge. "Maybe we're supposed to get lost then find something unexpected along the way."

Odessa raised an eyebrow. "You've got a weird way of thinking about things."

Before Mita could reply, a soft voice came from behind them. "Are you planning on solving the first clue, or are you just gonna stand around and act mysterious?"

Mita turned to find **Zyran** leaning against one of the old stone walls, his arms crossed and a cocky smirk playing on his lips. He was alone now, his team, including her roommate, seemingly scattered, still searching high and low for clues, while he was chilling out. The guy had a reputation for not following the rules, but Mita couldn't tell whether he was just a nonchalant rebel or if he was trying too hard to seem cool.

"Not trying to act mysterious, just figuring out where the next clue is, but you might be too high above such petty tasks, your majesty," Mita shot back. Her sarcasm was sharp, but she could feel that weird tension in her stomach, the same feeling she had when she'd first encountered him. It was like a game of mental chess, and she wasn't sure if she was winning or losing. Why was it a competition in the first place? She already had a lot on her plate

Zyran rolled his eyes and pushed himself off the wall. "Well, good luck. You'll need it." He turned and walked away, disappearing into the aisles of books with a casual flick of his wrist.

Mita exhaled, relieved the weirdness was over. But she wasn't about to let him get to her. Not tonight.

"Focus, guys," Reed interrupted, pulling out the letter from earlier and holding it up like some kind of treasure map.

They all gathered around as Reed read aloud from the first clue again:

"The place where history and knowledge meet, where you'll find a place to sit and think. Seek out the room that's older than time."

"Okay," Mita said, tapping her finger against her chin. "It's clearly the library. But where exactly in the library? And why make it sound so ominous?"

"Because that's part of the fun," Reed replied, his eyes sparkling with that same adrenaline-fueled excitement. "The old, creepy vibe adds to it."

Suddenly, the same door from earlier that we thought the next clue was in creaked open, and **Cassian** stepped into view, his disoriented gaze wandering over the group.

"Hey, Cassian," Odessa greeted him, her tone flat but polite.

Cassian didn't seem to register her completely. "Are we looking for a treasure or just getting lost in here?" His voice was calm, too calm, as though the hunt itself didn't matter.

Reed's eyes gleamed. "Both, I think. But it looks like you're just lost."

Cassian just gave a lazy shrug, as if it didn't bother him at all. "I'll figure it out eventually. Or not." And then, without another word, he shuffled off into the darkness of the stacks.

"Okay, what was that about?" Mita murmured.

"I don't know," Reed said with a frown. "But I'm starting to think we're not the only ones who think we're lost."

Before Mita could respond, the next twist hit them all at once. A low hum filled the library, and the lights flickered again, more intensely this time, almost like a warning. Mita felt a strange buzz in her fingertips, as if the energy in the air had shifted.

Then a loud voice crackled through the speakers, making everyone jump.

"Alright, treasure hunters! Time for your next clue!" the voice announced, sounding like an excited game show host. "Your next location is *unexpected*. It's a place where ghosts have been known to roam... but not the scary kind. Look for the room that was once the *heart* of the university, the place where the old tradition still lingers. The clock is ticking!"

Mita's heart pounded faster. "What in the world is that supposed to be? Ghosts? Old traditions?" she muttered. The mist of it was settling into something more intense as the air in the library shifted, everyone thinking about the next clue, leaving an eerily quiet atmosphere with faint murmurs.

"Did they just say *ghosts*?" Odessa asked, her voice dripping with sarcasm.

"Yeah," Mita said, her eyes scanning the library. "And old traditions... Do you think it's the history department's hall?"

"Only one way to find out," Reed replied.

Just as they began to make their way toward the door, Mita caught sight of **Ethan**, his expression was unreadable as he stood in the doorway, a flicker of recognition flashing in his eyes when he spotted her.

"You're on the hunt too, huh?" Mita asked as though she didn't see him earlier, her tone light.

Ethan didn't smile. "Wouldn't miss it."

With that, he turned and walked off in the opposite direction.

As Mita, Reed, and Odessa made their way out of the library, the campus began to feel even more like a labyrinth, its darkened corners and hidden passageways suddenly alive with possibilities and dangers. The hunt was far from over, and Mita was ready to win this.

But there was something nagging at her mind. Was this just a game? Or was there more to it? She couldn't shake the feeling that this event was more than just a quirky bonding experience. The clues were getting weirder. The people around her—**Zyran**, **Ethan**, **Cassian**—all felt like pieces of a puzzle she hadn't even started to solve.

As they left the library and entered the night air, the hunt was on once again, and Mita was more determined than ever to figure it all out. She had her friends, her instincts, and the will to push through whatever weird clue came her way.

She only hoped she could trust the people she was with .

Meanwhile, further down the campus paths, **Rune** leaned against the wall outside the music department, his sharp gaze catching the last few moments of the group's retreat. His lips curled into a knowing smile. Whatever happened next, it was going to be *fun*.

But Mita wouldn't know the full game until the very end. And by then, it might just be too late.

Chapter 7: The Treasure Hunt – Racing Against Time

❧

The campus was alive with excitement, but it also felt like a maze, each turn leading deeper into the unknown. Mita's pulse quickened as she and Reed made their way toward the next location with Odessa close behind, their shoes crunching over gravel paths that seemed too quiet for an event this chaotic.

The latest clue led them to an old lecture hall at the far end of campus, tucked away behind ivy-covered walls. Mita wasn't sure what kind of ghosts they were talking about, but she definitely felt like she was walking into something that had been forgotten by time.

"Ghosts, huh?" Odessa muttered for the 10th time, following close behind. "This better not be another weird prank like the library."

Reed didn't reply. He was too focused on trying to decode the riddle.

They reached the door, only to find it locked. "This is weird," Mita said. "The room was supposed to be a part of the hunt? So why is it locked?"

"I'll figure it out," Reed said confidently. He pulled out a small keychain from his pocket and fiddled with it. "I have a few tricks up my sleeve."

Just as Reed was about to pick the lock, they heard footsteps. Mita turned, and there, standing at the edge of the hall, was **Zyran** leaning casually against a door frame.

"You look lost," he said, a lazy smirk on his face.

"You look like you don't have equilibrium in your legs," Mita shot back, not in the mood for his games. "We're looking for the next clue. And why are you everywhere but with your group?"

"Well," Zyran said, stepping forward, "it's simple. If you can't open the door, maybe you should try the window." he said, turning his back to us, walking away, before he then turns back to us, taking his time like the world waits with gaping breaths for every word from his mouth, "You think about your group and I'll do the same, hmm?" *This guy either has a smooth brain or selective memory; either way, he rubs me the wrong way.*

Reed gave him a look of annoyance. "Not helpful, dude."

But Mita had already been annoyed by the whole thing, and now him. She started walking around the side of the building, ignoring him, and sure enough, she found a slightly ajar window. Without waiting for anyone to say anything, she slipped through. The others seeming to have followed her. The lecture hall was dusty, filled with rows of old desks and chairs that looked as though they hadn't been used in years.

The next clue was taped to the chalkboard. Mita grabbed it eagerly.

"The heart is not in the building, but beneath the stone. Follow the footsteps where the old ones roam."

"Seriously?" Odessa groaned. "We've got to go *underground* now?"

"I guess so," Mita said. "Let's go."

As they moved across campus for the third time toward the underground tunnels, which was an eerie section of the university. Mita caught sight of **Cassian**, away from his group, again, looking as aloof and disconnected as ever, near the entrance of the tunnels. *Why is everyone everywhere but with their groups?*

"Not surprised to see you here," she muttered as she walked past him.

Cassian looked up at her, blinking slowly. "The tunnels? Yeah, I've heard it's a good place to get lost, and I'm good." He turned and disappeared into the shadows, leaving Mita feeling more unsettled than before. *Was that a*

35

joke or sarcasm?

Reed led the way through the narrow, dimly lit corridors, while Mita couldn't shake the feeling that someone was watching them. They passed graffiti-covered stone walls and flickering lights, following a trail of chalk markings that had to be part of the game that indicated the way and turns for them to take, as rumor has it, the tunnels were so huge they couldn't even allow for anyone to get lost, not even just for laughs and giggles.

That's the only help we get from these people? Mita thought as she looked at the chalked arrows on the walls

Eventually, they reached an old, heavy door with a large lock on it. Mita's heart skipped a beat. Something was unnerving about the place, like it wasn't just part of the game.

"We need a code," Reed said, stepping back. "It's probably hidden somewhere close."

Just as he said that, **Ethan** appeared with the other member of his group as Cassian was everywhere but with them, just like Zyran. The flickering overhead light barely lit Ethan's stern face.

"You guys figured it out yet?" he asked.

Reed didn't answer. He was scanning the walls. The silence between them grew thick, but before Mita could speak, Ethan's gaze shifted to her. "I'm going to find another way in. See you on the flip side," he said before slipping back into the darkness.

Mita felt uneasy. "Let's get this done," Odessa urged. "This place is giving me the creeps."

After a few moments of searching, Mita found the code, hidden beneath a loose stone in the wall. Her fingers worked quickly, pressing the numbers one by one. The lock clicked, and the door creaked open.

Inside, they found a dusty stone room with a long table covered in candles, old maps, and mysterious symbols on the walls. A large chest sat in the center of the room, its lock rusted and ready to open.

Mita approached it cautiously, her mind racing. This was the final step. Behind that chest lay the *treasure,* the end of the game.

But as she knelt to unlock it, a familiar voice stopped her.

"Not so fast."

Rune emerged from the shadows, his dark eyes glinting with mischief. "You really think it's going to be that easy?"

Other players, including Ethan and his partner returning after their probably failed attempts, Amerei, her team, and some other freshmen and less than a handful of upperclassmen, rushed into the room, seeming to finally find the clues for themselves.

Mita's heart skipped. "What do you mean? This *is* the last clue."

"I'm afraid not," Rune said, sauntering toward them. "You've all still got one more test to win."

His voice was laced with that familiar sarcasm. "The real treasure isn't the prize. It's the experience... and the *surprises* along the way," he said, walking right past the others who had made it in after. Before Mita could respond, the door slammed shut behind him, and the lights flickered once again. Leaving them all stunned and feeling duped into this joke of a treasure hunt.

Meanwhile, Mita and the others were brooding over the prank the seniors had pulled on them. At the front of campus, the other students were gathering for the final leg of the hunt. The **pizza party,** but no one was in the mood to celebrate yet, not until the other students solved the final riddle.

Mita's team was about to face the ultimate twist, and only one question was on her mind: *Who could she trust in this twisted game?*

It was time to figure it out or risk losing everything.

Chapter 8: The Final Test

Mita stood frozen in the candlelit room, the heavy air pressing against her chest. Rune's cryptic words hung in the air, thick with mystery.

"The real treasure isn't the prize. It's the experience… and the surprises along the way," Rune's voice rang out in her thoughts, repeating what he had just said before he left them with a bunch of questions swirling in their minds. His words still filled the room like a charged storm, even though he wasn't there physically.

Reed was the first to speak, his voice tight with frustration. "What does he mean? This is it, right? The last clue? We solved everything!" he said, basically repeating what Mita had said earlier.

The sound of Rune's breath came through the speakers in the room, before his words indicated his exasperation with either the situation or the questions they asked, and Mita knew that it was the latter. To think they can be exasperated when Mita and the rest of the players were the victims here. "You thought the treasure hunt was just about solving puzzles and following clues? No, no. The final test isn't about what you find… It's about what you can leave behind, right, Mita?"

It was as if she could feel his dark eyes catching hers in the dim light as he spoke. "It's about what you're willing to sacrifice."

Mita felt her pulse spike. Was this part of the game? Or was it something else entirely?

Reed stepped forward, the muscles in his jaw tightening. "You're saying we're not done? That we have to… *sacrifice* something? You're joking, right?"

Rune was silent, building the suspense in the room on purpose before his voice came through. "I'm not joking." To Mita, everything about his words felt calculated and deliberate. "I can give you a hint though… It's not about figuring out the last clue. It's about who you *trust* and what you *choose* to leave behind in the end."

Mita took a step back, trying to make sense of his words. **Leave behind**? Her mind flashed to her phone, to her life at home, to Joshua's messages reminding her to hold onto her faith and to *not let the environment shape her*.

No one spoke for a moment, each person lost in their thoughts.

Finally, Odessa broke the silence. "So, what now? Are we supposed to just… give something up?"

Rune said nothing for a long time, then, "You'll find out. Trust me, the game doesn't end until you learn something about yourself."

Mita's head swirled with confusion and doubt. **What did that even mean?** She had no idea what she was supposed to leave behind. Was it a piece of her personality? Something she'd been holding onto for comfort? Her faith?People in this room?

Suddenly, a voice echoed through the room from the speaker, different from Rune's voice. **"The choice is yours. Find the key. The real treasure lies within."**

The lights flickered once again, casting strange shadows on the walls. Mita's heartbeat thundered in her ears as she scanned the room. There, hidden under one of the chairs, was a small metal key. It gleamed in the faint candlelight.

Her breath caught. She rushed to it, grabbing it in her hand before anyone else could. The key felt oddly warm, like it had been waiting for her. She turned it over, the strange engraving on it sending a shiver down her spine.

It wasn't just a key. It was a *symbol*.

With the key in hand, she turned back to the group of students in the room, consisting of both freshmen and sophomores. "I think… I think I found the key," she said quietly.

Reed looked at her, brows furrowed. "That doesn't look like part of the game."

Mita didn't care. "It doesn't matter. It's part of the clue." She held it up. "We need to trust what we've learned here. We're not just playing a game; we're being tested. And I think this is what Rune was talking about."

Odessa crossed her arms, skeptical. "You really think this little key is the answer?"

"It's a start," Mita said, more sure of herself than she'd been all night.

Rune watched them closely through the security camera, his smirk still present, as though he knew they didn't.

"You've figured it out," he said, his voice coming through the speakers mystic as ever but almost reluctant. "You've found the key, but the question remains, what does *it unlock?*"

"The door, obviously," Odessa said to everyone at large in the room.

The sound of footsteps echoed outside the door, but before anyone could move, the door swung open by itself.

A figure appeared in the doorway, a masked student holding sealed envelopes. The student first handed it over to Mita, then did so for the other students without a word, and then disappeared back into the shadows through the doors.

The envelope was simple and unmarked, slightly different from the ones before. Mita ripped it open. Inside was a single sheet of paper, with a question written in neat handwriting:

"What are you willing to give up to find the treasure?"

Her heart sank. The puzzle was more personal than she'd imagined.

She glanced up at the others, who were all watching her intently; they also did not know what to do. For the first time that night, everything felt too real. The stakes weren't just about winning a prize anymore. It was about what she was truly willing to sacrifice.

"Looks like it's not just about the treasure," Mita muttered. "It's about who we are and what we leave behind."

Rune's voice was back, but now sharper than before. "You've got it now. The treasure is not just a thing. It's an experience. A lesson."

What was he, a master of ceremonies? she thought

The others stared at her, the silence pressing in.

Mita exhaled slowly, the weight of the moment sinking in. She realized then that it wasn't about proving something to anyone or solving a series of cryptic clues. It was about understanding herself, what mattered most to her, and what she wasn't willing to let go of.

The room suddenly felt lighter, like the air had shifted. She looked down at the key again, feeling the strange sense of clarity it brought. **It wasn't just a key to a door. It was a key to understanding.**

With a deep breath, she turned to the group.

"Let's go," Mita said quietly but firmly. "It's time to end this."

The Final Reveal

When Mita and the rest of the students finally reached the last destination, the entire campus seemed to breathe in anticipation. The treasure was waiting. But what they didn't know was that it wasn't about finding something physical at all; it was about the relationships they'll form, the lessons they'll learn, and the moments they'll share together.

As they arrived at the back of the Quad, near the student union, the place where everything had started. The booths and all the excitement from earlier tonight had long been packed up, and the cleaning crew was making their rounds, leaving them confused as to where everyone went.

The doors of the nearby building swung open at that moment; two students standing in the huge entrance way were signaling them to come in. Upon entering, there was an enormous pizza party, complete with loud music, games, and a giant banner that read, **"The Treasure is the Journey."**

Mita felt a strange sense of peace as the weight of the night lifted. She didn't have to choose between who she was and what she wanted. The game had just shown her how to balance it all.

"I told you the real treasure is the experience. What are you willing to sacrifice on the new journey of uni life?" the familiar voice cut through her thoughts like a knife, "Will you give yourself up to the environment, or will you offer up your environment to be yourself? Find out who you are if you haven't and build or reinforce who you already are; this is the purpose of this event." Rune's voice cut through the crowd beside her, causing her to turn. Making eye contact with him, he gave Mita a knowing smile, not breaking their gaze, before continuing "My personal advice would be for you all gather here, especially freshmen, find a department or a club thats different from your major to see what you could like and what you're interested in, and the trick of today is all of you just won the prize to start paving the path ahead of you, Welcome to Diadromi University."

Breaking eye contact with Rune, not even bothering to define what this tension between them was, Mita turned to join her friends at their table, too overwhelmed to have another conversation with Rune or about this entire treasure hunt. After taking a couple of pizza slices, placing them on her plate, deserving this treat; she sat back and enjoyed her meal. She knew one thing for sure: the treasure wasn't a prize.

And fortunately and unfortunately, this was just the beginning.

Chapter 9: Finding Balance

The weeks since the treasure hunt had flown by, but for Mita, it felt like time had slowed to a crawl. The excitement, the laughter, and the adventure were all still vivid memories. Yet something was lingering beneath the surface, a heaviness that wouldn't leave her alone. **Nightmares—maybe** "nightmares" was a strong word; they were more like dreams that were discomforting and uncomfortable but not horrific. She couldn't shake them for the life of her.

Sometimes, she would wake up, drenched in sweat, her heart racing as if the events from the subconscious had come to life again. Other nights, she would lie awake for hours, staring at the ceiling, wrestling with the question that had been plaguing her mind since that final, cryptic clue.

Was balance even possible? Was having your cake and eating it too ever really okay?

Mita had thought she could manage it all: her faith, the newfound freedom of university life, and the friendships she was building. But it felt like pieces of herself were slipping through her fingers. The constant pull between the wild side of university life and the quiet, steady faith she held was a tug-of-war in her soul.

She tried to push it away, to keep going, but the questions wouldn't stop. What did it mean to be a Christian in this new world? Was she allowed to fit in with her peers while still keeping her values intact? Could she still experience life, freedom, adventure, and friendship without compromising who she was created to be?

One of the things that had helped her was the Christian club. After receiving the flyer at the student council event, Mita had been hesitant at first. But she'd made her way there one evening, sitting in the back, quietly observing the group. There was something comforting about the way they gathered, openly sharing thoughts, laughing, and supporting each other. She hadn't gone back again since that first time, but something in her kept urging her to go back.

Maybe it was time. Perhaps it was time to make that decision, to go back.

Mita found herself sitting in her sociology class one afternoon, her mind wandering as she stared at the back of Odessa's head, deep in thought. The lecture felt distant, like background noise. Ethan, Mr. *'grounded'*, was sitting next to her and must have seen the war between her eyes.

"What's going on with you?" he had asked, and she didn't reply, noticing the quiet hesitation written across her face when he mentioned it. He continued, "Something's on your mind. Care to confide in me?"

Mita had almost dismissed the thought, but the sincere look in his eyes made her fortified walls crumble, and before she could think to gather her words, they were already spilling out of her. "I don't know, I just... I've been thinking about going back to this Christian club. But sometimes I feel like I don't belong there. I don't know if I'm doing this whole faith thing right. I don't know if I'm enough or if I even *fit the convention.*"

He raised an eyebrow, and his gaze softened. "Mita. It's not about being enough. It's about being real. We're made to be enough through Jesus. Without him, well, we're all a mess, just trying to get it right."

Her eyes widened, surprised by his words. She didn't know what she had expected from Ethan, but it was not that. "Wait, you... You think that too? You believe in all of that?"

He'd surprised her more than once recently, especially after the treasure hunt. There was something about him, something steady and thoughtful that Mita couldn't quite place. Though she hadn't expected him to be the type to even care about anything spiritual, so his response had completely caught her off guard.

Ethan gave her a small, knowing smile. "I'm not perfect. I don't have everything figured out, but Jesus does. That's why we have salvation; he died on the cross and rose three days later, so we are forgiven by his blood. He is the way, the truth, and the life." His voice was steady, calm, like he had said this a thousand times. He leaned back in his chair, our lecture completely forgotten. "Don't overthink it. You don't need to have it all together. Just show up."

Mita couldn't help but smile a little at the simplicity of his words. He made it sound so... easy. She appreciated that.

Maybe I'm not alone in this, she thought. Ethan's unexpected support had lifted a small weight off her shoulders.

The class ended, and Mita gathered her things, her mind buzzing with the conversation she had with Ethan earlier. As the students were all gathering their stuff, she glanced at Odessa, who was packing her bag in the row in front of her.

"I'm going to this Christian group tonight, you wanna tag along?" Mita said casually, testing the waters.

Odessa paused, looking up with a raised brow. "Oh. I don't know if I'm up for all that. I mean, you do you. But it's not really my thing. You know?"

Mita nodded. She'd expected that answer. Odessa had always been a bit... distant when it came to matters of faith, even if she never overtly dismissed it. They both respected each other's differences.

"I'll go alone then," Mita said, trying to sound nonchalant about it, but she couldn't hide the tinge of relief that had settled in her chest, not at the fact that Odessa wasn't tagging along but at the fact that she could say it out loud to someone who could be considered a friend and not be judged.

"Alright," Odessa said, giving her a small wave. "I'll catch you later."

Mita didn't waste another second. She turned, heading to Ethan, who was waiting by the door with his backpack slung over one shoulder.

"You going to the club?" she asked, hesitating for just a moment.

Ethan nodded, adjusting his backpack. "Yeah, thought I'd go with you?"

"You're serious?" she asked, surprised. She had thought he'd just said that to be polite, but Ethan seemed totally genuine.

He shrugged. "Yeah, why not? As I said, I'm not perfect, but I'm always down for some real conversation and some biblical debates."

They both exited the building of their sociology class, heading to the student union to walk to the Christian group meeting. Mita couldn't help feeling a little less alone in the world.

The campus was still buzzing with activity as they made their way across the courtyard. But as they neared the entrance to the club room in the student union building, Mita's heart skipped a beat when she saw a familiar face, Zyran.

Of course.

Zyran, the annoying leaning-on-everything guy from the treasure hunt. She hadn't seen him since that night, but his sudden appearance here made the evening feel... strange. He stood by the door, leaning casually against the wall, a mischievous smile on his lips as he spotted her and Ethan.

"Well, well," Zyran said, his voice smooth and teasing. "Look who's here. Didn't think I'd see you at one of these meetings."

Mita raised an eyebrow. "You're here too?" but it wasn't really a question.

Zyran just gave her a shrug, his posture effortlessly cool. "Why not? They've got good snacks, and it's about my fav celeb, Jesus. Thought it would be great."

Ethan looked between the two of them, a slight smirk on his face. "Seems like you two know each other."

"Yeah," Mita said, keeping her voice casual to dial down her annoyance with Zyran's presence. "We met during the treasure hunt."

Zyran chuckled lightly. "Good times. Can't believe you survived that night. Most people would've bailed when the lights went out."

Mita shook her head, amused despite herself. "You say that like it was some kind of test. It was just a game," she said. She could hear the denial even in her own voice.

Zyran tilted his head, his eyes narrowing slightly. "Everything's a test, though, isn't it? Life, faith... It's all part of something bigger."

Mita was so taken aback; she was rendered speechless for a moment

46

because he was right. There was something about his words that made her think deeper than she wanted to. But this wasn't the time to dig into it.

"Well, yeah," Mita said, before quickly adding, "Well, we are all here now. We might as well see what this week's meeting's all about."

As they stepped inside, Mita couldn't help but feel the weight of the moment, **the weight of choices**, of being where she was supposed to be, of navigating life in a place where things weren't always so clear, but those things weren't so burdening right now.

Because tonight, she made the first right step in the direction of her purpose.

Chapter 10: Uncharted Territory

As the evening sun dipped behind the buildings on campus, casting long shadows across the courtyard, Mita followed Ethan and Zyran into the medium-sized meeting room where the Christian club gathered for meetings. It was a cozy space with soft, golden lights from the late evening sun spilling through the windows; a chalkboard on one wall and a whiteboard on the other filled with Bible verses written in neat, careful handwriting; and rows of folding chairs set up in a semi-circle with bean bags all around. Some kids even look like they brought their own seats and blankets, like it was a sleepover. The sound of their soft chatter and laughter filled the room, but there was a quietness in the room too, an unspoken understanding among those who had come to gather.

Mita felt a little out of place at first, but something about the atmosphere made her feel safer than she had expected. Ethan took the seat beside her, his usual relaxed demeanor offering her a sense of calm.

As they settled in, the door at the front of the room opened, and a woman stepped in, tall and confident, with a warm smile and a quiet authority that instantly commanded the group's attention. She had shoulder-length dark hair, sharp, kind eyes, and a presence that felt like she could light up an entire room. She wore a simple blouse and jeans, but there was something about her that felt like she had a hundred different stories to tell, each one powerful in its own right.

"Good evening, everyone," she said with a bright, welcoming voice. "I'm Ruth Robbison, and I'll be leading tonight's study. For those of you who don't know me, I've been working with this group for a few years now, helping to guide those who are new to their faith, mentoring those who have been in the faith, and being there even for those who are just curious. I'm excited to dive into God's word tonight with all of you."

Mita exchanged a glance with Ethan, her nerves now a mix of curiosity and anticipation. Ruth had this ease about her that made Mita want to listen, to pay attention to every word that came from her mouth. This was different from what she experienced the first time she came; she finally saw it for what it was: a group of students gathered not just to socialize but to explore something much deeper.

Ruth cleared her throat and walked to the chalkboard behind her. "Tonight, we'll be looking at John Chapter 1," she said, turning to face the group. "It's a beautiful chapter that introduces us to the heart of the Gospel. It's where we meet Jesus—not just as a man, but as the Word of God, the divine Logos. This chapter is rich with meaning and invites us into a deeper understanding of who Jesus is."

Mita was intrigued. John 1 was a chapter she had read before, but it had always felt like a lot to unpack. She had never really sat down and thought about its depth before this.

Ruth's presence seemed to pull everyone's attention, and the way she spoke made everything feel so much more accessible, like she was unraveling a mystery piece by piece.

Ruth began to explain, turning back to the board to write down a verse. "Let's start with the first few verses—John 1:1-5: '*In the beginning was the Word, and the Word was with God, and the Word was God. He was with God in the beginning. All things were created through him, and apart from him not one thing was created that has been created. In him was life, and that life was the light of men. The light shines in the darkness, and yet the darkness did not overcome it.*'"

Ruth paused, allowing the group to digest the words. "This is powerful," she said softly. "John begins with a profound statement that we don't often stop to consider. 'In the beginning was the Word.' If you're familiar with the opening lines of Genesis, you'll notice the connection. This is a deliberate echo of that first line in Genesis, 'In the beginning, God created the heavens and the earth.' John is telling us that the Word was there from the very start of everything—**the Word** being Jesus himself."

Mita's brow furrowed slightly. **Jesus was the Word?** She had always thought of Jesus as the man who walked on earth, the one who performed miracles, the one who died for their sins. But the idea that he had existed from the very beginning of time, that he was somehow part of creation itself, was a concept that felt different.

Ruth continued, "John is emphasizing that Jesus wasn't just a human being who arrived at a point in history. No, Jesus is the **Word**, and through him, everything was created. For God the Father fulfilled the creation of the world with the Word, and God the Son, Jesus, is the Word. Therefore, making Jesus the foundation of creation. All things that exist came into being because of him—**including us.** And through him, we have life, life that shines like a light in the darkness."

There were quiet hums of agreement, and a few *'amens'* sounded in the room. Mita looked around, her mind racing. **Light in the darkness.** The idea of Jesus being the light seemed poetic, yet so meaningful. She thought of her own life—her search for balance, her struggles, and the nightmares that still crept in when the room fell silent at night. Could it be that Jesus was the answer to all that darkness? Could he really be the light that darkness can't overcome?

Ruth's voice broke through her thoughts. "The next part of this passage says something profound: 'The light shines in the darkness, and the darkness has not overcome it.' What does that mean for us today?" Ruth paused, scanning the group. "It's saying that no matter how dark the world gets, no matter how lost we feel, there is a light that **cannot be extinguished.** The light is Jesus, and that's the hope we ought to have in Jesus that he can't be overcome."

Mita felt a stir inside her. It wasn't just the hope Ruth spoke of. It was the sense that maybe faith wasn't so distant after all. Perhaps she wasn't so far from the light.

Ruth moved on, writing down the next verse. "Let's continue to verses 6-8: *'There was a man sent from God, whose name was John. He came as a witness, to bear witness about the light, that all might believe through him. He was not the light, but came to bear witness about the light.'*" Ruth looked up. "Here we have the introduction of John the Baptist, someone whom the Lord sent to prepare the way for Jesus. John wasn't the light himself, but he was pointing others toward it. This speaks to us as well. We, too, are called to bear witness to the light—to bear witness to Jesus, to share the good news with those who haven't seen it yet."

Mita felt her chest tighten at the thought. **Am I supposed to be a witness?** She wasn't sure how she could be or what she should even bear witness to, precisely, but the more Ruth spoke, the more she realized the answer wasn't so much in what she did but in who she was. **Could she really share the light with others? Could she live out her faith boldly without the fear of being judged?**

As the evening went on, Ruth continued to walk them through the chapter, exploring the deeper meanings of verses 9-14, where John talks about the coming of the true light, the Word becoming flesh and dwelling among us. By the end of the study, Mita felt a mix of awe and peace.

Ruth wrapped up the evening with a final thought. "John 1 reminds us that Jesus is the foundation of everything. He's not just a good teacher or a figure from history—he's the divine Word, the light in the darkness. And we, as his followers, are called to walk in that light, to be his hands and feet in the world, and to share the hope we've found in him."

The room was quiet for a moment, and Mita realized that, somehow, for the first time in a while, she felt lighter. Maybe it was Ruth's words, or maybe it was the quiet sense of community around her, but something had shifted. The weight she had carried for so long—uncertainty, fear, loneliness—felt a little less heavy.

She looked around the room and then glanced at Ethan beside her, sitting quietly, a small smile on his face, as though he, too, had been touched by the study. Zyran, surprisingly, had his head down, his usual sarcasm absent for the night. It was strange to think that just a few weeks ago, they had all been strangers. But now, they shared something more, a glimpse of understanding, a flicker of light.

As Mita left the meeting, her heart was still a little heavy with all the things she didn't understand. But she felt a spark of something new, something hopeful. *Maybe this was the balance she had been looking for.*

And maybe she could find her way through the darkness after all.

Chapter 11: Ethan's First Night

Ethan stood in front of his new dorm room, the sound of students talking, laughing, and moving in drifting around him. It was the first day of college, and while the campus was buzzing with excitement, he felt oddly… at peace? The air was thick with anticipation, but Ethan was someone who thrived on stillness. He wasn't the type to get swept away by the noise. His heart wasn't racing; it was steady, like a calm river navigating the twists and turns of a rocky terrain.

The hallways were packed, packed with strangers who were about to become friends, or maybe just faces in a crowd. Some students greeted each other like long-lost relatives; others stood awkwardly by their doors, unsure of how to begin their new journey. Ethan did, however, feel a pang of nervousness, but it didn't linger. He had learned long ago that feeling a little bit of discomfort was a good thing. It meant he was growing and adapting.

He took a deep breath, gathering his thoughts. *This is it,* he thought, glancing around his room. The bed wasn't made yet, and the desk was littered with textbooks and unpacked boxes, but it didn't matter. Ethan wasn't the kind of guy who needed everything in order to feel at home. He could make do with what he had.

"Hey, Ethan! You coming to the get-together tonight?" Aseal's voice broke through his reverie; they were friends from high school who applied for the same school and got in together. He turned to see him standing in the doorway to his own room. He had an easy smile on his face, but there was an eagerness in his eyes that suggested he wasn't gonna give up easily.

"Yeah, sure. I'll swing by," Ethan said, his voice low and steady, just like the rhythm of his thoughts. It was his first night, after all, and he wasn't the type to go into things half-heartedly. Even if the idea of a dorm hangout made him feel a little out of his element, he wasn't going to shy away from it.

Aseal raised an eyebrow, clearly surprised by Ethan's easy acceptance. As he had always known him as the "lone wolf" type. The kind of person who would pass on the social events and bury himself in his studies. Ethan didn't blame him; he was a quiet observer, but that didn't mean he was detached. In fact, he believed that sometimes, the best way to connect with others was to give them the space to reveal themselves.

As evening fell, Ethan found himself in the dorm's shared common building. The lights were dim, and the atmosphere was buzzing with the kind of nervous energy only freshmen could bring to the first night of college. Students clustered in small groups, some chatting animatedly, others nursing solo cups, all of them trying to figure out how to belong, and it was kind of painful for him to watch, but he stood near the door for a moment, scanning the room.

There was a girl in the corner with purple hair—a color that stood out even in a room full of color. She was laughing with a group; her voice carried across to him. It was light but full of warmth, and Ethan couldn't help but notice how easily she fit into the crowd, how comfortable she seemed in her own skin. It was hard to miss the way her eyes flickered toward him. Maybe it was because he was standing off to the side, quietly observing everyone, or perhaps it was because she could feel his eyes on her.

"Hey, Ethan!" Aseal's voice rang out, breaking the moment between him and the stranger across the room. Nodding, he made his way across the room to his roommate and friend, weaving through the groups of people.

"Purple-haired, huh," Aseal stated, unbothered, causing Ethan to glance in the stranger from ealier before turning to look at Aseal grinning, "Ethan, I love you, man, but if you're gonna stare at a girl, at least be nonchalant about it." Aseal said, "I wasn't that obvious, was I? I barely came through the door," Ethan complained, bewildered at how his friend had caught him in such an embarrassing act. He knew Aseal would be nagging him about it for weeks to come. "You were as obvious as a cow in a dog's pen (house)," using his head to signal in the direction of the girl Ethan had been eyeing, he continued. "Her name's Anika. She's a theater major. You'll like her. She's kind of... a spark plug."

Ethan chuckled softly, more at himself, actually, not knowing what to do with this newfound information the Aseal somehow acquired. He didn't usually get caught up in the whirlwind energy of others, but there was something disarming about Anika's unselfconsciousness. It reminded him of how his own faith helped him remain grounded—he didn't have to be loud to be seen, and Anika, it seemed, was a testament to that. She didn't demand attention, but she seemed to draw it all the same.

He walked over to her, offering a quiet smile as he approached. Anika raised an eyebrow, clearly studying him for a moment. She must've sensed something about him because the slight smile on her face was unmistakeable.

"Ethan, right?" she asked, her voice steady but curious.

"That's me," he replied with a small nod, not bothering to question how she knew his name.

"Well, welcome to the chaos, I guess," she said with a grin, gesturing to the crowd before offering him a drink from the serving table they were now both standing beside. "I'm Anika. And if I could be as forthcoming, I was wondering when you'd come up to me."

"I wasn't sure if I should," Ethan said, his eyes scanning the room. "plus the whole university thing feels a little... overwhelming."

Anika laughed, the sound light and unguarded. "I get that. It's a lot to take in all at once. But you'll get used to it. Besides, you don't have to dive into the deep end if you're not ready. Just... take things as they come."

That was something Ethan could appreciate. He wasn't the type to dive headfirst into anything, especially not when it came to people. But he was willing to give this whole "new beginning" a chance. He took the drink she had offered him, taking a small sip, letting the flavor roll on his tongue.

55

"I guess that's the plan," he said, looking around the room. The air was thick with the weight of newness—new faces, new surroundings, and new challenges. But he wasn't intimidated. He had been here before, in different places, with different faces. College was just another step in his journey. And he had faith in the process.

Anika leaned against the table, a knowing smile playing on her lips. "I don't think you're as out of place as you think you are," she said. "I can tell. You've got this calm about you. Like… you know what you're doing, even when you're not sure what's next."

Ethan smiled, looking down at her. "I guess I just try to take it one step at a time."

"That's all anyone can do," she agreed.

And for the first time that night, Ethan felt a small flicker of something warm inside him—a quiet hope that maybe this was the start of something good.

Chapter 12: The Class of Introduction

Ethan Pov

The classroom buzzed with the usual first-day energy. People shuffled in, adjusting their bags and trying to find the perfect seat, and I could hear snippets of nervous chatter as everyone sized each other up. I had to admit, the feeling of being surrounded by all these new faces—people from different walks of life, with different goals, different stories, was exciting. But it wasn't overwhelming. I wasn't the type to get anxious in new situations, and besides, I had learned long ago that confidence didn't come from forcing yourself into the spotlight; it came from being grounded in who you were. I'd learned to trust that.

Professor Lawson stepped up to the front of the room, adjusting his glasses with a quiet professionalism. He had that calm energy that made him seem like someone who had been doing this for years—and probably had. His voice was welcoming as he addressed us.

"Alright, everyone," he said, his voice steady, "Welcome to college math. I'm Professor Lawson, and I'll be guiding you through this semester. We'll be covering everything from algebra to calculus, so if any of that sounds like a foreign language to you, don't panic. We'll take it step by step."

There was a collective sigh of relief from the room. I wasn't sure how the rest of the class felt about math, but I knew I could handle it. It might be a challenge, but I'd come prepared. I always did my best to take things in stride, and that confidence helped me stay calm when others were panicking.

"Before we dive into the material, I'd like to get to know you all a bit better." Professor Lawson continued, " I know, I know, it's the first day, and the last thing you probably want to do is stand up and talk about yourselves," he chuckled, "but bear with me. Just give your name, what you're studying, and one word that best describes you"

I looked around the room, wondering how each person would define themselves. For me, it was simple. I didn't need to think too hard about it. I stood up, straightened my shirt, and smiled at the class.

"I'm Ethan," I said, my voice calm and sure. "I'm studying business, and I'd describe myself as... grounded."

I could see a few people nodding, and I felt the familiar comfort of knowing I didn't need to say more. I didn't need to explain myself, what I said was enough. I'd been through enough in life to know that staying true to who you were was all that really mattered. I could walk into any room and feel at peace, knowing my faith, my values, and my heart were the foundation of everything I did.

The next student after me stood with this almost otherworldly grace, and when she spoke, her voice was smooth and confident.

"Andromeda," she said, voice clear and deliberate, "I'm studying medicine. I'd describe myself as... above it all."

I didn't want to judge her, I knew better than to assume things based on first impressions—but that was definitely a bold choice of words. Still, I had to admit there was something about her presence that made it hard not to pay attention. People like her seemed to have an ease with themselves that I respected, even if I didn't completely understand it.

The next person had this easy-going vibe about him, almost like he'd lived his whole life on vacation. There was no rush, no urgency in his voice.

"I'm Reed," he said, leaning casually against the desk, "I'm studying environmental science, and I'd describe myself as... free-spirited."

It was clear to me that Reed was the type who didn't sweat the small stuff. His laid-back attitude was something I admired. He seemed comfortable with himself in a way that wasn't arrogant, just… relaxed. There's something admirable about being able to go with the flow, especially in a world that's often so fast-paced.

Up next was a guy in the same row. He barely seemed to care, shrugging as he stood and muttering, "Cassan. Undecided. I don't know. Whatever."

Some people might've seen him as indifferent, but I didn't judge him for it. Sometimes it was hard to know what you wanted, especially when everything in life felt like it was being thrown at you at once. He wasn't rude, just quiet, and there was a depth to him that I could sense even if he didn't want to show it.

Next was a girl at the next end of the row. She entered conversation with the kind of confidence that felt like a spotlight had followed her in. She stood tall, her posture perfect, her outfit flawless.

"Odessa," she said, almost too smoothly, "I'm studying communications. I'd describe myself as… unapologetically confident."

There was no doubt in my mind that she believed that wholeheartedly. I didn't mind confidence—it was good, as long as it didn't cross into arrogance. Odessa's confidence was a bit more intense than I was used to, but I had a feeling she'd earned it in her own way.

The next girl didn't stand as confidently as some of the others. But when she spoke, there was a humor and self-assurance in her words that made me smile.

"I'm Mita," she said, giving a small but playful grin. "I'm studying digital marketing. And I'd describe myself as… 'underestimated but always right.'"

It made the class chuckle, and I couldn't help but appreciate her humor. There was a sharpness to her wit, a way of not taking herself too seriously, even though I could tell she was a lot sharper than most people gave her credit for. I liked that about her. She had a subtle strength, the kind that didn't demand attention but deserved it nonetheless.

After the introductions, Professor Lawson welcomed Merrick. And when Merrick walked in, the atmosphere in the room shifted. Tall, dark-haired, and impossibly good-looking, Merrick had that aura about him that made everyone take notice. But it wasn't just his looks; it was the way he carried himself. He had a quiet confidence that I could respect. There was something genuine about the way he interacted with the class. He didn't need to make a grand entrance. He just *was*.

"Everyone, meet Merrick Hughes," Professor Lawson said with a smile. "He's been helping out with this class for a while now, and we're lucky to have him."

Merrick smiled back, his presence steady and calm. "Hey, everyone," he said, his voice warm but not overwhelming. "Looking forward to working with you all. Feel free to ask questions or come by my haunts if you need any help with the material."

As I watched him, I couldn't help but appreciate how easy he made it seem. He didn't need to be flashy or overly charismatic to connect with people. It was a kind of humility wrapped in confidence, something I thought I could learn from.

The class was definitely shaping up to be interesting. But no matter what happened, I knew one thing: I was here for a reason. This was my time to grow, to challenge myself, and to live out my faith in the best way I knew how—by staying grounded and walking in truth. I wasn't here to impress anyone. I was just here to be me.

Chapter 13: Prepping for the Event

The lectures for the day ended, and the room slowly began to empty out, the buzz of students chattering about their classes, schedules, and the usual first-week small talk filling the air. I grabbed my bag, slinging it over my shoulder, and made my way out of the classroom. There was something about the first few days of college; the excitement, the nerves, the promise of new opportunities—that always made me feel both grounded and a little restless at the same time.

Today wasn't just about classes, though. I had something else on my mind, something I'd volunteered for on a whim at the start of the semester: the student council event tonight.

I wasn't really the "join-the-club" type, not because I didn't like people or the idea of being involved, but because I always wanted to make sure that anything I committed to was something I could pour myself into fully. But when the opportunity came up to help out with the student council event, I saw it as a chance to connect with people, to get a feel for campus life, and maybe make a positive impact.

I wasn't the type to jump into the spotlight, rather. I liked to quietly help behind the scenes, offering whatever I could. It's why I volunteered to handle some of the logistics for tonight's event. Not a big role, but it was enough to keep me busy, which was exactly what I needed. I needed to be productive; I needed something to anchor me while I settled into this new routine.

I headed back to my dorm, the familiar path a small comfort. My room was a little messy, but that's the way I liked it—organized chaos. I threw my bag down on my bed and started rummaging through the pile of clothes strewn around the room. I had just enough time to get myself together before I needed to sign in for duty, but I knew I needed time to focus before taking off.

First, I grabbed my planner, flipping through the pages until I found the event details. *The student council had organized a welcome event for new students at the quad, complete with food, games, and some entertainment. They were expecting a decent turnout, and I needed to make sure everything ran smoothly with the smaller things.* I jotted down the things I still needed to handle:

1. confirming the food order
2. and coordinating with a few volunteers who were in charge of the setup.

But honestly, my mind kept drifting. I kept thinking about Anika. It wasn't that I had a crush on her, or at least I wasn't sure if I did. But there was something about her. She has this kind of quiet strength that I found really intriguing and that way of making you feel like you didn't have to try too hard. Her playfulness, the ease of talking to her, and a genuine confidence that she wasn't just playing around or saying stuff to make you feel better.

I shook my head, trying to focus. Maybe it was just the fact that I was still figuring out what kind of guy I wanted to be in college, or maybe I was overthinking things. Either way, tonight's event was what I needed to focus on right now. No distractions, meaning no thoughts of a girl with purple hair that I barely know.

I threw on a simple but presentable shirt, a plain blue button-up with the sleeves rolled up—along with my favorite pair of well-worn jeans. I made sure everything was neat enough; I didn't have to be fancy, but I always liked to look like I had my act together. My mom used to joke that I had a "quiet professional" vibe, and I guess I'd adopted that over the years.

With a quick glance in the mirror, I gave myself a nod of approval. I looked good enough to go, and I was feeling good, too. Even though I wasn't sure what the event would bring, I was ready to give it my best. Besides, it wasn't about impressing anyone; it was about building connections, being part of something bigger than myself, and maybe, in some small way, doing some good for the people around me.

Before I left, I prayed briefly. It wasn't anything fancy or long, just a quick moment to center myself, asking the Lord for peace, for patience, and for the ability to be present. As I tended to overthink things, especially in new situations, so it was helpful for me to remind myself that I was doing my best and that was enough.

The hallway of the dorm was busier now as other students returned from their classes, their laughter echoing off the walls. I caught glimpses of familiar faces, but my mind was focused on the task at hand. As I walked towards the quad, I saw the volunteer crew setting up the tables, moving chairs around, and working together like a well-oiled machine.

The event was still a few hours away, but things had to be ready early. I checked in with the head volunteer, Mark, who was coordinating the food.

"Hey, Mark," I said, giving him a quick handshake. "Need any help?"

He looked up from his clipboard and smiled. "Hey, Ethan! Actually, yeah, we're just about to get the food here in ten minutes. Can you make sure the drinks table is set up? We're still waiting on the soda delivery, but the juice should be here any minute."

"Got it," I said. I quickly jogged over to where the drinks station would be set up and started organizing the space, making sure the cups, ice, and napkins were all in place. As I worked, I found myself humming a little to the background music that was already playing.

The atmosphere was relaxed, but there was a quiet excitement in the air.

I kept checking my watch. I still had some time before things kicked off, but as I scanned the area, I realized I was more excited than I thought I'd be. Maybe it was the idea of seeing the new students, of having a role to play, or maybe it was just the thought of meeting more people who were just as uncertain and excited as I was. I wanted to be there for them, in whatever small way I could, and this event seemed like the perfect opportunity.

As people started filtering in, I made my rounds, making sure everything was in place and that the volunteers were on track. I smiled and exchanged pleasantries, asking how their days had been and encouraging them to enjoy the event. It wasn't a big job, but it felt good to know that I was making a small difference.

When the event finally kicked off, the rest of the student body filled the area with easy chatter, and everyone was mingling, trying to find a place to settle in.

I was just starting to relax, feeling like everything was going well, when I saw Anika walk in with a group of people. She was looking around, her eyes scanning the area just like she had in the dorm's shared common building meet-up.

I found myself pausing for a moment, hoping she would look at me, but quickly shook it off. There was no need to get all wrapped up in it, reminding myself I had a job to do.

I grabbed a drink from the table and walked toward the back to check on the decorations, but as I passed by the group, Anika's eyes met mine. She gave me a small, knowing smile. A silent acknowledgment. I didn't know why, but it made me feel... good. Like maybe I wasn't just blending into the background here.

I smiled back, keeping things casual, and moved on.

This was just the beginning of everything; yes, there are a lot of faces, and there will be a lot of moments like this. But one thing was for sure: This was a chance to meet new people, do something good, and stay grounded, just like I promised myself I would.

Chapter 14: Ethan's account of the treasure hunt night

As they arrived at the place of the latest clues, Ethan felt something clicked into place. The tension in the air vanished, leaving only the hum of conversation and the soft thrum of music. The doors swung open to reveal something unexpected: a pizza party. The kind of cheesy, boisterous, all-American college gathering that you'd seen in every coming-of-age movie ever made. There was loud music, flashing lights, people dancing like they had something to prove, and a banner that read: "The Treasure is the Journey."

Ethan stood there for a moment, taking in the scene.

It was almost comical—like a cheesy marketing stunt designed to remind everyone that college wasn't about the grades or the internships, but about the *experience*. Sure, it was a bit over the top, but he wasn't bothered. He'd always had a complicated relationship with expectations. He knew enough not to let them cloud the moment.

Rune arrived, giving the same speech he had back in the tunnels. "The real treasure is the experience,", his tone almost too sure of itself. *"What are you willing to sacrifice on the new journey of uni life? Will you give up yourself to the environment, or will you give up your environment to be yourself?"*

Ethan had heard those kinds of speeches before. Too many times. It wasn't new, but it still carried a weight. It was the kind of message that would stick with you in the long run. The one you'd recall when you were standing on the precipice of your life, wondering if you'd made the right choices.

He wasn't sure about the rest of the group, but for him, it had always been a question of depth of faith. The treasure hunt had been a metaphor for life. Everyone was looking for a shortcut, a map to the perfect future, but the truth was simpler: *the path itself was the treasure.*

Cassian was leaning against the wall, arms crossed, staring out at the crowd as if this whole party was beneath him. Ethan had never been sure if Cassian was just naturally disdainful or if he wore that indifference as armor, but the guy was a master at being unreadable. Still, Ethan could see a flicker of understanding in his eyes—something had clicked for him, too. Cassian, for all his aloofness, wasn't immune to the deeper truths of the night.

"Do you get it?" Aseal asked, suddenly standing next to him, looking uncharacteristically serious for once.

Ethan glanced at him, the question catching him off guard. "G-Get what?"

Aseal hesitated for a second, running a hand through his hair. "That this... all of it wasn't about winning a stupid prize? It's about what happens next. The whole 'find yourself' thing." His voice trailed off, uncertain.

Ethan gave him a slow, deliberate smile. "Yeah, I get it. Sometimes you don't find what you're looking for. Sometimes, you find something better. The journey. That's the real treasure, at least that's what they said."

Aseal's brow furrowed, then a grin broke across his face. "You make it sound so easy."

"Not easy," Ethan replied. "Just... the way it is. Faith isn't about knowing all the answers. It's about trusting the process, even when you don't know where it's taking you."

Aseal nodded, though Ethan could see the wheels turning in his head, trying to make sense of the words, but he knew it was too much for his friend to unpack in one night. Maybe it would take a few more late-night talks before Aseal understood that *living* was the treasure, not the perfect ending.

As for the others, Reed and his team were already laughing and dancing, caught up in the revelry of it all. There was no competition anymore. The pieces had fallen into place, and it was like a collective sigh of relief in the atmosphere.

"I told you," a random guy said with that knowing tone, sitting between Aseal and Ethan. Ethan assumed it was an upperclassman who was involved in the planning of the treasure hunt. "Find a department, a club, something that's different from your major. The trick of today was that you won the prize to start paving the path ahead of you. Welcome to Diadromi University."

For the first time in what seemed like weeks, Ethan felt the weight lift off his shoulders just a touch. There was no prize at the end of the night, just a snapshot in time where they'd all learned something crucial about themselves. Some of them would remember it for years; some of them would forget by next semester. But for Ethan, this was just another chapter in the long book of life—a chapter that would lead to something else.

He didn't know exactly where it would lead, but that was the point.

For a moment, he stood alone, watching the others, and felt... content. Not because he had all the answers, but because he finally realized that the answers didn't matter. The process was enough. Life was the treasure, and maybe that was what Rune had been trying to tell them all along.

With a quiet sigh, Ethan turned back to the group and made his way toward the pizza table. There were still some slices left.

Chapter 15:Ethan's POV

The week had felt like a blur. Between classes, late-night study sessions, and random bursts of socializing, it felt like the moments when everything slowed down, when it was just him and his thoughts, had become rare.

That afternoon in sociology class, I'd noticed it; this girl, Mita, was having an obvious quiet struggle; it was the way she was just sitting here, but looked like she was miles away. Something was bothering her. I could feel it, and I didn't want to let it slide for some reason, even though it wasn't my business.

"What's going on with you?" I asked, keeping my tone light

She'd almost seemed like she would shrug me off, but she didn't. She'd opened up.

"I don't know, I just... I've been thinking about going back to this Christian club. But sometimes I feel like I don't belong. I don't know if I'm doing this whole faith thing right. and I don't know if I'm enough, or if I even fit the convention."

I could hear the weight in her voice. She wasn't looking for some canned response.

So I said what I knew.

"Mita. It's not about being enough. It's about being real. We're made to be enough through Jesus. Without him, we're all a mess, just trying to get it right."

It wasn't some perfect speech. It wasn't about sounding profound or even polished. It was just the truth, plain and simple.

I didn't want to complicate it, nor did I want to come off strong

But I could tell she was surprised by the simplicity of it. Maybe she was expecting something more complicated, maybe because life *felt* complicated. I didn't blame her. Faith, especially in a place like this, felt like it should be a lot harder than it actually was.

When she asked, *"Wait, you... you think that too? You believe in all of that?"* It kind of made me chuckle inwardly.

What had she expected?

"Yeah," I said. *"I'm not perfect. I don't have everything figured out, but Jesus does. That's why we have salvation. He died on the cross, rose three days later, so we could be forgiven. He is the way, the truth, and the life."* My words were steady, just stating the facts, no drama. It was just… truth. It had to be.

I gave her a small shrug. *"Don't overthink it. You don't need to have it all together. Just show up."*

And maybe that was the part that people missed. You didn't have to *have it all together* to be a part of something real. You didn't need a perfect faith, perfect thoughts, perfect anything. You just had to show up, show up to Jesus, to the people around you, to the messiness of life, and say, "Here I am."

Mita seemed a little less tense after that. It was kind of funny—how easy it was to get lost in your own head and make things way more complicated than they had to be.

We walked out of class together, and she casually mentioned going to the Christian group that night.

She seemed surprised, and for a second, when I had said I would go with her to the club, maybe she thought I'd just said what I'd had in class just to be polite. But nah. I wasn't the type to say things I didn't mean. And I wasn't the type to let someone do something that mattered alone.

"You serious?" she asked, a little uncertain.

"Yeah, why not?" I shrugged, keeping it chill. *"Like I said, I'm not perfect, but I'm always down for some real conversation and biblical debates."*

Real conversation. That was what we both needed, wasn't it? The kind that didn't try to sugarcoat things, didn't gloss over the hard stuff. The kind that made you feel seen, heard, and understood, even if you didn't have all the answers.

That's what being in the presence of God does.

As we walked across campus, the mood was light, but Mita's pace seemed to pick up, like she was suddenly in a hurry to get to the meeting. I couldn't blame her. It was kind of a big deal, taking that step, opening yourself up to something bigger than what you could see in front of you.

Chapter 16: Ethan's reflection

The evening air had a crispness to it as Ethan and Mita stepped out of the meeting room, the sky was now a deepening shade of purple, and the night had begun to settle in. It was the kind of night that made you feel like you were stepping into something bigger than yourself, a feeling Ethan was currently living.

He stretched his arms out, feeling the quiet hum of peace from the study still lingering in him. Tonight had been different. It wasn't the typical casual hangout or the usual lighthearted chat about life. No, tonight was something that felt deeper, more grounding. It wasn't just about reading Bible verses; it was about understanding them in a way that was real, practical.

Ethan looked over at Mita, who was walking beside him, her eyes fixed on the path ahead. He could tell by the look on her face that something had clicked for her tonight and still was. She seemed more thoughtful than usual, quieter, but in a way that felt… right. As if some light was shed on her unspoken doubts, fears, and uncertainties were just a little less heavy.

That was what the study had been about, right? Light in the darkness. That was what Ruth had said. The words had struck Ethan too, but for him, they didn't feel new, they felt like a reminder. Something deep inside him that he'd known for a while, but needed to hear again.

"The light shines in the darkness, and the darkness did not overcome it."

Ethan repeated the verse in his mind. He'd heard it before, many times, but tonight it felt like it had a weight to it that he hadn't noticed before. A kind of certainty he couldn't shake.

When Ruth had spoken about Jesus being the *Word*—not just a teacher, not just a man who had walked on earth—it felt like a fresh perspective on something he'd grown up with. The idea that Jesus was *the Word* from the very beginning, that everything had been created through Him, that He wasn't just part of history but *the beginning of everything*, hit Ethan in a way he couldn't quite articulate.

It was like the pieces of a puzzle had shifted into place. Jesus wasn't just some figure to look up to. He wasn't just some guy with a story to tell. He was the reason everything existed in the first place. Everything. The whole world, the universe, *us*—made through Him.

Genesis 1 verse 26 "**Let US make man in OUR image according to OUR likeness...**" makes a lot more sense to him now.

It wasn't just the intellectual realization of it all; it was more than that. It was a personal thing, how he especially made us in his likeness, as if he was aiming to form a relationship with us from the beginning of time, and not just with the Exodus of the Israelites.

Ethan thought about his own journey, how he'd wandered through life, figuring things out, not always understanding where he fit in. He'd never really *needed* to fully understand why Jesus was the center of everything. He just knew He was. And tonight, for the first time, he could see it more clearly than ever before. Jesus wasn't just the light. He *was* the reason there was light in the first place. The light that couldn't be extinguished, even in the darkest times.

As Ruth had said, the light shines, and the darkness has not overcome it. There was something unshakable about that.

Ethan had always had an easygoing attitude toward his faith. It was part of who he was, how he saw the world. He wasn't overly intellectual about it, but tonight made him realize that understanding—deep, unshakable understanding—was something that needed to be embedded in him. Ruth's words had made him realize how much of his peace, his balance, came from the fact that he *believed* in something unmovable. That, even when the world felt chaotic, there was a light that had always been there, and it wasn't going anywhere.

It wasn't just about knowing the right answers. It was about living with the certainty that the light, the hope in Jesus, was real and present in every moment, no matter what came, and we should live like we know it

.

The thing was, Ethan had seen that light in Mita tonight. It had been subtle, but he could tell that something had shifted for her. When Ruth had talked about John the Baptist, about how John came to bear witness to the light, Ethan could almost see the wheels turning in Mita's head. He could sense it.

Ethan smiled to himself. He didn't know all the answers for her, but he knew one thing: faith didn't have to be perfect to be real. Ruth had emphasized that Jesus wasn't just a figure from history, but was the foundation of everything. And that was what was so powerful about it all. The idea of sharing that light with others wasn't about getting everything right. It was about being a witness to the truth, to the hope that came from Jesus.

For Ethan, that was something he could do. He could *be* a witness, not because he had everything figured out, but because he believed in the light and yearned to live in that light. He knew it would change him for the better, and if he could point even one person toward it, that would be enough.

He glanced over at Mita again. She was still quiet, but he could see a shift in her, an openness that wasn't there before. Her curiosity had grown, and there was a flicker of hope in her that he hadn't seen before. Maybe she didn't have all the answers yet, but he could tell that tonight, she had taken a leap in something that she needed.

That's all it took—one step toward the light.

As they walked in silence toward the campus dorms, Ethan felt the familiar weight of peace settling on him. It was more than just knowing the truth. It was knowing that Jesus was the foundation of it all: the Word, the light, the reason for everything. And no matter what else came, that light would never be overcome.

Maybe Mita wasn't there yet, but he could see the spark in her. And perhaps she was on the edge of finding her own way through the darkness too.

And that thought made the night feel even brighter.

Ethan entered the Male dormitory, his mind still back in the meeting room

The quiet of his dorm room was a welcome contrast to the lively buzz of campus. Ethan eased the door shut behind him, careful not to disturb Aseal, who was probably already fast asleep. Peeping through the crack to Aseal's room, Ethan saw him sprawled across the bed with his headphones still on, faint beats leaking out of his earphones. The room smelled like leftover pizza and the faint trace of something herbal. It was familiar, comfortable, exactly what Ethan needed after the evening's study.

Opening the door to his room, glanced over at his desk where his Bible sat, tucked between his journal and a few random textbooks. He'd left in such a rush for class earlier that evening, forgetting to grab both. The Bible and the journal had stayed behind, not knowing he would need both, but there was no real use crying over spilled milk. Besides, his mind was still buzzing from what Ruth had shared during the study, and he couldn't wait to sit down and really *dive in*.

Ethan walked over to his desk, flicked on the small desk lamp, and pulled both items toward him. His fingers brushed the leather cover of his Bible, the edges worn from frequent use. He opened it to John 1, the chapter they had studied tonight.

He hadn't had the chance to fully process everything Ruth had said. He had been too wrapped up in the moment, too caught up in the flow of the group, the way Mita seemed so lost in thought after everything was said. But now, alone with his thoughts, he could hear the words echoing in his mind. *"In the beginning was the Word..."*

Ethan set his journal beside his Bible, cracked it open before taking a deep breath. It was late, later than he'd intended to stay up, but his heart felt stirred. He couldn't wait to dig deeper into the Word, to understand it for himself, to let the Holy Spirit guide him into a fuller understanding of what it meant for his life.

He started with the first few verses of John 1, the ones that had stood out to him in the study:

"In the beginning was the Word, and the Word was with God, and the Word was God."

Jesus, the Word, was with God *from the beginning*. Ethan paused, running his hand through his hair as the weight of it sank in. *The Word was God.*

The thought felt vast. Jesus wasn't just a part of God's plan that happened to take form in human history; He had always *been*. He was present before the world began, shaping all of it. How could something so vast, so eternal, be tied so intimately to his own life? Jesus wasn't some figure locked in history; he wasn't just a part of creation. He was the Creator. He had been there all this time, bringing order and life into existence. He was foundational, from before time even existed.

Ethan jotted down some thoughts in his journal, trying to make sense of it all.

"Jesus as the Word, the eternal God who holds the fabric of the universe in place. Through Him, everything exists. Nothing is made without Him. That's mind-blowing. This isn't just a man who lived. This is God in the flesh, before the beginning of time."

Ethan flipped to Genesis and read the first verses, then back to John, and he felt something shift in his heart. It was so beautiful how Jesus Christ, the Creator of the universe, was reaching out to him, and how he made Himself known, coming into the world He had formed.

He closed his eyes for a moment, imagining the vastness of it, the scope of it, and his heart felt both humbled and amazed. It was hard to fathom the depth of what that meant.

Then, he moved on to verse 4:

"In him was life, and the life was the light of men."

It struck him. Life itself, *true* life, was found in Jesus, not just in existence, but in a deeper, more meaningful sense. The light that Jesus carried wasn't just about shining brightly in the darkness of the world. It was about a *life* that could not be extinguished, a life that conquered even death.

Ethan thought about how easy it was to get lost in the distractions of daily life, how the weight of school, relationships, and the confusion of figuring out his purpose often clouded his vision. But Jesus, the Word, the Creator, was the source of the true life he longed for. And this light, it wasn't just about external circumstances. It was something internal, something *within* that could guide him through the darkness of the life *he* lived.

He scribbled more notes in his journal, the words flowing easily as he meditated:

"Jesus is the life. The life we're all searching for. The peace that we crave in the chaos. His light is the hope we need. It's not a light that can be extinguished by the things of this world."

He couldn't help but smile at the truth of it. It was something he had always known in a way, but tonight, it was brought across with more clarity and boldness. It felt like the pieces were aligning correctly.

After hours of reading, reflecting, and praying, he turned to the last section he had marked earlier, verses 6-8:

"There was a man sent from God, whose name was John. He came as a witness, to bear witness about the light, that all might believe through him. He was not the light, but came to bear witness about the light."

The role of John the Baptist stood out to him now. John was called to prepare the way for Jesus, to point to the light but not be the light himself. That was his purpose. It wasn't about drawing attention to himself, but pointing others to Jesus.

And in a way, that was a calling that Ethan felt for his own life. It wasn't about being perfect or having it all figured out. It was about living as a witness to the light. About allowing his life, his actions, his words, and the way he navigated his struggles to point back to Jesus.

It wasn't just about knowing the light existed. It was about *living* that light out in a world that so often felt dark and lost.

He paused, took a deep breath, and prayed softly:

"God, I want to understand this more. I want to let Your light shine through me. Help me see what it means to live as a witness, to share the hope I have in You. Guide me, Holy Spirit, and help me be more like Jesus in every area of my life. Let this light fill me up and spill over into the world around me. In Jesus name, Amen."

He sat there in the quiet of his room for a few more moments, letting the words of the prayer settle. He didn't have all the answers yet. But he felt a renewed sense of purpose, a deeper understanding of the Word that had come to life in a way he hadn't expected.

As he closed his Bible and journal, sliding them gently to the corner of his desk, he realized the hours had slipped by faster than he thought. It was nearly 3 a.m., but somehow, he felt more awake than ever. Ultimately, the light he had been reading about had started to work its way deeper into his heart than before.

Chapter 17: A Morning in Motion

❧❧❧

The soft hum of early morning was a gentle invitation for Ethan to rise from the quiet cocoon of his bed. With a glance at his clock, he saw he had a few hours before his afternoon classes for the weekend. Perfect. It had been a while since he had taken a proper morning jog, and with the way his mind was still buzzing from last night's study, he knew it would help clear his thoughts. It was a chance to pray, to center himself, to just let his feet hit the pavement and talk to God as he went.

He pulled on his favorite athletic gear: a comfortable hoodie and joggers, a pair of running sneakers, and, of course, his headphones. He slipped his miniature journal into his pocket because he had both just in case something came to mind during a run. It wasn't that he expected divine revelations whenever he went on his jogs, but after last night's study, he was open to whatever God might whisper into his.

Stepping outside, he inhaled the crisp morning air. The campus was just waking up, quiet but full of promise. The buildings were still casting long, slanted shadows from the rising sun. Ethan fell into a comfortable rhythm, letting his feet pound against the pavement as his thoughts turned to God.

"Thanks for today, Lord," he started his prayer, breathing steadily. "Thanks for the study last night, for Mita, for the weird kid with attitude yesterday, and for the club. I don't know what's ahead, but I trust You've got it in hand. Help me keep my eyes open to where You want me to go. In Jesus' name, amen."

As he jogged through the quiet streets of the campus, he thought about his life, the friends he had made so far, and the opportunities—both the ones he'd been given and the ones he hadn't. He wanted to move forward; he just wasn't sure exactly where that forward led.

He turned the corner, heading towards the arts department, where Aseal usually had his morning classes. Ethan had yet to explore much of the campus; he'd been so focused on the routine of classes, dorm life, and getting through the basics of college that he hadn't taken time to roam. But he figured a little adventure wouldn't hurt today, especially if he could find Aseal.

As he jogged along the building's stone steps, the sound of voices caught his attention. Shouting, but not in anger, more like...commands meant for guidance leaking from near the empty entryway of the art building....

".....Be *more empathetic! Feel more! Softer eyes, softer! Please!*"

Curious, Ethan slowed his pace and came to a stop outside the door. Peeking in, he saw a small group of students practicing a scene for what looked like a drama piece. He was given the view of the back entrance at the front of the room, just behind the last row in the audience. The room was a large, yet intimate thrust theater with a polished wooden floor, with adequate seating for an audience, and a few lights flickering overhead. The atmosphere in that space felt alive and electric, watching them from where he stood.

A voice rang out again, this time with more authority, but still warm: "*Longing gaze, longing... Look at him like he's the last thing that has your affection.*"

Ethan blinked, a bit surprised by the intensity of the directions. He leaned in slightly closer, drawn in by the energy in the room. The male student acting alongside his female counterpart were on stage, and from the looks of it, the director was speaking to the male student. He was being told to soften his gaze when he looked at his scene partner, as if she were his everything. The scene seemed filled with desire? Need? Love?-

Before he could finish his thought, his eyes drifted to the woman directing the actors; his heart gave a jolt.

It was her.

Anika.

The girl from the dorm's common building. The one with the vibrant purple hair, who had caught his attention without even trying.

She stood at the front of the room; he could only catch a glimpse of her profile before her back was turned to him. Hands on her hips, her eyes sharp but gentle, guiding the actors with an intensity that was both alluring and intense at the same time. Her features were all sharp angles and soft curves; her eyes, for the brief second he caught sight of them, were twinkling with the energy of someone who knew exactly what they were doing. Her purple hair framed her face perfectly, and the way she moved, graceful but confident, left Ethan momentarily breathless. She wasn't just directing; she was *living* in the moment. It was like the room itself was caught in the pull of her presence.

As the actors paused for a break, Anika turned to talk to someone else. Ethan, still standing at the door, caught her eye.

And then, *she waved.*

He blinked. *Did I look like a stalker standing here?* The sudden thought popped into his head

A second later, she was jogging toward him, her smile a little too mischievous for him to ignore; nothing about her could be easily ignored. She slowed as she approached him, still breathing a little heavily from her mini run up the stairs in the aisle from the stage.

"Hey, you," she said, her voice warm and genuine. "Fancy seeing you here. You stalking me?"

Nailed it, he thought

Ethan laughed, slightly caught off guard. "Stalking you? No way. I was just....well, I was jogging, and then I heard all the commotion in here."

She raised an eyebrow. "Commotion? This *is* art, my friend. It's passion, it's heart, *it's* life."

He chuckled again. There was something about the way she spoke, so effortlessly confident in her passion. She was the kind of person whose zeal was engraved in her bones, which was unwarrantedly attractive to Ethan.

"You're doing an amazing job," he added. "I mean, it's really impressive, watching you lead this. It's like... you're totally in your element."

Anika smiled, her expression softening. "Thanks. That means a lot, really," she said, looking up at him for a second longer than necessary. before breaking eye contact, turning back to gesture to the scene behind her as if also taking in the sight. "Honestly, I live for moments like these. My favorite part of all of this is getting people to feel something real, something they didn't think they could do. It's like... magic."

Ethan nodded, watching her closely. "I can tell. It's contagious, honestly. I kind of want to jump in and be part of it."

"Well," she said with a teasing smile, "if you're feeling inspired, I could always use an extra hand." Her eyes glinted mischievously. "But I'm guessing you're more of a spectator? "

Ethan raised his eyebrow in mock defense. "I'm more of a... *cheerleader*."

"Good choice," she said, still smiling. "It's a *fun* job. And believe me, I could use all the encouragement I can get around here."

They both laughed. Ethan noticed how her entire demeanor shifted when she was in this environment; she was confident but also genuinely *kind*. It made her even more magnetic, in a way he hadn't expected and didn't want.

"I actually came here to look for my friend," he said, trying to focus now. "Aseal. Do you know him? He has a class in the arts building this morning."

Her eyes brightened at the name. "Aseal? Oh yeah, I know him; everyone knows Aseal by now. He's cool. That guy is always in a good mood. I haven't seen him around yet today, though."

"I don't really know where to look for him," Ethan admitted, shrugging, still looking at her, hoping he doesn't come off as a creep, but he couldn't draw his eyes from her face but managed to pull his gaze from her before continuing. "Still getting used to the campus. I should probably—"

Before he could finish, he heard a whistle from above. He looked up, half-expecting to see someone else.

"Aseal?" he called out, recognizing the familiar face from above.

From the balcony, Aseal waved down at him, grinning widely. "Yo, Ethan!

Is that you?"

"Who else would it be?" Ethan answered,

"Romeo?…" Looks like you've got company," Aseal said, now leaning against the upstairs railing, looking down at both of them. "See what I did there? No? Ethan, dude, if you're going to flirt with theater, at least know what's in production."

Anika snickered, clearly catching on to what was happening.

Ethan rolled his eyes, laughing. "You're gonna tease me now? Really?"

"Oh, you've got a *lot* of teasing coming your way, young man," Aseal called back. "But first, come up here; I have something to show you. Anika, could I borrow your boyfriend?"

"I mean, he's your friend," she said, rolling her eyes, but the smile on her lips was definitely not as discreet as she thought it was.

Ethan tried not to read into what had just happened and said his goodbye to Anika and made his way up the stairs to join his friend.

Later that Morning:

After a quick shower back at the dorm, Ethan felt ready. His mind felt more focused, but his thoughts kept drifting after the brief but significant encounter with Anika. He shoved those aside before diving into his Bible study, reflecting on the night before, and finished preparing for his classes.

Before heading out, he said a quiet prayer—*"Lord, protect me today. Help me stay focused in class, and keep me on the path you want me to walk. Not my will but yours be done, in Jesus' name. Amen.*

Then, with a deep breath, he grabbed his bag and left his dorm, feeling lighter and a little more hopeful. Whatever today held, he was ready.

Chapter 18: A Quiet Peace and New Beginnings

Mita returned to her dorm room after the Bible study that night feeling... different. There was a sense of calm that she hadn't experienced in a while, as something deep inside her had shifted. She closed her room door behind her and leaned against it for a moment, just breathing. Then, with a deep exhale, she walked over to her desk, pulled out her journal, and opened it to a fresh page. The words from John 1 were still fresh in her mind, and she wanted to capture everything before it slipped away.

She grabbed her highlighter and flipped through her Bible, finding John chapter 1. She could still feel the warmth of Ruth's voice, the way she spoke about the light shining in the darkness, about Jesus being the Word that existed from the very beginning.

The Word became flesh and dwelt among us. Mita marked that verse immediately, tracing the highlighter slowly over the words as if sealing them into her heart.

She paused after that. There was so much that had stood out to her, so much to consider. She fought the urge to highlight the entire chapter; after all, it was all meaningful, wasn't it? But then she reminded herself that highlighting everything wouldn't help her focus on the most important truths. Instead, she picked a few other verses, ones that seemed to speak directly to the state of her heart, like when it talked about Jesus bringing life and light, and the verse where the darkness couldn't overcome the light.

When she was done marking the verses, she leaned back in her chair and closed her eyes for a moment. She felt something stirring deep inside her, something she couldn't quite name, but it felt like hope, like peace.

God, show me Your way. Guide me, in Jesus name, amen," she whispered silently.

She prayed quietly, talking to God about everything that had been weighing on her heart: her dreams, her fears, her doubts. And then, she did something she hadn't done in a long time: she rebuked the darkness. The things that haunted her thoughts, the shadows that lingered around her at night. She didn't want any part of them anymore.

"I rebuke the kingdom of darkness, in the name of Jesus," she prayed firmly, her voice steady. *"I close every door I've opened, knowingly or unknowingly. I take authority over every thought and feeling that's not from You and bind them and send them back to the pits of hell. Fill me with Your peace, God, and surround me with Your light in Jesus name, amen."*

She felt the weight lift slightly after she said that. Her shoulders felt lighter, like a burden had been taken off her. The tension in her body, the knots in her stomach, began to unravel.

By the time she finished praying in the name of Jesus, she felt a deep peace. The kind of peace she hadn't felt in a while. There was no nightmare looming over her. No fear. Just quiet, still peace.

She went to bed feeling safe, something that had become rare for her lately. For what felt like centuries, Mita fell asleep without the terror of nightmares chasing her. She slept through the night, wrapped in the quiet comfort of God's presence.

The next morning, Mita woke up feeling more rested than she had in weeks. She took a deep breath, looking up at the ceiling of her dorm room, and, with a smile, said a quick prayer to start the day: *Lord, cover me in the blood of Jesus Christ. Keep me safe today; protect my heart and mind and my way and my feet today. Guide me in everything I do in Jesus name, amen.*

Her first class of the day was a digital marketing workshop, and honestly, it went pretty well. She found herself actually understanding the material. She wasn't scrambling to catch up or pretending she understood what was going on. She felt engaged, and when the professor asked a question, she raised her hand, offering her thoughts. It was a small victory, but it felt big to her.

After class, Mita was walking across campus to her next class, Academic Writing, when she heard her name called. She turned, surprised but not shocked to see Reed.

"Hey, Mita!" Reed grinned at her from a distance and made his way toward her, his hands shoved into the pockets of his denim jacket. His curly hair was a little messy, but somehow it only made him look more laid-back, more approachable. "I didn't think we would walk together for class. What good deed did I do for such luck?" he said, grinning with his carefree demeanor on full display. When she didn't respond, he continued, "I'm messing with you, what's up? How was your week?" he added playfully, bumping her shoulder.

She smiled. "Oh, it was great, thanks for asking," she said, a calm silence spreading between them before she added, "I guess we might have more run-ins like this, since we both have this class on Saturdays?"

Reed's eyes scanned her for a moment, an eyebrow quirking up. "Something's different about you today... You're glowing, spill. What's up?"

Mita chuckled nervously. "Glowing? Maybe I just got a good night's sleep for once."

. "Uh-huh, sure." Read replied, narrowing his eyes tilting his head to the side. "Honestly, you do look *way* more cheerful than usual. What happened? Did you finally break free from the shackles of sarcasm?"

Mita laughed, rolling her eyes. "I don't know about all that. But I am feeling better, I guess. You could say I'm trying to focus on... different things."

Reed grinned, clearly enjoying this interaction. "Different things, huh? What kind of different things?"

Mita hesitated, wondering if she should dive into it. The last thing she wanted was to get too personal with Reed. But there was something about his easy-going energy that made it hard to resist.

"I don't know… just, you know, focusing on positivity and… faith," she said, unsure of how much she wanted to share.

Reed's eyebrows shot up, surprised. "Wait, hold up—faith? You're telling me you're on the 'faith train' now?"

Mita shrugged, looking at the ground for a moment. "I mean… yeah. I don't know what it all means yet, but I've been feeling… different. Like things are starting to make sense."

Reed studied her for a moment. "Okay, okay. I like this. You know, I've heard that people who get closer to Jesus end up feeling better about life, feeling more peaceful… maybe that's what's going on with you?"

Mita's heart skipped a beat at his words. She wanted to ask him about himself, about his faith or his perspective on all of it, but before she could speak, the bell for class rang, cutting the moment short.

"Well, I guess we're in this together. Let's see what this lecture's all about," Mita said with a smile as they walked toward the classroom.

The class began, and midway through the 1 hour, the professor explained that there would be a group project. Mita and Reed exchanged a glance when he mentioned that students would be working in pairs. And not to her surprise, the professor assigned Mita and Reed to work together.

Reed's grin widened as he looked at her profile, bracing his head in his hands. "Looks like you're stuck with me. You good with that?"

Mita shrugged, casting a sideways glance at him. "I guess I'll survive. But no distractions, alright, Matt Rife? We've actually have to get this work done."

"Distractions?" Reed teased, reaching out to take a few strands of her hair into his grasp before brushing it behind her shoulder. "Who said anything about distractions? I'm just here to get the project done and look good while doing it."

Mita rolled her eyes, but she couldn't help but smile at his sense of humor.

The professor gave the class their project topic: the pair was supposed to write a research essay on the effects of digital media on consumer behavior. Mita wasn't exactly thrilled about the topic, but at least she had Reed to work with.

"The deadline is in two weeks today," the professor announced, and Mita took a deep breath, asking God for patience.

Two weeks?! How was that humanly possible? Does he think I have no life or other classes?

"We'll meet up and figure out what to do," she said to Reed, who was already scribbling down notes, probably thinking of how he could turn this project into some kind of joke.

As the class ended, Odessa, who was also in this class, got up quickly and walked over to a girl she was paired with. Mita and Reed were left standing there waiting for her, the hallway buzzing with students leaving class.

"So, coffee tomorrow?" he asked, his tone light but suggestive.

Mita raised an eyebrow, skeptical, at his sudden diligence. "You actually want to meet up and work on it this weekend?"

Reed's grin crossed his arm over his chest, looking down at her directly. "Oh yeah. It's only two weeks that can pass in the blink of an eye, and …I'm in it for the coffee *and* the project, of course. But we can make it fun, right? I mean, *I* will be there, so that's a given."

Mita couldn't help but laugh at his cockiness. "We'll see tomorrow."

"Tomorrow," Reed confirmed, winking at her.

With a smile, Mita nodded before turning away. She did not bother to wait for Odessa, as her next class was on the other side of campus, and besides, she had Reed as company.

Mita made her way to her next destination for the day, but she couldn't help but feel a little excited for tomorrow, as the thought of working with Reed doesn't seem to be so bad after all.

Chapter 19: Sunday Surprises and New Connections

Sunday morning came with a peaceful rhythm. Mita woke up early, feeling rested and at ease. She spent the next hour with God, reading through her Bible and reflecting on the verses she'd highlighted in John 1. The words about the Word becoming flesh, about the light that shines in the darkness, seemed to grow deeper in her heart each time she read them. The peace from the Bible study still lingered, like a warm blanket around her.

After her quiet time with the Lord, she made her way to the kitchen, curious to see if Amerei was awake yet. As she stepped into the bright, sunlit space, she spotted Amerei, her now-best friend and roommate, dancing and humming along to a song playing on her speaker. Mita paused for a moment, watching her friend sway with such joy, her short curly hair swaying with each beat. The kitchen was never without the happy, carefree energy that Mita always admired in Amerei.

"Morning!" Mita called over the music, a smile tugging at her lips.

Amerei spun around, eyes sparkling. "Hi, Mita! Good morning," she grinned. "You'll never guess what's on my itinerary today!" Her words rushed out like she couldn't contain them any longer.

Mita raised an eyebrow, intrigued. "Try me."

Amerei giggled like a schoolgirl, her voice a mix of excitement and disbelief.

"Okay, so you remember that hot guy, the math TA, Merrick Hughes? You told me about a while back, the one who looks like he stepped out of a Vogue magazine cover shoot?"

Mita's eyes widened. "Yeah, *that* guy. The walking model. What about him?"

"He asked me out! Like, officially asked me out. We're going out today at 3!" Amerei bounced on her toes, her face practically glowing.

Mita couldn't help but smile, genuinely happy for her. "What?! That's crazy amazing! I'm so happy for you! But wait, don't mean to be a party pooper, girl, but be careful, okay? remember to share your location with me at all times, just in case."

Amerei's smile faltered slightly, but she nodded in agreement. "Yeah, yeah. I'll be careful. But I'm so excited! I'm really looking forward to it."

"Good! But don't forget, Hot or not, always trust your instincts, alright? And have fun, enjoy yourself. And tell me *everything* when you get back."

Mita grabbed a seat at the kitchen counter, her mind racing with all the excitement Amerei was feeling. "I'm actually heading out to meet Reed in a little bit. We have a group project together," she said casually, knowing it would pique Amerei's interest.

"Oh, yeah? Who else is going to be there? Andromeda? Odessa?" Amerei asked, giving her a knowing look, placing down a plate in front of Mita.

Mita shook her head and thanked her for breakfast. "Nah. Just me and Reed. It's a paired-up project, and Andromeda isn't in my class, and Odessa's paired with someone else." she answered before lowering her head in prayer to say grace.

Amerei raised an eyebrow but remained silent, giving Mita time to finish her prayer before continuing. "Ohh. So no one else is going to be there. *Just* you and Reed?" She smirked playfully, swatting Mita's arm across the kitchen island.

Mita rolled her eyes, her cheeks flushing. "Oww and yes, *just* Reed and me. We're working on a *research essay*. Nothing to see there," she said, holding her probably bruised arm.

Amerei's grin grew wider. "I see. I see. So it's just a *study* date, huh?"

Mita gave her a pointed look. "It's not like that. We're working on a project together. Simple as that."

Amerei leaned forward, bracing herself against the kitchen counter, narrowing her eyes at Mita. "Hmm, sure. You and Reed, all alone... I saw how he was looking at you during the student council event, and how you two clicked during that treasure hunt. There's definitely something there."

Mita crossed her arms, trying to remain unfazed, but the thought of Reed still lingered in the edge of her thoughts. "It was a team thing; we *had* to click. It's nothing like what is going through your head, alright, Miss Matchmaker."

Amerei laughed and rolled her eyes. "Okay, okay. We'll see how 'nothing' it is after you both have coffee and do some *research* together. Let me guess, you're wearing your usual 'too-cool-for-school' style, right?"

Mita smirked. "Well, yeah. Wait a minute, what's wrong with the way I dress? Too cool for school? That's lame!"

"Nothing at all, but *I* want to help. You know how we're total opposites in style, right?" Amerei asked, twirling a finger through her hair. "It's obvious you two aren't *just* meeting up for a group project, and you want to show up looking like a slouch?"

Mita blinked. "A slouch?! I think I dress just fine, thank you very much, and we are meeting up because of the project," Mita said, slightly offended but amused.

Amerei snickered. "Oh, of course, honey, I'm not saying it's bad, just that it's... well... not exactly 'make-a-good-impression' material. Ah, ah, ah, let me lend you something from my closet. It'll balance out your vibe and keep it cool. Trust me."

Mita's mouth dropped open. "Oh no. I know what this is. You want to dress me up so that Reed thinks I'm, what? Desperate or something?"

Amerei's laughter was melodic as she waved a hand dismissively in the air. "No, no, no! Not at all. Just want to help you look... I don't know, a little more *stylish*, but still 'Mita'."

Mita shook her head, but relented. "Fine, fine. Pick out a top. But only a top. I'm not turning into you, okay?"

Amerei clapped her hands, jumping up to grab a few things from her closet. She returned holding a flowy, lavender blouse, soft and feminine but with a relaxed, casual vibe that still screamed style. It had delicate details at the collar and sleeves, with a slight ruffle at the edges, the kind of top that looked effortless yet chic.

"You're going to look amazing in this. Just trust me," Amerei said, handing the top to her friend.

Mita looked at it and then back at Amerei. "Alright, alright. But I'm keeping my pants and sneakers. Don't even think about it."

Amerei laughed. "Deal. You're welcome!"

Mita quickly showered and changed into the blouse and paired it with her usual slim-fit jeans and white sneakers, comfortable yet stylish. She looked in the mirror, adjusting the top, and nodded. "Okay, I admit it. This actually works. You know what you're doing, Amerei."

"Of course I do," Amerei grinned, giving her a wink. "Now go out there and have fun with your *study date*."

Mita grabbed her bag, checking her phone one last time. "Alright. You have fun with Merrick. And remember to share your location with me."

Amerei waved her off, already buzzing with excitement for her own date. "Will do! Enjoy yourself! And tell me everything when you get back!"

Mita made her way to the coffee shop to meet Reed, feeling a strange mix of nerves and excitement. She blamed it on Amerei for putting thoughts in her head. The day was warm, and the campus was buzzing with activity. She loved the feeling of stepping out into the world, especially when she was so sure of the direction she was heading.

When she arrived at the coffee shop, she spotted Reed immediately. He was sitting at a table by the window, already looking like he was in his element: comfortable, confident, and just... *Reed*. He looked up when she approached, giving her a small smile.

"Hey, you made it!" he said, his smile broadening. "Well, don't you look even more beautiful today?"

Mita raised an eyebrow, noticing how his stare lingered a little longer than it usually did. Was it the shirt? Did it make her look more... *put-together?*

"Thanks," she said, taking the seat across from him. "But actually, I think the credit goes to Amerei. She picked this top out for me."

"Ahh, so that's what's different today. But you look fine in whatever you usually wear, though. But if you are going to mirror some of her style to impress me, I won't complain, because that means I was on your mind all morning," Reed chuckled, taking a sip of his coffee. "I like it. It's... refreshing."

Mita rolled her eyes playfully. "You're not going to let me live this down, are you?"

He gave her a wicked grin. "I don't think I'll ever forget it. But alright, let's get to business. We've got a project to work on, right?"

Mita smiled. It wasn't a date, but there was something about Reed's easygoing nature that made the whole thing feel less like "work" and more like a hangout to Mita.

"Darn Amerei and her stupid assumptions," she thought

And with that, the coffee shop turned into their little meeting place; ideas flowed, research was done, and laughter bubbled between them as the hours passed.

As the sun started to set, Mita realized that maybe there was more to Reed than just a study partner, and again she blamed Amerei for these thoughts and her confusing feelings. But who knew? Maybe she was beginning to actually enjoy the connection between them more than she had expected.

Chapter 20: A Life in the Balance

The coffee shop was quieter now; the hum of low conversations and the clinking of cups in the background as Mita focused on her work was a wonderful ambiance, but her heart wasn't fully in it anymore, though. The project they were doing together, Reed and she, was slipping away, almost forgotten as she watched him consumed in his work. It was rare to see him other than carefree, laughing, or just carrying on with animated conversations, but in this moment, he was just so… *there*, so *present*. She tried to keep her focus on the work in front of her, but every time she glanced up, her eyes found him. Of course, he *was* sitting in front of her, but when her eyes saw him sitting there, they captured something different about him each time.

He had this way of looking at the world, like it was his to conquer. He was one of those people who always seemed to be in motion, even when sitting still. His hands danced as he talked, expressive and confident, drawing patterns in the air that matched the flow of his words. He was funny, his remarks always tinged with a sarcasm that Mita found disarmingly charming. And those smirks, my gosh. The kind of smirks that made it impossible not to be *aware* of him.

She felt a flutter in her chest each time he teased her, each time he caught her eye with that playful glint. He was *dangerous* in the best way, a little too easy to get lost in. And now, as the minutes passed and the weight of the day hung in the air, she couldn't stop thinking about him even though he was right in front of her.

Amerei had warned her. *You're starting to like him.* And for the first time, she had the urge to strangle her friend.

Mita had laughed it off, chalking it up to her imagination. She and Reed were just study partners, nothing more, because she didn't have the time for this to be anything more. But now? Now she wasn't so sure; maybe if the opportunity did present itself, she would be more amenable, but if it didn't, she wouldn't force something that was out of timing or, worse, not meant to be.

As they wrapped up their study session, the chatter in the coffee shop faded into the background. Mita's fingers tapped lightly on the table, her attention pulled once again to Reed's expressive face.

But then, the remnants of an argument in the corner of the shop caught her attention.

It was a couple, their voices rising above the murmur in the shop, causing everyone to glance sideways at them from time to time. The girl was saying something harsh, but Mita couldn't catch what she was saying, her voice tinged with anger and fear, while the guy shouted back, each word laced with bitterness. Mita could feel the tension in the air. People were now looking at them nervously as their volume started to rise in the shop, but no one was stepping in to intervene.

She glanced at Reed, who seemed to notice it too. He raised an eyebrow, then shrugged.

"Guess I'll go check it out, another damsel in distress needing my knightly duties," he said with a half-grin, realizing the exaggerated look she gave him as he went on. "It's not the first time I've played mediator."

Mita bit her lip. She wasn't sure what it was, but there was something about that moment that made her chest tighten. It wasn't just his words; it was the way he cared, the way he was willing to help out another girl in an

94

uncomfortable situation, and the way he took responsibility when things got out of hand that made Mita see him in an even more desirable light. She wasn't sure if she preferred that or not.

She watched him stand and walk over to the couple, his voice low but firm as he tried to reason with them. She felt a pang in her chest.

Why do I always let my emotions get ahead of me? she thought, her eyes fixed on his figure.

Reed was trying to calm the girl down, his hands up in a gesture of peace, his posture relaxed but assertive. Mita couldn't hear the words, but she could see the girl's tense shoulders gradually begin to loosen. She seemed to be listening. The guy, though, was a different story. His face was red, his eyes full of rage.

Suddenly, the guy shoved Reed.

Mita's breath caught in her throat. Seeing Reed stumble back, hitting the table behind him, made her heart constrict. The guy's voice boomed louder than before in the shop.

"You're not gonna tell me what to do, man! What are you, my dad?" the guy shouted, stepping forward aggressively.

Mita's eyes widened, her heart skipping a beat. Reed stood his ground, trying to keep the peace, but it was clear that the guy wasn't backing down.

Before Mita could process what was happening, the guy shoved Reed again, harder this time. Reed lost his balance and slammed into the table once again, knocking over the cups and sending papers flying.

"*Stop it!*" Mita heard herself shout before she even realized she'd spoken.

But the guy didn't stop. He shoved Reed once more.

Mita couldn't believe it. The atmosphere in the coffee shop shifted, the air thick with tension. Reed wasn't the kind of guy to back down. She knew that. But she never imagined he wouldn't fight back in a time like this.

And then—*it happened.*

Reed, once calm and composed, lost it. His face twisted into something fierce, something raw. Without warning, he lunged at the guy, knocking him back with a force that was both shocking and terrifying. The guy didn't even have a chance to react before Reed had him pinned against the wall, his body taut with anger.

Mita's hands gripped the table as she watched in horror. Her heart pounded in her chest.

The girl screamed.

And then something happened that Mita could never have anticipated.

The guy reached into his jacket pocket. It happened so fast. One moment, he was struggling under Reed's grip, and the next, he pulled out a knife.

Reed didn't see it coming.

PLAYLIST- HONESTLY,WE NEED JESUS BY TERRIAN

The guy lunged, and in a flash of silver, the blade sank deep into Reed's stomach.

Mita's scream echoed in the room.

Everything froze. Reed's eyes went wide with shock, and in disbelief, he released the guy. He looked down at the blood seeping from his side, the knife still lodged in his body. His hands shook as they hovered over the wound, seeming like his body was finally realizing what was happening. His legs gave out, making him collide with the floor with such a loud thud, landing on the wound, further sinking the knife into him.

"*No...*" Mita whispered, her voice breaking. She rushed forward without thinking, dropping to her knees beside him, her hands shaking as she rolled him fully on his back, pressing down on the wound around the knife that was still lodged in him. Blood oozed through her fingers, warm and sticky. She tried to hold it in, but it was impossible.

"Reed," she whispered, her voice choked with emotion. "Reed, stay with me."

But his eyes, his eyes were losing their focus. The smirk that had so often been there, the teasing light in his gaze, was gone. His face was pale, and his breathing was ragged.

The girl who had been arguing with him now stood frozen, a look of horror on her face. Her boyfriend, now unconscious, lay in a heap on the floor. The crowd around them stood still, paralyzed, unsure of what to do.

Mita's hands trembled as she pressed harder against Reed's wound. "Please, don't leave me," she sobbed. "Please, Reed."

But Reed, his eyes hazy, managed to murmur, "You know… you're really beautiful, Mita," his voice slurred, as though he was somewhere far away. "I really… like your shirt… but I really like you… more…"

Mita's heart shattered. Tears streamed down her face as she pressed harder on the wound, trying to stem the blood flow. She didn't know what to do; nothing was working. The blood was seeping through her fingers, through her pants, soaking her into a cold, stark reality. The world around her felt like it was falling apart.

His breathing was slowing, his hand weakly gripping hers.

"Please, Reed," she sobbed, her voice breaking as she cried out. "Please stay with me. Please don't go."

She looked around desperately, but no one was helping. The people who had been mere spectators moments ago were now too frozen, too paralyzed by fear. Mita pulled out her phone with shaking hands, trying to unlock it, her fingers too slick to get a grip. In desperation, she pressed the power button, sending out an SOS message to her emergency contacts. She didn't care if her mom would give her a lecture. She didn't care about anything else right now.

"Help me… please," she cried into the empty space around her.

Reed's hand slipped from hers, but just before it fell, he looked at her one last time, a weak smile tugging at the corner of his lips. His eyes locked with hers, his voice barely a whisper, "I'm sorry… I should've."

And then his eyes closed, and Mita's heart broke into a million pieces.

"*No!*" she screamed, but it was too late. Reed was slipping away from her.

She couldn't stop him.

She couldn't stop the blood.

And as the paramedics arrived, rushing to his side, Mita sat there, frozen. Bloodied. Broken. Her whole world is slipping away with every heartbeat.

And as the paramedics worked on Reed, she looked around the coffee shop, remembering how just a few minutes ago they had been sitting together, laughing, studying. Now, everything was wrong. The world felt unfair, and all she could think was how *unbelievably unfair* it was that Reed *of all people was* fighting for his life.

"Please," Mita whispered to the heavens, "please, God… save him."

The day had taken a turn that no one could have ever anticipated.

And as the paramedics moved Reed away, her body still frozen in place, Mita whispered between sobs, *"I need you, Jesus. Please. Please save him."*

Chapter 21: The Silence After the Storm

The world felt like it was moving in slow motion. Everything around Mita was muffled, distant, like she was underwater. The paramedics were taking Reed away, their hands working frantically, their voices filled with commands, but none of it reached her. She couldn't understand their words. She couldn't understand *anything* anymore.

Her eyes remained locked on the stretcher, on Reed's pale face, his body partially covered in blood, his eyes closed like he was already too far gone. Mita's hand was still outstretched, as if she could reach him, pull him back from wherever he was slipping away to. She wanted to scream, to cry out for him, but her voice was lost in the chasm of shock that had swallowed her whole.

Her knees felt like they were going to give out, but she didn't move. She couldn't. Every muscle in her body felt like it was made of lead, heavy and useless. She stared at the space where Reed had been; his absence from the spot where his blood was still on the floor made the whole situation feel more suffocating than anything. The reality of the situation was starting to set in, but it didn't feel real. It couldn't be real. Not *Reed*.

No, not him, her mind kept repeating, but there was nothing she could do to stop the truth from crashing down on her.

Mita glanced around the coffee shop, at the people who had been so oblivious only moments ago. Some were still standing frozen, others were awkwardly shifting, not knowing how to react. A few had begun whispering, talking in hushed voices, but none of it mattered. All she cared about was Reed, and in that moment, it felt like everyone else had faded into the background, like their lives didn't matter. All she wanted was him. All she needed was for him to be ok.

Her body trembled, as a sob finally broke from her throat, raw and gut-wrenching, as she slowly lowered herself to the ground, still covered in his blood, unable to tear her eyes away from the door through which the paramedics had carried him.

She had been *so* aware of him before, hadn't she? The way he moved, the way his eyes sparkled with that mischievous light. The way he'd made her feel, alive, seen, like she'd mattered. The flirtations, the jokes, the moments where he *chose* her in the midst of all the people. It had all felt so... *right*.

But now, it felt like her world had been ripped out from under her.

How could this happen?

Mita didn't even realize she was crying until her tears had blurred her vision. She couldn't stop. The floodgates had opened, and there was no turning back.

"Please, God..." she whispered between sobs. "Please don't take him. Don't take him from me. and if not from me, from this world, just please don't take him." Her voice cracked, and she felt her chest tighten, like it was closing in on her, suffocating her. She could feel her heart breaking into pieces, each one sharper than the last. The pain—*the raw, unbearable pain-* was so much that she didn't know how to handle it. She couldn't breathe.

Her mind raced; a few memories she had of Reed flashed before her eyes like a slideshow: the way he'd smiled at her, the playful banter they shared, his kind heart, the way he always seemed to know how to make everything and everyone around him feel better, even on their worst days. It was too soon in the semester for this. He was *so full of life*, so alive. And now... now he was fighting for it.

Mita's hands, still covered in his blood, shook as she tried to gather her thoughts. She didn't know what to do with herself. She didn't know how to move forward. All she could think about was the sound of his last words.

"You're really beautiful, Mita. I really like your shirt, but I really like you more..."

That *wasn't* how it was supposed to end. That wasn't how it was supposed to be.

She had so many questions for him. So many things she still wanted to say, but now, now it was too late; they had a group project to hand in together, darn it.

Through her haze of tears, Mita heard the sound of footsteps approaching. She didn't look up. She couldn't. She couldn't face anyone right now. She wanted to be alone with her pain, alone with the grief that was already threatening to swallow her whole.

But someone sat next to her. It was Odessa. She wrapped her arms around her, pulling mita into a tight hug.

"Shhh... it's okay, Mita," she whispered, her voice soft but as unsteady as Mita felt shrouded with emotion. "We're going to be okay. Just breathe, okay? Just breathe."

Mita's sobs only grew louder. She couldn't stop herself. She couldn't hold it in. The grief was too much. She needed to scream, to cry, to let it all out.

But Odessa didn't let go. She just held her tighter, offering her the comfort she couldn't give herself.

"I can't... I can't do this. He's... he's... *gone*, Dessa He's gone..." Mita choked, her words barely comprehensible through her sobs.

"No. Mita," Odessa said shakily but determined. "He's not gone. He's still fighting. You hear me? He's still fighting."

The words should have offered some comfort, but they didn't. Mita could feel the distance between what she wanted to be true and the painful reality of what was actually happening. She didn't want to hear it. She didn't want hope. Not yet. She wasn't ready to hope again, not after watching Reed's life, his blood spill onto the floor through her finger.

"I... I don't know how to... I don't know how to go back to how it was, not..." Mita whispered, broken. "...not after what happened in my arms, to him, in front of me. I don't know if I can."

Odessa didn't respond immediately. She just held her, her presence a steady anchor in the storm.

After a long moment, Odessa spoke softly, her voice laced with love and sadness. "I'm not going to lie to you, Mita. It's going to be hard. And it's okay to feel lost, to feel like you don't know how to go on, heck, I feel lost right now." Odessa's voice broke, "But what I know is that you *will*. You'll get through this. You'll fight for Reed, we all will, even if he can't fight right now."

Mita wiped her face with her sleeve, still trembling, feeling the weight of the world on her shoulders. But Odessa was right. She had to keep pushing, keep fighting. For Reed. For herself. She couldn't let his fight be in vain. She had to *believe*.

"Don't you dare say goodbye to him, Mita," Odessa whispered, almost as though she could read her mind. "Not now. Not when he's still fighting for his life. You have to believe, look at me, okay? You have to. *For him.*"

Mita nodded, her tears still flowing, her body shaking with the weight of the moment.

"I don't know if I can," she whispered, her voice barely audible. "I don't know if I can keep fighting, much less start."

Odessa pulled back slightly, tears running down her own face, holding Mita by her shoulders, her eyes soft but determined.

"You *can*. You just have to take it one breath at a time. And you'll have me, you'll have all of us, *we'll be here for each other.*"

Mita clung to her friend, the only constant in the sea of chaos around her. But as the minutes dragged on, and the silence began to settle in after the chaos, after the campus police and the official police came and questioned her, one thought kept repeating in her mind:

What if it's too late?

And that was a question she wasn't ready to answer just yet.

Not when everything felt like it was slipping away.

The paramedics had taken Reed away, the police had left, and the coffee shop was slowly returning to some semblance of normal, though it was closing up for the day. But for Mita, nothing would ever be the same.

. . . .

The quiet beep of the machines was the only sound in the room as Mita sat beside Reed's bed. His pale face was the image of fragility, and for a moment, it felt like everything was suspended in time. His mother and sisters had left the room to give her some space, but Mita couldn't bring herself to move. Every part of her, every inch of her body, wanted to be there for him. She wasn't sure if he could hear her, but she couldn't help but talk to him anyway.

He was in surgery, and doctors said it went well. But, he was in a coma due to a lack of oxygen to the brain and may or may not have some minor damage; nothing was evident on the tests they ran. According to them, it would explain the coma.

They also said he had some underlying illness that contributed to his body going into sleep mode. The doctor described his coma as his body trying to repair and restore any possible invisible damage. But it's just all down to time, and if he was willing to wake up.

"Reed," she whispered, her voice hoarse. "I know you're in there. I know you're fighting. I need you to pull through this. Please. I need you to come back to us. We all do."

She gently took his hand in hers, her fingers trembling against his cool skin.

He was still alive. He was still here. That had to count for something.

The minutes dragged by like hours, and still, Reed didn't stir. Mita felt a heaviness in her chest, like the weight of the world was pressing down on her. It was too much. She had been through so much in these last few months, too many highs and too many lows. And now, with Reed here, struggling for his life, she didn't know how much more she could take.

Her thoughts wandered back to the coffee shop. To the fight. To Reed jumping in to stop the violence. It was just so *unfair*. He didn't deserve this. He was a good person. He was always so full of life, always making people laugh, always so free-spirited and carefree. He didn't deserve to be lying here in a hospital bed, unconscious, fighting for his life. The whole ordeal made her feel angry, but mostly… it made her feel helpless.

She took a deep breath, trying to steady herself.

This wasn't the time to fall apart. Not yet, at least.

Suddenly, there was a soft knock at the door, and Mita's heart skipped a beat at the sudden disturbance. She looked up to see Marcus, Reed's older brother, standing in the doorway, his expression unreadable. He looked tired, like someone who had been holding it together for too long and was finally starting to crack.

"Can I come in?" Marcus asked softly, his voice quiet as if he didn't want to disturb Reed's fragile state.

Mita nodded, gesturing for him to enter. "Of course."

He stepped inside, his eyes briefly glancing at Reed before settling on Mita. She could see the weight of his emotions in his gaze: anger, maybe pain, and even a hint of confusion. But there was something else, too. Something softer. His eyes flickered to Reed again, and for a brief moment, Mita thought she saw a flicker of hope there.

"I just spoke with the police," Marcus said, his voice rough. "They're still going through the footage from the coffee shop, trying rule intent or whatever. As if the intention wasn't clear as day." he finished but said the last part under his breath like he didn't mean it for anyone ears particularly.

Mita nodded, her throat tight.

"Do you need anything?" Marcus asked after a moment. "Is there anything I can do?"

Mita shook her head slowly, her hands still gripping Reed's. " Isn't that my line" Mita said finally looking at him, she saw a hint of a smile before it was lost under his mask of grief. "Just… just pray. That's all we can do right now. Just pray that he wakes up."

Marcus nodded silently, his lips pressing into a thin line. He walked over to the window, his back turned to Mita, she allowed her gaze to linger on him; she could see the tension in his posture, the way he was loosely holding himself together as if any at moment he might break. She couldn't even begin to imagine what it was like for him, for Reed's family. *This wasn't how it was supposed to be.*

The next few hours passed in a blur of soft conversations and worried glances. Mita could feel the hours stretching thin around her, every second feeling like an eternity.

At one point, Marcus left to speak with the doctors again, and Mita was left alone with Reed and his sisters, who had returned to the room some time back, and were both off sleeping on the couch in the corner, exhausted. The room felt overwhelmingly quiet, almost suffocating in its stillness. She squeezed Reed's hand again, willing him to wake up. To look at her and smile that smirky, confident grin of his wore. The same grin that had teased her and made her laugh a couple of hours ago.

But now, there was nothing but silence.

"Reed... please," she whispered, her voice catching in her throat. "You're too strong for this. You can't leave us now. Not like this."

A single tear slipped down her cheek, and she quickly wiped it away, frustrated with herself. She wasn't sure how much longer she could keep it together.

The door opened again, and Mita didn't look up. But the voice that spoke next made her heart stop.

"Are you Mita?"

It wasn't Marcus.

Mita slowly turned, her head spinning. Standing in the doorway was none other than Reed's mother. Her eyes were red-rimmed from crying. She looked tired, worn down by the events of the last few hours, but her gaze never wavered from Mita's.

"I just wanted to thank you," Reed's mother said softly, her voice trembling slightly. "For being there. For being with him at that time. It means more to us than you know."

I understand what she mean, but why are talking like he is already dead.

Mita didn't know what to say. She couldn't form the words that were appropriate for that moment. All she could do was nod, her throat too tight for anything else. She didn't deserve their gratitude. She hadn't done anything. All she had done was... sat there and watch it happened.

"It wasn't... wasn't anything, we were there to do a group project," Mita whispered, her voice barely audible. "I just... I just want him to wake up." her voice cracking on the last part.

Reed's mother's eyes softened, and she stepped into the room, her hand gently resting on Mita's shoulder. "I know," she said, her voice steady now. "We all do. But don't give up hope. As long as he's breathing, as long as he's fighting... there's still a chance."

Mita nodded, the words sinking in, but they didn't do much to ease the overwhelming feeling of dread in her chest. Reed was *alive*, but for how long? And would he be the same when he woke up?

"Thank you," Mita whispered, finally able to choke out the words.

Reed's mother smiled faintly, a tear escaping down her cheek. "You're family now," she said softly. "And we take care of our own."

That night, Mita couldn't sleep. She stayed in her dorm room, curled up in bed, but sleep didn't come. She kept thinking about Reed. Thinking about how much she wished she could take away his pain. How she wished she could make it all go away.

But all she could do was wait. And pray.

God, please don't take him from us.

Chapter 22: Moving Forward

The campus buzzed with the usual noise of students chatting in between classes, laughter echoing in the halls, and the faint shuffle of sneakers on the pavement outside. It was a typical day. Yet for Mita, nothing felt typical.

Since the stabbing, the days blurred into each other like smudges of ink on paper, her mind still grappling with the reality of what had happened. Reed's absence was like an empty space in the middle of her chest, one she couldn't quite fill. And yet, somehow, she had learned to breathe around it.

The hospital visits became part of her routine now; she'd leave after her classes, freshen up in her room, then head over there any time her schedule could afford. Something was soothing in the monotony of it, sitting by the reeds beside the side in the evenings. The beeping of the heart monitor, the soft shuffle of nurses' footsteps on the outside of the room in the corridors, and the low hum of fluorescent lights somehow became part of the background noise of her life.

She sat down next to Reed's bed one afternoon, the sun casting long shadows through the window. His face still looked so pale, his body still, seeming lifeless under the covers. The doctors had said that Reed could hear her, even though he couldn't respond, and Mita clung to that hope. She couldn't change the fact that he was comatose, but she could still talk to him and still share what she was learning.

She opened her Bible and flipped to Matthew 6.

"Therefore, I tell you, do not be anxious about your life..." Mita murmured quietly, her voice steady but filled with emotion.

As she read, she spoke the words like they were her own personal prayer. Like she was reminding herself, as much as Reed, that in this moment, she didn't have to have all the answers.

*"...***But seek first the kingdom of God and His righteousness, and all these things will be added to you.***"*

She closed her Bible and sat back, gazing out the window.

"Do you hear that, Reed? I don't know what God is doing. I don't. But I know He's here with us...with you. I trust that He's working in all of this somehow."

It was a prayer she'd learned to speak not just for Reed but for herself. She'd been doing a lot of that lately, speaking faith into the emptiness.

Maybe that's what faith is, she thought, *not knowing but still trusting, not understanding but still obeying.*

As the weeks passed, Mita slowly found herself adjusting to life again, like a clock finally clicking back into rhythm. She continued attending her classes, even though sometimes the weight of the world felt like it was pressing in on her chest. She saw the concerned looks from friends and classmates, but it didn't bother her as much as it used to.

Ethan, ever the faithful friend, made sure to check in with her during the breaks between classes. He'd smile, hands shoved deep into his pockets, and lean against the desk.

"How's Reed?" he asked one day, his voice soft with concern.

Mita smiled. It wasn't a smile filled with joy, but one that held a candle towards gratitude for his concern. "Still the same," she said. "I've been talking to him. Reading to him even."

Ethan nodded. "That's good. You know, I was thinking, maybe next time, I could go with you. I could pray with you. You shouldn't have to do this alone."

The offer was warm, and Mita appreciated it more than she could express. "Thank you, Ethan. However, I think I'm starting to be okay with it. The silence. I mean."

Ethan looked at her for a moment, searching her face, probably for any indication of deception, but must not have found none. he relented. Then he smiled that easy, kind smile that always seemed to make her feel just a little bit better. "That's good. I'm glad you're finding peace in the midst of this. We're all praying for him, you know?"

Mita nodded, her heart swelling. Ethan's faith had grown stronger, too, and it made her feel less alone in this journey. Every week, they met at the Christian fellowship gatherings, just like before.

"Isn't that exactly what I said?" Zyran grinned, leaning against the door frame of the study room Mita and Ethan occupied, his typical mischievous gleam in his eye. "You *did* bring the wrong notes to that one exam, figured you *would* need prayer so that *doesn't* happen again ."

Mita rolled her eyes, feeling the familiar warmth in her chest at his antics. Zyran had always been the one to try to cheer her up when things felt heavy lately. Even if it meant annoying her a little, when they first met, they never took a liking to each other, but now no one could know that if they didn't know them beforehand.

"I didn't bring the wrong notes," she argued, fighting back a smile. "You just *think* you know everything."

Zyran snickered. "I'm basically a walking encyclopedia. You should've listened to me!"

"And what would I do without you, Zyran?" Mita teased.

He shrugged, grinning. "Well, probably *not* pass your exams with flying colors."

Mita shook her head, the laughter bubbling in her chest. She was starting to feel like herself again.

"How's everything going with Merrick?" Mita asked one afternoon, after class let out, she spotted Amerei walking toward the student union. Amerei hadn't been hovering over Mita so much of late; she had taken Mita's advice to focus on herself and Merrick, though she always made sure to check in on Mita, at times.

"It's great," Amerei said, her voice warm with affection. "You know, it's still a little complicated, you know, ups and downs and differences, but we're getting there."

Mita smiled, nodding. "I'm glad. You deserve happiness, Amerei. Don't forget that."

Amerei smiled softly. "I don't plan to. But hey, how are you *really* doing lately? I don't know if you're a great actress with an amazing mask or if you are actually OK, so I want you to tell me honestly so that I don't assume you are well when, in fact, you're suffering behind closed doors."

Mita paused, considering the question. She'd been asked so many times if she was okay, but this time, she answered honestly.

"I'm healing," Mita said. "It's slow, but I'm getting there. I've learned a lot… about my faith and building it, about trusting God, about… letting go and giving it to him. It's not easy, but I am trying."

Amerei gave her a sideways look. "I'm glad you have your faith. Even if I don't get it, I'm glad it's helping you."

Mita appreciated that. Amerei might not have shared her faith, but she supported it. That meant more than Mita could ever put into words.

Mita walked into the hospital room, another day, feeling the familiar mix of emotions: hope, sorrow, and a quiet acceptance. Reed still hadn't woken up, but she hadn't stopped praying. And she hadn't stopped talking to him.

"Reed," she said softly, sitting in the chair beside his bed. "I'm still here. I'm not going anywhere. And so are you," she chuckled at herself, that last bit was kinda dark

She opened her Bible again, this time turning to Isaiah 59. As she read the words aloud, her voice calm but firm, she felt the strength of God's promises wash over her.

"Behold, the Lord's hand is not shortened that it cannot save, or his ear dull that it cannot hear…"

Mita knew that Reed couldn't respond, couldn't even move. But in the silence, she knew her faith was still growing. It was becoming something unshakable, something that could withstand the hardest of storms if she believed.

"Don't worry, Reed. God is working. And I'm going to keep trusting Him."

She leaned back in her chair, the weight of her textbooks heavy on her lap.

Exams were approaching, and she would study with Reed just like she had before, except now, they were in a hospital. Even though Reed was silent, even though life had taken a turn she hadn't expected, Mita knew that her journey was far from over. And she would walk it with faith, no matter how long it took.

It wasn't the life she'd imagined, but it was her life. And Mita was learning to live it with grace, faith, and a love that would never let go.

Chapter 23: Prayer, Paths, and Purple Hair

Ethan's Pov

The early morning air always felt different. Quiet, calm, like the whole world was still asleep, and I was the only one who had time to think. I'd always been a runner, keeping my mind clear with a prayer jog at dawn any morning that I could, but today, it wasn't just about clearing my head. I had more on my mind than usual.

Mita. She hadn't been herself lately. She hadn't been attending our Christian fellowship meetings much, and sometimes she didn't come to class. It's like she's disappearing slowly after that incident with Reed. And it wasn't just the fact that Reed was in a coma that had her distant. I knew there was something bigger at play. Something I couldn't figure out.

And so, I found myself out on a path on campus, running harder than usual, trying to run away from the knot of worry in my stomach.

"God, please take care of Mita," I whispered between breaths. *"I don't know what's going on with her, but she's hurting even if she is good at masking it. Please, help her find peace in all this. And if it is in your will, heal Reed. Lord, there is nothing impossible for you, and if we have you, we have all we need to make a mountain move in faith with the authority you have given us. Let your will be done on earth as it is in heaven. In Jesus name I pray, amen."*

I ran harder, as if my feet could outrun the worries plaguing me, but it only chased me down harder, twisting in my chest.

Eventually, I ended up near the art building. My feet stopped before I even realized it. It wasn't the usual path I ran, but my legs had taken me here, so I paused for a moment, catching my breath before heading toward the grand structure.

The Arts building had always felt peaceful. It was where I could find Aseal, and honestly, to be in the artist's space whenever I felt like I needed a break from everything was liberating past time. Walking past some of the showrooms and even the art gallery distracted my mind from the issues swirling in my head, and having a friend who does just that, paintings and art, and being able to sit down and watch him in his element whenever I could back in the dorm was exhilarating. Just watching his artistic skills flow through him onto the canvas was therapy in itself. But today, as I made my way into the building, there was no loud music blaring from practice rooms, no chatter from art students. It was quiet, eerily so.

I stepped inside, drawn to the familiar quiet corner where I had once found Aseal before, the literature nook at the end of the hall.

Instead of Aseal, I saw *her* again.

Her purple hair was the first thing that came into view.

Anika.

She was sitting by herself, her head tilted slightly as she stared out the window; more's the pity that I wasn't able to see the expression she wore as her back was turned to me. I hesitated for a moment, unsure whether I should interrupt her solitude, but before I could make up my mind, she turned and looked right at me as though she could sense she was being watched. She was momentarily stunned before waving me over. I made my way over to her, trying to hide how my soul was smiling in her presence.

"Hey," she said softly, offering a smile that was warm but tired.

"Hey," I replied, a little caught off guard by how peaceful she looked.

I wasn't sure if I should sit down, but my legs were sore from the run, and I figured the worst she could do was tell me to go away.

I sat down across from her, though not too close. I was still sweaty from my run and didn't want to make her uncomfortable.

She tilted her head and narrowed her eyes, giving me a small smile. "You're sitting too far away. Why?"

I let out a little nervous chuckle, rubbing the back of my neck, trying my best to avoid looking right at her. "Uh, because I'm sweaty," I admitted, feeling slightly embarrassed.

Anika's lips twitched, like she was holding back a full-on grin. "And you think I care about that?"

I hesitated at first before a seat two spaces from her, leaving enough room to fit another. "I guess not," I said, trying to keep my voice light.

"You're looking for something," she said after a beat, her voice calm but piercing, as she could read right through me. "Something's bothering you, Ethan. You wanna talk about it?"

I took a deep breath to think about it. It wasn't like I couldn't talk to Anika, she was one of the few people who didn't make me feel like I had to have it all figured out. Still, I didn't want to weigh her down with all of my worries, but the truth was, I couldn't shake the thought of Mita.

"I'm worried about Mita, one of my friends. You heard about the stabbing of a kid from our school. Both of them are in my class, not the perpetrator. I meant she was there when it happened. He was in her arms and since then..." I finally said, leaning back against the wall as I talked, really let the situation turn over in my mind. "She's been distant. Not always attending class, and not showing up for club meetings... She's been acting like she's carrying the world on her shoulders. And I know that is a traumatic experience for her, for anyone in her shoes. I just... I don't know how to help her. I am not sure if I'm being a good friend. I am really worried."

Anika's expression softened, and she turned her eyes to the window once more for a moment, like she was processing what I said. "You are an amazing friend, first of all," she said quietly, still looking out the window. "As you've said, it is a traumatic experience; we are unable to comprehend it as we ourselves didn't experience what she did, and even if we did, we are different; we can experience the same thing and cope and react differently, as one experience can affect many differently. So relax," she said, finally glancing back at him, "she is just trying to cope, to learn how to fit this into her life, and figure out how to move forward despite what happened. As onlookers, we are not helpful if we hover over her, asking her questions about how she is doing, when she may not even know herself, and with her not know how to answer, we kinda force her to give a casual 'yeah, I'm OK' response to not worry the people who care, so as not to be a burden when she isn't actually OK. People recovering from grief are fragile; one wrong word and they can shatter. So give her space, give her time," she continued, "she will get through this, she just needs time, and you just do what you do for her out of love and pray for her, OK?"

I couldn't help but feel a little relieved that Anika understood. She always seemed to get it, even when I felt like I was drowning in confusion.

"I just want her to know I'm here," I muttered, staring down at my hands. "But I don't want to push her if she's not ready to talk. You know? I don't even know what she's going through. I don't think she even wants anyone to know."

Anika looked at me, her expression thoughtful. "You're right," she said. "This Mita girl seems strong, but... that doesn't mean she's okay. Sometimes, people don't know how to reach out for help, especially when they're afraid of burdening others. What happened to your friend, Reed... It shook her up more than you probably know. But if she doesn't come out, you've got to respect that. You can't force her to heal on your timeline."

I nodded, a little embarrassed by how obvious the answer seemed when she said it out loud. I'd been so wrapped up in worrying about how to help her, I'd forgotten to just give her space.

"I'll do as you said, pray for her," I added. "I just... I don't know what else to do."

Anika's smile deepened. "Prayer's good. I've been praying too, you know," she said, squeezing my hand gently. "I know you're not alone in this. And neither is Mita. God works in mysterious ways, and He's always there."

I felt my chest tighten slightly, but in a good way. I hadn't realized how much I needed someone to say that until she said it.

I looked at her, really looked at her, for the first time in a long while. "Thanks, Anika. You have no idea how much that helps."

She gave me a small, encouraging smile, and the moment felt… right. She wasn't just a friend, not anymore. There was something else, something more that I couldn't quite put into words yet. Maybe it was the way she made me feel like I wasn't the only one with questions, with doubts. Maybe it was the quiet understanding between us, or the way she held my hand without saying much. But it felt like God was doing something here, too.

After a while, I cleared my throat, pulling myself back from my thoughts. "You should come to one of the meetings," I said, more confident now. "I'd really like it if you did. I think it might help. We'd be able to pray together, talk about faith, and… well, anything."

Anika raised an eyebrow, still holding my hand. "I'll think about it," she said after a long pause, her voice playful but soft. "I don't know if I'm ready for all that yet. But I'll consider it."

I couldn't help but smile. "That's better than a no," I said, leaning back against the wall, feeling lighter than I had all week. "You know, I think you'd be good for Mita. You've got this way of… calming people down."

Anika chuckled softly. "I guess we all need a little calm in our lives right now."

The next few weeks were a blur of finals, group projects, and surprisingly, growth. I didn't see Mita as often as I'd hoped, but I noticed the small changes. She started showing up at meetings again. Not every week, but more than she had been since the incident. And when she did come, there was a new sense of peace about her, like she was starting to trust that everything would be okay in time.

And in the midst of all of this, I found myself growing too. I kept praying. I kept asking, seeking, knocking, like it says in Matthew 7:7-12. And the more I prayed, the more I realized that the answers weren't always immediate, but they were always there.

"Ask, and it will be given to you; seek, and you will find; knock, and it will be opened to you."

The more I understood that, the more I felt my own faith deepening. I

116

didn't have to know how or when things would change. I just had to trust that God would open the doors when He was ready.

And He was doing it, even when I couldn't see it.

I wasn't alone. Mita wasn't alone. And neither was Anika.

Chapter 24: In the Quiet of the Storm

Coming home should've felt like a complete victory. She should've been extremely excited, bursting with joy to see her mom again, to step into the space that always felt like hers. But there was a heaviness that Mita couldn't shake. She felt it every time her mind wandered to her friend Reed. It had only been a little over a month since the stabbing. The memory of it still lingered like a bad smell, clinging to the air she breathed in her memories.

Mita couldn't stop replaying that night in her head: the panic, the helplessness, the evenings spent at his bedside. What if she could've done more? What if, somehow, she could've stopped it from happening? What if it had been her, not Reed? These thoughts had become like ghosts, haunting her every waking moment. She couldn't escape them, even if she tried to lose herself in the comfort of her mom's house.

Mita made her way to her room, closing the door behind her as if the walls could protect her from everything she was feeling. She sat down on the bed of her childhood, the quiet of the room almost suffocating. She had come home for Christmas after finals and had basically run out of her dorm without informing her roommate and her other friends that she was leaving. She'd just left, as if being in her room on that campus any longer would suck her very life force from her, so she ran when Joshua texted her to say he had arrived on her campus to bring her home for the holidays, only to drop her off and not spend it with her and Mom. The thoughts she believed she had escaped from on her campus seemed to have followed her back home. It was only the Christmas lights twinkling on the windowsill that brought some sense of peace.

She reached for her Bible, her fingers tracing over the lightly worn pages, and found herself in Matthew 11:28-30. She had opened to this passage countless times over the past few weeks, but each time, the words felt different.

"Come to me, all you who are weary and burdened, and I will give you rest. Take my yoke upon you and learn from me, for I am gentle and humble in heart, and you will find rest for your souls. For my yoke is easy and my burden is light."

Tears began to sting her eyes as the words sank in. *Rest for your souls.* She didn't even know how long it had been since her soul had felt at peace since the incident. She had been carrying too much weight, not just her own but Reed's and maybe even some of the world's. How could she keep carrying it all alone?

She closed her eyes, breathing in deep, and let herself *feel* in this moment. She wasn't responsible for Reed being in the hospital. She wasn't the one who had chosen the cruel path he had found himself on. And God wasn't punishing her for it, either. But somehow, she had convinced herself that maybe He was, that maybe her friend's pain was a consequence of her own failing in some way.

Mita's mind wandered to something she had learned in one of her theology classes back at school, how easy it was for people to convince themselves that bad things happened because they deserved it. Society was obsessed with the idea of punishment being tied to wrongdoings, but what if it wasn't that simple?

What if life were just messy? What if things happened, bad things, cruel things, because we lived in a broken world?

She thought about the people she had met in her life, the ones who were constantly angry, who had walls so high they couldn't see over them anymore. She thought about how many people walked around pretending to have it all together when they were falling apart on the inside. How many wore masks of pride, hiding their fear, their vulnerability, afraid to admit that they weren't fine?

Mita had been one of those people, in a way. She had carried the weight of what she thought was her own guilt, convinced that if she could just hold everything together, she would stop the world from falling apart.

But God didn't work like that. She wasn't meant to carry it all alone. He was there, ready to take the load off, if only she would let Him.

As Mita sat there in the silence, she could almost hear the waves crashing in her mind, much like the waves Peter must've felt when he stepped out of the boat to walk toward Jesus. She could feel the weight of them pressing against her chest, threatening to pull her under. What if she stepped wrong? What if she couldn't keep her balance?

Peter's mistake had been simple. He had looked around. He had been distracted by the chaos, by the storm, instead of focusing on the one who could calm it.

Mita understood that now. It wasn't that the storms wouldn't come. They would. But when she kept her eyes fixed on Jesus, she could walk through them, too.

The guilt was slowly starting to fade. She had been carrying it for so long that she forgot what it felt like to be free of it. But today, today, she finally felt that release.

Christmas was just around the corner. It should've felt empty, with Joshua and Ruach both gone, but in some strange way, it didn't. Maybe because she was starting to understand what it meant to have peace even in the absence of the things she thought she needed.

She didn't have all the answers. She didn't know what would happen with Reed or how she could make sense of everything that had been going wrong in the world. But she knew one thing for sure: she didn't have to face it alone.

Her resolution for the year ahead wasn't about fixing herself or trying to make everything perfect. It was about growing. Growing in her relationship with Jesus. Learning to trust Him more, to be patient with herself, to love others better, and to have peace even in the storm.

Mita lay down on her bed, the Christmas lights still twinkling softly in the dark, and whispered a prayer, her voice steady for the first time in a long while.

"God, I want to walk on the water with you. I'll keep my eyes on you, even if the waves are big. I'll trust you, even if I can't see the way ahead, Abba. Let not my will but your will be done in my life in Jesus' name, amen."

She closed her eyes, finally feeling the weight of the world lift off her shoulders. As the tears roll down her face. Finally accepting that it wasn't her fault, nor was it her burden to carry. And for the first time in what felt like forever, she let herself be at peace with that.

The new year was coming, and Mita was ready to face it with Jesus beside her.

Chapter 25: The Unexpected

The hum of the campus echoed with the usual buzz of students greeting their peers and friends as they were returning from winter break. Mita stepped out of the busyness of the corridors and into the quiet of her dorm room, taking in the space that felt like home but also foreign after the break. It was a new year, a new semester, and, in a way, a new chapter of her life.

As she pushed open the door to her room, she suddenly realized the silence. Empty. Her roommate, Amerei, wasn't back yet.

"Guess I get the place to myself for a bit," Mita muttered, setting her bag down by her desk. The room felt cold, not in temperature, but in that way that only an empty space can feel.

She had a plan. The first thing she would do when she saw Amerei was apologize. Her sudden disappearance before the break had been selfish, and Mita knew it. She hadn't explained anything to anyone, not her friends, not Amerei, and it was time to do things right.

After dropping off her things, Mita headed to the hospital. She hadn't been able to stop thinking about Reed. Her mind kept drifting to the image of him lying in that sterile hospital bed, a place she'd never thought she'd find him at the start of the school year. But, no matter how many times she replayed the events of that evening in her head, it always ended the same: with Reed in that coma.

The hospital was eerily quiet when she arrived, the scent of antiseptic thick in the air. Mita walked through the maze of corridors, decoration still covering the walls, but her thoughts were occupied with what she would say when she saw him.

She stood in the entranceway of his room for a while, watching the steady rise and fall of his chest and the soft beep of machines in the background. She stayed there for a while before making her way to his bedside, pulling out a chair and her Bible, and silently read a passage she'd come across during her winter break:

"The Lord is close to the brokenhearted and saves those who are crushed in spirit." (Psalm 34:18)

Mita got up from his bedside and walked over to the window in his room. Closing her eyes, she rested her forehead against the cool glass of the window. "I don't know what to say, Reed. I just… I hope you can feel something, anything." She paused, swallowing hard. "I'm learning, too. I'm learning how to let go of the things I can't control. And I can't control when you wake up. Even though I knew I wasn't God from the beginning and couldn't make you open your eyes, I had been living like I could do just that all semester. Still, I can't, and because I know I am not God, I will live with my action reflecting just that, that I am not God, knowing that in his time everything is made and done perfectly. I hope you wake up. I really do. But I am trusting in his will and timing, not my own."

She whispered one last prayer before heading out of the room, unsure if Reed could hear her words at that moment or if they were just falling into the silence.

As Mita walked back to her dorm, she spotted Ethan leaning against a pillar outside the shared dorm common building, his eyes lighting up when he saw her.

"Mita!" he called, pushing off the pillar and walking toward her with a grin. "Long time no see."

"Hey, Ethan," she greeted him back, smiling. "How have you been?"

"I've been good. Busy, but good. How about you? Your Christmas, alright?" His eyes softened, searching hers for something; he probably still worried about her.

She nodded; she could feel the smile stretching across her lips at his concern for her. It was almost adorable. "Yeah, it was good. Got some time to rest, you know? But..." She hesitated, the guilt creeping back in. "I'm sorry I left without telling anyone. It was kind of abrupt."

Ethan gave a little wave of his hand, dismissing her apology. "I kinda picked up that you needed to leave. I wasn't upset or anything. But it's great to see you back."

"Thanks," she replied, feeling a warmth spread through her at his understanding. "I'll be at the Christian Club meet-up at the end of the week, though."

He raised an eyebrow. "You sure about that? You're not avoiding us?" he joked

She chuckled. "No, I'll be there. I promise."

"Good, I'll see you then," he said, before waving and heading off, calling over his shoulder, "But seriously, good to have you back."

When Mita returned to her dorm, Amerei was already back, lounging in the living room. She was sprawled across the couch, chatting on the phone with someone, but she immediately sat up when she saw Mita.

"Mita! You're back! How was break?" Amerei beamed, setting the phone down and standing to give Mita a hug.

Mita hesitated for just a moment before pulling her in tighter. "Hey, Amerei. Actually, there's something I need to say first."

Amerei tilted her head up at her. "What's up?"

"I'm sorry. I left without saying anything. I know it was sudden. I just... I had to get away. My mind was..." She searched for the right words. "My thoughts were poisoning me. I just needed space to figure things out. I should've told you, and I'm really sorry for just disappearing."

Amerei's face softened as she reached up to cup Mita's face. "Mita, don't worry about it. I get it. You don't have to apologize. It's your space, your head space. I'm just glad you're okay."

"Yeah," Mita said quietly, relieved. "I'm… I'm getting there,"

"So how was it? How was your break? Did you find peace or something like that, like with your faith?" Amerei asked, settling back down on the couch and crossing her legs.

Mita hesitated, then nodded. "I did. I learned a lot. I spent a lot of time reading, trying to work through some stuff. And… I've been thinking about Reed, too. I don't know. I feel like I'm on a journey right now. Not sure where it leads, but I do feel much lighter."

"That's good," Amerei said, nodding approvingly.

"And how's everything with you and Merrick? Still going strong?" Mita asked, changing the topic

Amerei's face lit up at the mention of her boyfriend. "Oh, it's going great. Merrick's amazing. He's like the boyfriend 101 textbook example, honestly. He's attentive, always thinking of me. And…" She grinned, looking almost shy. "I kinda wonder if he's… too perfect. Like, is it okay for it to be this good?"

Mita laughed. "You're worried about it being too perfect? That's a new one."

"I don't know," Amerei said, shrugging. "I just feel like maybe it's too good to be true. But… I love every minute of it. He's perfect for me."

Mita smiled. "You deserve it, Amerei. You really do."

The two spent the next hour chatting; Amerei filled Mita in on her relationship with Merrick, and Mita listened intently, offering her best advice. She loved hearing her friend's stories; it was like a distraction from the messiness of her own life.

The next few days flew by, and before Mita knew it, the weekend was approaching. She wasn't in the same classes as Odessa and Andromeda anymore, but they had a group chat that was buzzing with plans to catch up. It felt nice, like old times. They agreed to meet up that weekend, their friendship picking up right where it had left off.

On Friday, Mita was walking across campus to her next class when she heard a voice that made her stop dead in her tracks.

"Hey, Mita!" Rune's voice called, smooth and warm, just like the night of the treasure hunt event, like a melody she couldn't escape.

Her heart skipped a beat as she turned to face him. Rune, the attractive guy from the music department, the one she remembered all too well.

"Oh, hey," she said, trying to hide the rush of nerves in her chest. "Long time no see."

"Yeah, it's been a while," Rune replied, his smile effortless. "How've you been? How was your Christmas?"

"It was… good," Mita replied, fighting the urge to feel flustered. "How about you?"

"Amazing," he said with a grin. "But hey, do you wanna come to the music club meet-up this weekend?"

Mita blinked, surprised by the sudden invitation. "Uh… this weekend? What time?"

"Six on Saturday," he replied, as if it was a given. "You free then?"

She hesitated, already making mental plans for her weekend, but she couldn't resist. "Yeah, I can make it," she said, letting out a breath

"Awesome," Rune said, smiling again. "See you there, Mita."

"Yeah, see you," she replied, her heart pounding as he walked off.

Later that evening, Mita made her way to the Christian Club meet-up. She was eager to see everyone again.

Ethan and Zyran were already there, with the usual dynamic between them that had Mita laughing before she even took a seat. But then the doors opened, and in walked Rune, as cool and confident as ever. He seemed to glide into the room like he had been coming here for years.

Ruth, the club leader, greeted him immediately. "Oh, Rune! Welcome! We were just about to start. Have a seat quickly. I can't wait to teach this lesson."

Mita's heart raced. *What was Rune doing here?*

Their eyes met for a split second. Rune waved, and she offered him a hesitant smile before quickly looking away. She tried to focus on the lesson, but her mind kept drifting to the one question that lingered: Why was Rune here?

Chapter 26: A Fresh Perspective on Luke 11:37-54

❧

It was another Friday evening at the Christian Club, and the group gathered around the small circle of folding chairs, bean bags, and blankets and along with snacks, in the dimly lit room. Ruth sat in the center, her Bible open in front of her. There was an air of anticipation as the topic for tonight's study was announced. This time, it wasn't just a generic lesson on love or grace; Ruth had chosen a passage from the Gospel of Luke—Luke 11:37-54. The energy in the room shifted as people settled into their seats, journals and pens at the ready.

Ruth said the opening prayer before taking a deep breath, her voice steady and calm, but carrying the weight of something deep. "Tonight," she began, "we're diving into a moment where Jesus challenges the spiritual leaders of His time. He had no problem confronting the hypocrisy and shallow religiosity that was happening in the hearts of those who thought they had it all figured out."

Mita sat up straighter, her pen hovering over her journal. Ethan, ever the studious one, had his nose buried deep in his own journal, looking up only occasionally when something caught his attention. Zyran, on the other hand, was tapping away at his phone, making notes in the little app he'd reserved for such things. Even Rune, whom she never saw at the meetings, was scribbling away in his little notebook. Ruth's words were piercing, and everyone was caught in the moment.

The Dinner Table—Luke 11:37-41

"The passage opened with a Pharisee inviting Jesus to dinner. The atmosphere was likely tense; after all, these Pharisees weren't the biggest fans of Jesus' way of thinking. They followed the letter of the law, but Jesus was known for doing things differently, challenging traditions, healing on the Sabbath, and even dining with sinners."

Ruth paused as she read aloud from the Bible, "**When Jesus had finished speaking, a Pharisee asked Him to eat with him. So He went in and reclined at the table.**"

She looked up from her Bible, locking eyes with everyone in the room. "This is where it starts. Jesus, despite knowing the Pharisee's rigid views, accepts the invitation. He enters their space, which is something we should take note of. Jesus wasn't just seeking the 'good' or 'bad' people; He was also willing to break bread with those who thought they were already 'righteous.'"

Zyran raised an eyebrow and looked up from his phone. "Wait, so Jesus knew this Pharisee wasn't really open to His message, but He went anyway?"

Ruth nodded, a smile tugging at the corners of her lips. "Exactly. He wasn't afraid of confrontation, nor was He scared of being around people who were spiritually blinded by their own self-righteousness. He went to them, to challenge them, to help them see what they couldn't."

Ethan, pausing from his note-taking, piped in, "So, what was Jesus' main problem with the Pharisee?"

"Good question," Ruth replied, flipping the page in her Bible. "The issue wasn't with their desire to be righteous; it was the *lack of heart* behind their actions. The Pharisees were obsessed with external cleanliness, but they neglected the inward transformation. They scrubbed their hands and cups to avoid being **_ceremonially_** unclean, but Jesus pointed out that their hearts were filthy."

She looked around the room, making eye contact with each of them. "Jesus

told the Pharisee, '***You clean the outside of the cup and dish, but inside you are
full of greed and wickedness. You foolish people! Did not the one who made
the outside make the inside also?***'" Ruth's voice softened as she spoke those
words. "The question is, what are we really cleaning? Are we so focused on
appearing 'righteous' on the outside that we neglect the transformation that
happens inside?"

Mita scribbled a note in her journal, her hand moving fast as she processed
Ruth's words. Ethan looked deep in thought, his pen hovering above his
journal. Zyran was furiously typing on his phone, the question clearly
striking a chord with him.

Chapter 27: The Woes to the Pharisees—Luke 11:42-44

Ruth's voice grew more intense as she read the next part, where Jesus calls out the Pharisees with a series of "woes." It wasn't just a gentle rebuke; Jesus didn't hold back.

"Woe to you Pharisees, because you give God a tenth of your mint, rue, and all other kinds of garden herbs, but you neglect justice and the love of God," Ruth read aloud. *"You should have practiced the latter without leaving the former undone. Woe to you Pharisees! You love the front seat in the synagogues and greetings in the marketplaces. Woe to you! You are like unmarked graves; the people who walk over them don't know it."*

She looked up and met the eyes of the group again. "Here's the thing: The Pharisees were good at checking boxes. They tithed down to their herb gardens, but their hearts were far from God. Isaiah even mentions it in chapter 29:13: *"The Lord said, These people approach me with their speeches to honor me with lip-service, yet their hearts are far from me, and human rules direct their worship of me."* The Pharisees focused on the minutiae of the law, missing the bigger picture: justice, mercy, and love for God and people."

Rune, who had been unusually quiet up until this point, spoke up. "So they were focused on small details but missed the heart of the law?"

Ruth nodded, her expression serious. "Exactly. Jesus was challenging them: 'You've got your rituals, your tithing, your outward displays of religion, but what about the weightier things? What about caring for the poor, standing up for what's right, and loving your neighbor? It's easy to focus on external actions, but true righteousness starts in the heart."

Zyran leaned forward, tapping his screen with a couple of questions. "Isn't it easy for us to do that too? Like, we go to church, we do the right things, but… are we living out the justice and the love Jesus talks about? And the love and justice we ask God for but never exercise on others?"

"That's exactly the point," Ruth replied. "We can easily slip into the trap of looking good on the outside without paying attention to our hearts. We need to examine ourselves daily and repent daily, for we do fall short of things we do not know: But the question is, are we living out the values of God's kingdom? Are we people of justice, mercy, and love, or are we just performing?"

The Teachers of the Law—Luke 11:45-54

As the conversation grew deeper, Ruth moved on to the last section of the passage, where Jesus turns His attention to the teachers of the law. These were the ones who not only didn't practice what they preached but also placed heavy burdens on others, making it difficult for them to find true freedom in God.

Jesus said, "***Woe to you because you load people down with burdens they can hardly carry, and you yourselves will not lift one finger to help them.***" Ruth emphasized the weight of those words. Jesus was furious at the way the teachers of the law added layers and layers of rules to the people's faith, without offering them any real help. They were content with making others miserable, all the while neglecting to walk in the very truth they were supposed to be teaching."

Rune sat back, rubbing his chin as if processing something. "So, this is more than just an issue of hypocrisy? It's like, when you have power, you can end up making things harder for people, instead of helping them find freedom?"

"Precisely," Ruth replied, with a nod. "It's easy for those in positions of power to oppress others, rather than serve them. Jesus was calling out the teachers of the law for their hypocrisy, but He was also showing that *true leadership*, true righteousness, is about helping others walk in freedom, not making their journey harder. "

The Closing Reflection

Ruth paused for a moment, letting the room settle into silence. She closed her Bible gently and looked at each person around her. "Tonight's passage is challenging. It's not just about pointing fingers at the Pharisees or the teachers of the law; it's about asking ourselves,

'Are we living in a way that reflects the heart of God? Are we more concerned with being right or with loving others the way Jesus did?'"

Mita closed her journal slowly, a thoughtful expression on her face. Ethan seemed deep in thought as well, looking up at the ceiling, while Zyran typed out a final note on his phone. Even Rune was looking pensively at his book, the weight of Jesus' words settling in.

As Ruth closed the meeting, she left the group with a final thought: "Let's remember that true righteousness isn't about what we do on the outside that others can see, it's about our hearts, our motivations, and how we love others. which can't always be displayed, what are we doing to honor the Lord when no one is looking?"

After the closing prayer and dismissal, the group dispersed quietly, each person reflecting on the passage in their own way. The challenge of living authentically and humbly in the kingdom of God felt real, as it could change their lives if they let it.

Chapter 28: The Unexpected Walk

As the group began to pack up after the Christian Club meeting, Rune lingered in the background, looking like he was trying to decide whether or not to approach Mita. He had been quiet throughout the meeting, only speaking up once or twice, maybe thrice, but now, as the room emptied, he made his move. Mita was already deep in conversation with Ethan and Zyran, laughing lightly as they made their way out, but Rune didn't hesitate. He walked over to them, his casual stride purposeful.

"Hey, Mita," he called out, his voice smooth, yet just enough to pull her attention away from her friends.

Mita turned, raising an eyebrow. "Rune? What's up?"

"I was wondering… if I could have you for a minute?" he asked, a playful yet sincere glint in his eyes.

Mita shot a quick glance at Ethan and Zyran, who were already heading toward the exit with her in tow. "Alright, guess I'll catch you guys later," she said, smiling before quickly excusing herself from the group toward Rune.

As they walked toward the exit together, Mita couldn't help but ask, "So, why exactly are you here tonight, anyway? Have you been coming here for a while now?"

Rune, a little caught off guard by her directness, smiled. "Yeah, why? he asked Mita

Just then, Ruth, who had been quietly walking behind them, overheard the conversation. Her eyes twinkled as she joined in, "Yup, Rune was a bit of a surprise guest in our club, but he's been showing up pretty consistently. Who would've thought?"

Rune continued, "Did you forget our deal before winter break that if I came to the Christian club, you would come to the music club? I kept my end of the deal; I mean, I did agree to it."

So that's why he randomly invited me to the music club; I didn't even remember the deal until he mentioned it, she thought

Mita let out a soft laugh, her eyes sparkling with surprise. "I'm surprised you actually came, Rune."

Rune chuckled, shrugging nonchalantly. "Well, now, why would I break out our little bargain now? That would be a bit reckless of me, wouldn't it?" he said in feigned bewilderment.

Mita rolled her eyes playfully. "Now, I suppose I have to show up at the music club, huh?"

"Hope so," Rune said, his voice lightly hopeful but with a playful undertone.

Mita bumped his shoulder lightly with hers, teasing him. "We'll see."

"Ouch," Rune responded dramatically, stumbling a bit. "You trying to kill me, Mita?"

She laughed, her eyes crinkling at the edges. "If I wanted to kill you, I'd do it with kindness, don't worry," she said, not caring how corny it sounded.

They both fell into a comfortable silence as they walked out of the building. Mita's thoughts were racing, and yet, she was at ease. Rune had a way of making everything feel laid-back and effortless. She had always found him a little intimidating, but there was something about his charm and how much he felt comfortable just being himself that gave her leave to do the same without any pretenses.

"So, where are you headed?" Rune asked casually, breaking the silence as they walked down a pathway, the streetlamps casting soft pools of light around them.

"My dorm," Mita replied, glancing at the darkened surroundings. "It's a little late, and it's kind of sketchy out here."

Without missing a beat, Rune turned to her. "How about I walk you there? I don't mind."

Mita smiled, genuinely appreciative. "Yeah, sure. I'd like that."

And so, they continued their walk, talking about nothing in particular. At least, it didn't feel particularly important, just two people walking side by side under the dim street lights, laughing occasionally and making small talk. But there was something about the way Rune made her feel like she mattered in a world full of noise. He wasn't flashy and wasn't trying too hard, but everything about him, his confidence, his gentleness, and the way he respected boundaries without overthinking things, was incredibly magnetic, and his good looks were a bonus.

Mita had to admit to herself, even if she didn't say it out loud: she liked being in his company. She liked it more than she had expected. Rune was that rare combination of being utterly *himself*, with no effort to fit into the mold anyone else had set, but at the same time, he respected her enough not to push things too far. He wasn't just another guy looking for a way in; he was someone who valued her comfort. He was someone who kept his promises, apparently.

As they reached her dorm building, Mita felt that familiar tug of uncertainty, the warmth of his presence suddenly being replaced by the quiet, solitary world inside. Rune paused in front of the entrance, turning to face her.

"Well," he said with a small grin, "here you are."

Mita smiled, looking up at him. "Thanks for walking me back."

"No problem," he said, his tone softer now, with a hint of sincerity. "Just... don't forget to pray?" He said it in a question, like that wasn't what he had planned to say.

Her heart fluttered just a little at his words. It was simple but kind, no matter how uncertainly he said it.

"I won't," she replied with a nod, her voice quiet but warm. "Thanks, Rune."

With a final smile, Rune stepped back and gestured towards her dorm building for her to go inside.

Watching her as she entered the building, he gave her a wave before turning to walk back in the direction they had come, disappearing into the darkness of the night.

Mita stood there for a moment, her hand still on the door as she watched him go. Something about the way he treated her, the respect he showed, the way he didn't rush things, made her feel a little warmth in her chest.

As she entered her dorm room, she found it empty. Amerei, her roommate, was nowhere to be seen, likely out with Merrick. Mita chuckled softly under her breath at the thought of Amerei's relationship with Merrick, her "101 Textbook" boyfriend, as Mita liked to call him. She decided that would be his code name from now on.

The couple was the epitome of opposites, but somehow, they made it work. The perfect code name for Merrick, really.

Mita put her bag down and, with a sigh, walked to the bathroom. She undressed and stepped into the warm shower, letting the water run over her skin as her thoughts drifted. Rune had been on her mind for the rest of the bath. He was attractive, sure, but it wasn't just his looks that had her thinking. It was the way he carried himself, with a quiet confidence that she found oddly alluring. He wasn't insecure or cocky; he was a gentleman, someone who kept his word and seemed to care about the people around him genuinely.

The lesson from Ruth's Bible study still lingered in her mind as well. Jesus' challenge to look inward and examine her heart had struck her deeply. Mita had always prided herself on being a good person, but tonight she'd been confronted with the reality that it wasn't just about what she *did* on the outside; it was about the condition of her heart.

She finished her shower, wrapped herself in a towel, and walked back to her room. After sitting down at her desk, she glanced out the window, lost in thought for a moment.

Before going to bed, Mita whispered a prayer, thanking God for the people in her life and asking for the strength to grow. She prayed for Rune, for wisdom in her own life, and for a heart that would be more like Jesus, gentle, kind, and honest.

When she finally climbed into bed, the room was quiet. Amerei still wasn't home, and the world outside her window was calm, dark, and peaceful. Rune's smile flashed in her mind once more, and as sleep began to settle over her, Mita couldn't help but feel like tonight had been the beginning of something new.

Chapter 29: Catching Up, Catching Vibes

The weekend rolled around quicker than expected, and the girls were more than ready to unwind after not seeing each other during winter break. The weather was still cold, but warmer than the weeks prior; the streets buzzed with energy, everyone still under the haze of the holidays, while Mita and Amerei were about to meet up with the rest of the crew.

Mita was always into comfort over everything, but today? She was feeling a bit more…experimental. Her usual baggy jeans hung just right around her hips, paired with a beautiful off-the-shoulder full-length top, blended with her chunky sneakers, which were neither too chunky nor too thin. Her hair was pulled into a messy bun at the base of her skull, a few strands escaping and framing her face with that effortless kind of look, adding a jacket and scarf to ward off the cold.

Amerei, on the other hand, was the definition of feminine grace. She had that *girl-next-door* vibe but with a chic twist. Her white asymmetrical blouse hugged her soft curves, and a denim skirt with a slight flare gave her the perfect balance of playfulness and polish, with two pairs of skin-coloured thick stockings. The heels? Just enough to make her legs look a mile long without making her look too 'done up', and a matching jacket and scarf. Her curls, now a couple of inches longer than last semester, bounced as she walked.

The two girls were meeting Odessa and Andromeda at a local restaurant near campus for dinner and drinks. Odessa had texted earlier, telling them she'd already arrived.

As they entered the restaurant, it didn't take long to spot her.

Odessa was sitting at the table, already sipping on her drink. She wore a silky black dress that clung to her curves, showing just enough skin to tease without being too revealing. A pair of strappy heels elevated the look, and her makeup was flawless, natural, with a hint of smoky eyes that screamed mystery. Her long, dark hair cascaded over her shoulders, a perfect pair to her dark skin. The moment the girls walked in, she glanced up, flashing them a dazzling grin.

Mita and Amerei took their seats, exchanging glances, already aware that Odessa's presence had already drawn some attention, even though she was oblivious to it. A young handsome waiter with tousled dark hair and a Chad of a jawline came over, handing them the menus, exchanging pleasantries with the girls before glancing at Odessa, where his lingering smile became a bit brighter. He came back and handed the other girls their starter drinks, his eyes lingering just a tad too much once more to Odessa before leaving our table. She, however, didn't even seem to notice the first time or the second; she was sipping her cocktail without a second thought.

Mita and Amerei exchanged yet another knowing look. They had both seen the guy checking out Odessa. But it wasn't the first time stuff like this happened. Odessa had a way of attracting attention without even trying, and neither Mita nor Amerei was about to entertain or respond to it; they didn't mind. If Odessa wasn't interested, neither would they be.

As if on cue, the phones buzzed. A message from Andromeda saying she was running a little late but was on her way. The girls kept the time by making small talk, sipping their drinks while the atmosphere buzzed around them. It was one of those rare days when good vibes and friends could finally blend.

A few minutes later, Andromeda walked in like she owned the place. Her outfit? Simple yet elegant, a well-tailored blazer over a cream-colored blouse, paired with dark skinny jeans and knee-high boots. Her hair was sleek, pulled back into a low ponytail, and her makeup was minimal but polished. She had that unforced confidence that made it seem like she was just *better* at life. Even when she smiled, it was like she was in control of the room, no matter where she was.

"Well, well, look who finally showed up," Odessa teased, raising an eyebrow at her friend.

Andromeda rolled her eyes, taking her seat. "Sorry, ladies. I got held up. You know how it is."

Odessa smirked, crossing her arms. "Of course I do. Drama, as usual."

Mita laughed, leaning back in her chair. "Speaking of drama... I need to apologize to all of you. I disappeared on everyone right before winter break, and I'm sorry about that."

"I knew something was off, we all did," Andromeda said, her voice softening. "But we get it. Things happen. I'm just happy seeing you look brighter."

"Yeah, we just want you to be okay," Odessa added, her usual flirtatious demeanor now completely genuine. "You're still our girl, no matter what."

Mita sighed deeply, her face softening. "It's been a lot... up here," she pointed to her head. "Just needed time to figure it out. I'm really sorry, though."

Amerei nodded in understanding, "We're just glad you're back, sweetie."

"Now, enough about that," Odessa cut in, her eyes glinting as she turned to Amerei. "How's everything going with Mr. Vogue Model, huh?"

The table went quiet as all eyes turned to Amerei, whose face flushed a pinkish hue. She fiddled with her fingers, trying to play it cool. "Well...it's going great. Actually, I think, but wait, don't bite my head off, but.... I think I might have fallen in love with him."

The others froze, blinking at her.

"Wait—hold up," Andromeda said, leaning forward in her seat. "You're serious?"

"Yeah," Amerei said, smiling softly. "I think I am."

Odessa's grin grew wider. "Awwww, look at you getting all romantic. I'm happy for you, babe." She reached over to hold Amerei's hand, her fingers making patterns on Amerei's knuckles.

"Thanks, guys," Amerei said, her voice tinged with something like relief. "It feels good to say it out loud."

"And what about you?" Mita asked, turning to Odessa. "Any love interests? Any new...conquests?"

Odessa shrugged, a playful smile on her lips. "Nope. Haven't had anyone blowing up my phone lately. But it's fine." She paused, looking around at them. "I'm kinda enjoying the peace."

"Yeah, well, if you're gonna pursue someone, just make sure they're not a creep, alright?" Mita said, staring blankly at Dessa, her tone dry.

"I'm not even looking," Odessa said, rolling her eyes. "If I want a hookup, I'm good with that. Just no weirdos, but they always find me."

"That's fair, and unfair," Andromeda agreed. "But moving on~, what about you, Mita?"

Mita paused.

Amerei suddenly gleamed as though she couldn't contain herself with the secret any longer, causing everyone at the table to look at her with varying degrees of confusion and interest. "Actually, I've got something to tell you guys..." she trailed off, biting her lip as she glanced excitedly at the others.

Odessa raised an eyebrow. "Oh? This is going to be good."

"Last night, I saw *someone* walking back to the dorm with *someone* giggling and being all cutesy," Amerei said, glancing at Mita. "You guys remember that guy from the student council event? The music major who told us about the treasure hunt?"

"Oh, honey, how could we forget *him?*" Odessa said with a smirk.

"Yeah, him. Well, I saw *Mita* with him, walking back to the dorms, all giggles and smiles."

"I wasn't giggling," Mita said, leaning forward, shocked. "And how would you know, you weren't even back when I got to the dorms."

"Well~, Merrick and I were out walking when I saw you heading to the dorms with the guy. What's his name again?" Amerei asked, tapping her chin, trying to rack her mind for it.

"His name is Rune, I think, he was the one giving out his speech about the journey being the prize," she said before turning to Mita to continue, "How did this even come about?"

Mita sighed, "Apparently I made a deal with him before winter break. I agreed to check out his music club if he came to one of my Christian club meetings last semester. So he came. Honestly, I didn't even remember about it until he mentioned it, and I wouldn't have expected him to even show up, but he did."

"Wait, you went to the music club?" Andromeda asked, surprised.

"No, I'm going tonight, though, but he has been going to my club since we made the deal, even in the middle of exams," Mita continued, still baffled at the revelation. "But get this, he was *actually* interested in what was said in the club. He asked questions, even took notes. Like, what?!"

"And?!" Odessa demanded, leaned in, clearly dying for more.

Mita chuckled. "He even offered to walk me to my dorm after, no strings attached. When we got to the dorm building, he didn't ask me for anything; he just told me to pray before bed."

"And you didn't kiss him?" Odessa challenged, raising an eyebrow.

"No! Why would I? Plus, he didn't give off the vibe that he expected anything like that. He was respectful and a perfect gentleman." Mita paused, a goofy smile spreading across her face. "He might even be husband material...OK, that sounds cringe saying that out loud, but he *is* giving that vibe though."

The table fell silent, everyone exchanging surprised glances.

"Wait, wait," Odessa said, leaning back in her chair. "So, you haven't slept with him yet? How is this even possible? Honey, you need to speed things up or someone else will, that someone being me!"

Andromeda rolled her eyes. "She's a Christian for cry out loud, Dessa, with Christian values, remember? Do you even know what that means?" Odessa actually paused before saying, "She goes to church and worships Jesus, duh, everyone knows that I'm not dumb". Odessa finished sounding very sure that her answer was obvious.

"It means Dessa. They neither sleep with each other nor anyone else, as a matter of fact, until marriage, right Mita?" Andromeda finished before throwing a glare at Odessa, who just shrugged in response.

Mita grinned. "Yup, that's right."

"But isn't it hard, okay? What if he's not good in bed, and you find that out after you get married?" Odessa argued teasingly.

Amerei slapped her shoulder, "Dessa, stop teasing her," she joked. Mita wanted to explain, but the other girls jumped in, trying to change the topic with jokes and their tabloids of stories.

As her friends laughed, their happiness exuded around the table. Mita took a mental step back from the moment to look at the happenings around her, of her friends. Even though they didn't share her faith and wouldn't understand her perspectives, she knew even in this moment God was building her faith and resolve in his statutes. Knowing that God is in control is what makes life easier.

To explain that sex within marriage is the way God ordained his called vessels, his people, to live to protect ourselves from the seen and unseen things of this world, is not one easily received by non-believers. That sex is supposed to be in marriage, that it is **sacred**, **special**, **a connection between two people who are already joined as one flesh in vow under God**. But when done outside of marriage can cause Deleterious and Catastrophic harm to both parties, both physically and spiritually, and will stem down to future generations in their bloodline if it goes unrepentant for, and that is a whole other ball game.

She knew her friends wouldn't understand and weren't ready to digest that. They would even pass it off as an amazing fairy tale. But Life isn't about sex, nor was it a reward for *good men'* or *great guys'* either, and if I were to say that very thing, everyone would be like, *'Of course not, life is so much more than sex, and we shouldn't sleep just anybody.'*

But yet our actions don't line up with what our mouths say, **lip service,** is what the word of God calls it.

Example: A nice guy takes us out on an amazing date, and when he brings us home, we feel the need to kiss him to end it as a *'perfect night'*, or maybe

143

even have sex with them without a second thought. Others may prolong it to the third date, or maybe one month, perhaps two, others four, etc, *'but we are not forcing ourselves, though, right? No, why would we? We are our own people with our own independent voice, our body, our choice, right?'* Mita snickered to herself at how that thought alone would *rile* up about maybe 97% of the Earth's population, especially girls.

Still, the question is, <u>*why*</u>, why are we so OK giving ourselves away to each other, giving away our very bodies, which is the high form of trust and adoration to someone, but won't commit to said person, won't vow to love that person whom we trust with ourselves. As Mita thought this, she came up with the excuse she normally heard:

"I don't even know the guy, or we just met, or ... or we just aren't compatible'

Once she heard a girl say, and she quotes, *'he has other girls vying for his attention, plus I am not ready for that type of commitment,'* so, why are we then giving to such a high form of trust to people that can't be trusted.

To live in a world so desensitized to how special our bodies are, and how much damage other '**minor sins**' as they call it, can do, is sometimes mind-blowing.

Still, it's expected when you're living in a world so confused about how to breathe when he, God, already made it automatic in his name, not knowing they are only one prayer, one righteously willing heart away from being transformed in clarity and assurance, in that he is working all things together for our good, because if a serving God is not dead, then what is he doing?

Serving.

But before Mita could dive even deeper into her thoughts, the waiter returned. This time, he didn't just look at Odessa

They locked eyes. Odessa's playful smirk deepened, and the flirtation was palpable.

Amerei sighed as the waiter walked away. "Well, if he's not going to be the one to make the first move, you might as well pursue him, huh?"

"Ha." Odessa coughed out, her eyes still lingering on the waiter as he walked away. "I'll let you girls know if anything happens."

As the night continued, the group drifted deeper into conversation. Laughter echoed between bites of food and sips of drinks, and of course, teasing Odessa relentlessly about the handsome waiter. But time was creeping up on them, and Mita had to leave early for the music club. She said her goodbyes, promising to keep everyone updated in the group chat.

"Details, Mita. We want them all," Odessa called out as Mita got up to leave.

"Yeah, yeah, you'll get them soon enough," Mita shot back, blowing them a kiss.

As the sun set and the restaurant began to fill with customers, the remaining girls settled back into their seats, content and carefree. The night was just beginning for them.

Chapter 30: Notes and Prayers

The crisp air hit Mita's face as she stepped off the bus and onto campus. She paused for a moment, gathering her thoughts, looking up at the sky, her heart quiet but full of gratitude. The day had been full of twists and turns and emotions she had to untangle, and she couldn't help but feel a little overwhelmed. With a soft breath, Mita closed her eyes and whispered a prayer under her breath.

"God, thank You for protecting me today. For keeping me safe... for being with me even when I didn't know how to ask. Please guard my heart, keep my thoughts pure, and help me focus on You. Help me stay strong and avoid temptation. And... please, don't let me get distracted by things I don't need. In Jesus name, Amen."

Mita wasn't perfect; she knew that. But she trusted God to guide her, especially when it came to navigating the unpredictable waters of college life.

Walking toward the art building where she was supposed to meet Rune, she realized she hadn't thought things through. Where was this meeting being held? She had no clue. She didn't even have his contact info to ask.

"Well, that was smooth, Mita," she muttered to herself, shaking her head. "Why do you never think ahead?"

She paused at the main entrance of the arts building, about to turn around and head back to her dorm, when she heard a voice.

"You're lost, huh?"

She looked up, following the direction of the familiar voice. There was Rune, leaning against the stairwell, grinning at her with that mischievous glint in his eyes that she spotted even from this distance.

Mita couldn't help but curse herself at how he always seemed to catch her in these situations. She straightened, raising an eyebrow. "No, I think I'm just… trying to find my way." *Back to my room,* she finished; however, that last bit remained unsaid for obvious reasons.

"Uh-huh," Rune replied sarcastically, pushing off from the wall. "Come on up," he gestured toward the main staircase in the entryway of the building.

As she climbed the stairs toward him, Mita felt his gaze follow her, a little too intense for comfort, but at the same time, she couldn't help but feel a flutter in her chest. His eyes were always so… piercing. It was as if he were seeing right through her, at how much his gaze affected her. She didn't want to admit it, though.

When she finally stood before him at the top of the stairs, her face flushed as she caught him still staring at her, not even trying to hide it.

"What?" she said, trying to play it cool.

Rune didn't hesitate, his voice smooth as silk. "It's just that you look really… beautiful today."

Mita was caught off guard by the sudden compliment. It wasn't that she hated it, no, definitely not, but it just came out of nowhere and would logically explain why her pulse steered a bit off its regular path for a second.

"Uh…thanks. You look great, too," she replied, making it obvious how taken aback she was. Mita, in that moment, wanted to drive a tent peg through her own head, metaphorically, of course, for that tissue-thin excuse of a compliment.

She rubbed her neck awkwardly, unsure of what to say now. She hadn't expected to be complimented like that. Rune always had a way of making her feel…

special?

seen?

And heard when she didn't even ask for it?

No, definitely not more like different, maybe uncomfortable; yeah, let's go with that.

"So, where were you coming from earlier?" Rune asked, breaking the awkward silence.

Mita hesitated. "Oh, just some… stuff I had to do."

"Right, I figured." Rune paused before continuing, "Well, I'm glad you're here now."

Before she could respond, Rune reached forward, his fingers brushing against her hair. She froze for a second, feeling a strange jolt run through her. He wasn't being untoward, but she could still feel the heat spreading in her chest.

"What are you doing?" she asked, her voice tight.

He looked down at her, his eyes serious now, his hand still fiddling in her hair. "There's something in your hair."

Mita felt a little self-conscious and stupid for reacting like that as Rune gently tugged at a small twig or stick that had gotten tangled in her curls.

"Got it," Rune said quietly, his fingers lingering in her hair for a moment longer than necessary. He then tucked the stray strand of hair behind her ear with a careful touch.

Mita sucked in a silent breath for a moment, feeling the heat rise to her cheeks again. She bit her lip to hide the nervous laugh that threatened to spill out.

Rune smiled at her, his gaze a little more intense now, but with a warmth that made her feel safe. "You look even better when you smile," he added in that casual tone, like it was a casual 'good morning.'

Her heart tripped out of rhythm for the 100th time. "You don't have to say that. Compliments work when they are true." Mita said, sliding on her cap of sarcasm, the only defense she has in her current unexpected predicament.

He shrugged, his playful smile never leaving his face. "Maybe I do. And for your information, my compliments always work."

Mita's mind was racing. She wasn't used to this kind of attention, especially not in this way, so sweet, yet so... intimate.

She tried to focus, but his presence seemed to make it hard to think clearly. She glanced up at him again, and he didn't just look; he studied her with a predator's unwavering attention, heavy and deliberate. There were times when Mita couldn't tell the difference between a black kitten and a baby panther, but there was no denying it. Rune was interested in her, and she might return the gesture.

But, she reminded herself, *you've got to stay grounded.*

Rune, seemingly sensing her momentary hesitation, cleared his throat, shaking off whatever tension had built up around them, breaking it by redirecting their focus to the reason for her being there. "Shall we?" he said, his voice softer now as he motioned toward a door.

Mita nodded, trying to regain her composure. "Yeah,"

Rune led her into the room, and as soon as she stepped inside, her eyes widened in surprise. The room was filled with instruments: guitars, violins, cellos, and even a full drum set in the corner. There were a few people scattered around, all absorbed in what they were doing, but they seemed to know exactly what they were doing. Mita, on the other hand, felt completely out of place. This was the last thing she had expected to do when she came to college.

Rune noticed her hesitation and gave her a reassuring smile. "Don't worry. You're not the only newbie here. You're gonna love it."

He introduced her to everyone, and Mita forced herself to smile, feeling a little self-conscious as they all greeted her. She didn't quite know where to start as there was so much going on.

Rune walked her over to the grand piano, sitting down on the bench and patting the spot next to him. "Come on, let me show you around this beauty a bit."

Mita sat beside him, unsure of what to expect. Rune placed his fingers lightly on the keys, the notes filling the space between them. He explained the different types of notes, how they are grouped together, and how music could be both simple and complicated at the same time. He even let her try a few, though she was mostly focused on not embarrassing herself.

"You're a quick learner," he said after she managed a simple scale. "See? Told you it's not that hard."

Mita smiled, feeling a sense of accomplishment. She liked that she could learn something new, especially something that didn't involve textbooks or deadlines. And she liked how Rune was so patient with her. After more than a handful of awful notes, she saw a bit of improvement, just a bit.

As the night went on, she began to relax. The room was filled with laughter from others in the club and the soft clinks of instruments being played. She forgot about her worries for a while and just enjoyed being in the moment, surrounded by people who loved music as much as she did as of now.

Eventually, it was time to leave. Rune, being the gentleman he was, walked her back to her dorm once again, the two of them playfully bickering like siblings arguing over the stupidest of things, making each moment spent with him something Mita could enjoy, but in the back of her mind she was wondering if letting him in too close too soon, knowing how she felt toward him, was the smart thing to do, but the way he kept teasing her about her "amazing" piano skills, and how she kept throwing jabs back at him, melted everything. He was so easy to be around, and she felt so comfortable in his company. She didn't really have a solid case to build against *this,* whatever this was, to ask herself to stop whatever they were becoming, whatever *he* was becoming to her, before she couldn't.

When they reached her dorm, Rune turned to her with a grin, his voice gentle but firm. "Go inside quickly. It's cold out here."

Mita laughed, feeling a warm glow in her chest. "Thanks for walking me back."

"Of course." Rune looked down for a moment, his smile softening. "And remember, pray before bed, okay?"

"Will do," she said, returning the smile. "I'll talk to you later."

Rune didn't ask for a hug or a kiss. He didn't need to. He just gave her a nod, a quiet wave, and turned to leave.

Mita stood at the main entrance, watching him go for a moment before she finally stepped inside. The rotating door was still spinning, a trace of her entry into the building, after she went inside, heading to the elevator to culminate the vertical journey at her designated floor, then the door. She closed her room door behind her to officially end her day, feeling a strange sense of tranquility settle over her. She changed into her pajamas and knelt by her bed to pray once more.

"God, thank You for today. For Rune, for the music club, and for protecting me. I don't know what's going to happen next, but I trust You. Please guide me. Keep my heart and mind pure. In Jesus' name, Amen."

Mita lay back in bed, staring at the ceiling. She was tired, but her heart was light. Maybe she wasn't as lost as she thought.

And maybe, just maybe, Rune was more than just a guy who played music and made her heart flutter.

Chapter 31: The Weight of the Semester

The hustle of the new semester hit Mita like a tidal wave, crashing over her in waves of assignments, deadlines, and responsibilities. The initial thrill of starting fresh with new classes had quickly worn off, replaced by the heavy, relentless grind of university life. Mita didn't mind the challenge; she was used to working hard, but even she could feel the stress creeping in.

Between her lectures, club meetings, and trying to visit Reed at the hospital as often as she could, there was barely any time left for herself. Her days were a blur of books, notes, and half-drunk cups of coffee. By the time she got to the hospital, the only thing she could do was juggle between talking to Reed, who had still been in a coma for almost three months, and trying to finish her assignments. It was a delicate balance, but she was getting good at it, at least—that's what she told herself.

Mita leaned back in the soft plush chair by Reed's bed, her laptop open in front of her. Her fingers hovered over the keyboard, but her thoughts kept drifting. Reed's steady breathing and the beeping of the machines were the only sounds in the room, and Mita couldn't shake the feeling that she was losing touch with the world outside this sterile space. Her thoughts kept wandering to the things she couldn't control: assignments piling up, friends slipping away into their own busy schedules, and Reed, whose still body was a constant reminder that life was unpredictable.

She glanced over at him. His face was peaceful, the rise and fall of his chest the only proof he was alive. It hurt to see him like this, motionless, locked in a coma, but Mita refused to give up hope. He would wake up. *He has to.*

"Reed..." she whispered, though she didn't know if he could hear her. "I wish I could be here more. I'm sorry."

The guilt hit her every time she left the hospital, but she had to go back. The university wasn't going to wait. She had assignments to finish and meetings to attend. And then there was the music club, which she had promised to commit to.

It was hard to admit, but Mita didn't have time for everything anymore. She barely had time to see her friends.

Odessa was always off on school trips; whether it was for her media classes, visiting news companies, or working at a radio station, she was constantly on the go. Andromeda? She had all but disappeared. Mita hadn't seen her in person for weeks, and their texts had become sporadic at best. And then there was Amerei. They shared a dorm, but between the constant rush of school and sleep, they rarely even caught up with each other or had clashes, neither in the morning nor in the evening.

It felt like everyone was being swept away in different directions, and Mita had no choice but to go with the flow.

The semester was starting to feel like a blur of deadlines and expectations. There were days when Mita could barely remember what day it was, much less what her next class was about. She'd wake up, go through the motions, and crash into bed at night, her mind too tired to even think about her thoughts or feelings.

But there were small victories. Her Christian club meetings were always a source of peace and comfort. Even when the rest of her life was chaotic, she always felt grounded when she was with them. Those moments reminded her why she was here, why she was working so hard. Her faith was her anchor, and the club was her safe space.

And then there was the music club. The hours she spent there, whether it was playing piano or just listening to Rune and the others, gave her a sense of joy she hadn't realized she needed. Mita had started to get better at the piano, her fingers no longer stumbling over the keys. She still wasn't a professional, but she was starting to feel like she could create something beautiful on her own one day soon. That sense of progress kept her going. The club was more than just music; it was a place where she could learn, grow, and forget about the weight of everything else for a while.

But despite the progress, the pressure was beginning to catch up with her.

It was another late night in the hospital, and Mita was curled up in the chair next to Reed's bed, her textbook open but unread. The light from the small lamp on the desk cast a soft glow across the room, making everything feel surreal. The silence was deafening.

"God, I don't know how much longer I can keep this up," she whispered, resting her head against the back of the chair, staring up at the ceiling. *"Please, help me find balance. I just... I don't want to lose myself in all this."*

Within the next moment, she closed her eyes, praying intently; she prayed for Reed's health, for her friends, and for the strength to keep moving forward.

After a few minutes, the quiet sound of footsteps broke her reverie. She looked up to see a nurse stepping into the room, checking his vital signs, and making her rounds.

"How's he doing?" Mita asked softly.

The nurse gave her a reassuring smile. "Still the same. But we're hopeful. You've been a good friend, staying by his side like this. I know it means a lot to him."

Mita smiled weakly, her heart full but heavy at the same time. "Thank you. I just... I want him to wake up so bad and tell me himself." Trying not to make her voice break under her unspoken current of emotion

"I'm sure he knows you're here."

Mita nodded, her throat tight. "I hope so."

The nurse moved toward the door but paused before leaving. "If you ever need a break, don't hesitate to ask. We are here to keep an eye on him. You need rest, and by the looks of it," the nurse paused, indicating to the book in my lap and my laptop on the couch, charging, and the papers of the assignment scattered around it before continuing, "you *do* need your rest.

College is hectic, and I am talking from experience."

Mita looked up, startled. "I'm fine. Really. I just—" She hesitated, unsure of how to explain what she was feeling. "It's just hard to balance everything out, but I'll figure something out. But thank you."

The nurse smiled kindly before slipping out of the room, leaving Mita alone again. She let out a long breath, wiping away the tears that had started to well up in her eyes.

She missed her friends. She missed the feeling of normalcy. But for now, it was no use getting worked up over something she had no control over; she would focus on what she could control: visiting Reed, her faith, and the little moments of peace she found in her classes and her clubs.

The next morning, Mita was walking to her first class when she ran into Rune, as she always seemed to do since the semester started. He was carrying his guitar case, looking like he'd just rolled out of bed, but at the same time well put together; the smile on his face made it clear he was in a good mood.

"Hey, Mita!" Rune greeted her, his eyes sparkling. "How's it going?"

She couldn't help but grin. "Busy. I think the semester is trying to kill me."

"Oh, don't I know it," Rune said, dropping his guitar case at his feet. "But hey, don't forget to take breaks, alright? Don't work yourself too hard."

"I don't have a choice," Mita replied with a wry smile. "It's all assignments, all the time."

He tilted his head, raising an eyebrow. "How about tonight? You want to hit the music club again? We'll let you take a break from your assignments and actually *have* some fun for a change."

Mita hesitated. Her schedule was packed, but a part of her longed for the freedom to just... be.

"I don't know; I didn't even know y'all were meeting up today," she said. "I've got a lot to catch up on."

Rune's grin widened. "You're too serious, Mita. It's just one night. You deserve a break."

She looked at him for a moment, then laughed. "Fine. One night. I'll take

155

you up on it."

"Good." He gave her a playful wink. "Now promise me, no assignments allowed."

Mita shook her head, but the broad smile he always manages to pull from her stretched across her face. "Okay, deal."

For a moment, everything felt lighter. And that optimistic thought came to her once again that maybe, just maybe, she could learn to balance it all after all.

Back in her dorm later that night, post-club, Mita laid her head on her pillow after praying, feeling exhausted but strangely content. Her schedule was still overwhelming, and Reed was still in a coma. But she just needed to remember to take one step at a time.[1]

---

[1] (a/n; yes, I wrote that line intentionally),

Chapter 32: Ethan's Anika

❦

This semester has been brutal. Honestly, I don't think I've had a moment to breathe since the first week. The workload, the pressure, it's like an avalanche that just keeps rolling down the hill, and I'm doing everything I can just to stay on my feet. Assignments are stacking up, deadlines are coming in faster than I can keep track of, and don't get me started on the constant bombardment of group projects. It's as if the university has taken every ounce of energy and ambition I had left, wrung it out, and handed it back to me with an *"All the best; you're gonna need it!"* topped off with a smile.

But despite all the chaos, there's something that makes it all bearable—someone, actually. **Anika**.

I don't know exactly when it happened, but somewhere between the random study sessions and spontaneous Bible study hangouts, I started looking forward to seeing her, **a lot**. I guess you could say I'm developing feelings for her. But the thing is,

I'm not ready for that.

Not yet.

The semester's a mess, and honestly, I'm not sure how to juggle all the emotional stuff when everything else feels like it's spiraling out of control. I'm just trying to get through the days at this point, one assignment at a time, and most importantly, I know that I am not the man I need to be to lead and love one of God's daughters, and to be him, I need first to be a son of God wholly in order to become a man in Christ, ready to lead her lovingly and gently to Christ. A man of God is the goal, and unfortunately, that is not the current state I'm in, but I *am* working on that.

Still, whenever I'm with Anika, everything feels… like weightless. I can be myself with her; no superficial behavior, no putting on my best face. It's authentic with her; *I'm* authentic with her.

She's a theatre major, which, if you know anything about theatre people, you know she's practically always doing something. Rehearsals, performances, presentations, it never ends. But sometimes, when she gets a break from the chaos, that's when I get to hang out with her. I don't mind it, though. Honestly, it's a relief to just spend time with her. When she's preparing for a performance or working on some assignment, I'm usually around. It's not that I'm *hovering*; nothing of the sort. As a matter of fact, I'm working on my own assignments alongside her. I just like being near her, watching her work, and listening to her talk about what she's doing and what she is passionate about.

Sometimes, we'll talk about our classes or just laugh at the most random things. She's got this way of making me laugh, even when I'm stressed out. Her jokes aren't the kind that *try* to be funny; they just are. She has this effortless radiance about her, and when she smiles, *my gosh*, when she smiles, it's like everything else in the world stops. Yeah, I know it sounds cheesy, but it's true. It's like her presence makes all the noise of the semester fade into the background.

But beyond the laughter and jokes, she's different in other ways, too. Sometimes when we're sitting together, or when I'm walking her to class, we'll talk about deeper things. We'll share bits and pieces of our lives, stuff that's hard to talk about with other people. I've shared some of what I've learned in Bible study, and she's actually interested. She'll ask me questions or tell me about things she's thinking about. I never expected her to be so open to it, but she is. And when she asked me to pray for her, it felt… special. I don't know why, but it did.

The first time she asked me to pray for her, I wasn't sure how to respond. But I just did it. I prayed out loud, and she sat there quietly, listening in agreement to every word I said. The second time she asked me, it was when we were having our little hangout. She quietly asked me to pray on her behalf for her performance and a test she had coming up. It was simple, nothing huge, but it meant a lot to me that she trusted me with that. And when she joined me in prayer that one time, I felt like we were on the same wavelength. Like, maybe there's something more here than just friendship.

But, of course, I try not to overthink it. Because who am I kidding? With everything going on: work, classes, assignments, Reed in the hospital, and the pressure of just *being*, I don't need to add a relationship to the mix right now. It's not that I don't like Anika, because I do, a lot. It's more that, I need to keep my head in the game[2].

Still, it's hard to ignore the way she looks at me sometimes, or the way her voice softens when she asks me a question. There's a tenderness in the way she interacts with me. And sometimes, when she laughs or teases me, I feel this flutter in my chest that I can't quite explain. It's not like I'm *falling* for her, at least not yet. But I can tell that I'm getting attached to her. And that, for now, is a little terrifying on its own.

One of the things I like most about our friendship is how we can talk about everything and nothing all at once. In those moments, she has this way of making everything feel *manageable*. Her energy is contagious, and it was the only disease I was willing to be infected by if it meant I got to be around her

and feel like I could take on the world. Sounds like a win-win situation for me if we're being sincere here. There are nights when we show up at a meetup spot on weekends just to study together. We'll pull out our textbooks, sit side by side, and try to get some work done. But honestly? We end up talking more than studying.

There was one night, a couple of weeks ago, when we were sitting together, and she started telling me about her upcoming performance. She was

---

[2] (a/n: the real OGs know this one)

nervous, as usual, even though I knew she'd kill it. Anika was incredibly talented, but she still got nervous every time, like she didn't believe in her own ability. I told her she had nothing to worry about, but she just rolled her eyes, saying she was not buying it and that my opinion was biased and I was trying to butter her up.

"I'm serious, Anika," I said, trying to convey my sincerity. "You're going to do great. You always do."

She chuckled. "Thanks, Ethan. You always know how to make me feel better," she said, playfully tugging on a strand of my hair. It was a thing she does, and it was a thing I have come to more than like, if I am being honest again.

I shrugged, looking down at my notes, which I should have been studying. "I just speak the truth."

She smiled softly at me. "You're a good friend, you know that. E. Thank you for sticking around when you don't have to."

I looked at her, startled by the sudden nickname, but tried to play it off by thinking of something to deflect, but the truth spilled out despite my best efforts to cork the bottle of my emotions. "I *want* to stick around, Anika. You don't have to thank me."

Her eyes met mine for a brief moment, and something passed between us, something unspoken, but I quickly turned my attention back to my notes, trying to avoid making the moment weird.

But, for the rest of the night, the atmosphere had changed. There was an easy tension between us that I didn't know how to deal with. I liked being around her, I enjoyed laughing with her, and I relished how our friendship had deepened over time. But I wasn't sure what this meant for me. Or for us.

When we finally called it a night, she gave me a light hug. "Good luck with the Bible study stuff," she said, her voice soft and teasing. "Don't get too preachy, okay?"

I laughed, looking down at the top of her head, resisting the urge to run my fingers through purple strands of hair. "I won't make any promises."

As I walked back to my dorm, I couldn't help but feel a little giddy. A little *happier.*

There was something about Anika's presence that made everything seem a little more manageable. Even though the semester was still overwhelming, even though my mind was constantly racing with everything I had to do, I felt better when I was with this amazing friend of mine.

One day, I'd figure out what this thing with Anika meant. But for now, I was content just being in her orbit, watching her grow, supporting her, and trying to be the friend she needed. That was enough for me.

Chapter 33: The Trip and The Chuu

The semester was winding down, finally. The dreaded midterms were behind her, and while there were still assignments to tackle, the pressure felt less suffocating. Mita was using her newfound free time to spend more hours with Reed, who was still in the hospital, and to attend her club meetings, which had started to feel like a cozy routine. Between all the late-night study sessions and hospital visits, the music club had been one of the few constants that steadied her mental state.

One afternoon, during a music club meeting, the leader of the club stood in front of the group, looking more enthusiastic than usual. She cleared her throat to get everyone's attention before she began.

"Alright, everyone! I have exciting news! The music club is going on a trip! All expenses paid by the institution." She paused, watching the buzz of excitement ripple through the group. Mita leaned forward, immediately interested. "But," the leader continued, "there's a catch. We're splitting up into groups of three, and you will each be assigned to a genre of music to explore on this trip. "Kinda like a school trip but better," she said, trying to boost up the now dejected crowd

A collective groan went up from the group, but Mita was undeterred. She loved the idea of a trip, especially if it involved learning about music and seeing it come to life in a real-world setting.

"This is going to be a three-day, three-night trip, and you'll be visiting different companies and clubs that specialize in various genres of music. Your task will be to observe and document the instruments used in each genre, collect copies of music sheets, and note the differences in techniques, sound, and style in the genre you selected. In a week and a half, we'll all come back here, share our findings, and compare the music of different genres to understand their similarities and differences to each other."

Mita's eyes lit up. This was an opportunity to dive deeper into the world of music, and she was already excited about the possibility of exploring a new genre, maybe gospel or even classical.

The leader smiled, clearly excited by the anticipation in the room. "And don't forget, this trip isn't just about work! It's about making memories and having fun. We want you all to experience something new and learn things you didn't know before. So you can look back and say, '*Oh, you remember that trip we went on? Yeah, it was great, and so was our leader for making it possible.*' Because I made it happen." She gloated, checking her nails in feigned indifference before continuing. "So, I hope you're all up for the challenge. Let's make this trip one to remember." She received shouts of agreement in response.

The room filled with murmurs of excitement, everyone planning out their trip itinerary already, when the leader held up a bowl filled with pieces of paper. "Now, let's pick your genres! Each of you will pick a rep for your group; they will draw a slip from the bowl to know your genre."

Mita, still feeling the buzz of excitement, didn't really think much of the process. She was mostly focused on the piano in front of her, absently picking out chords as her thoughts raced about what genre she might end up with.

Suddenly, a voice broke through her thoughts.

"I volunteer," Rune said, grinning from where he stood beside the grand piano she was playing.

Mita blinked, looking up at him, but Rune was already walking over to the bowl, a comfortable smile on his face. She raised an eyebrow. Rune wasn't shy, that's for sure.

"Just pick a good one, please," she said more to herself and not to the one added member to their group as she turned back to her piano, though she wasn't really playing anymore. She was just... *waiting*.

A few moments later, Rune returned to their group, a slip of paper in hand. He looked at her and grinned, an almost mischievous glint in his eyes.

"Jazz," he said, his voice almost teasing.

Mita felt a small knot form in her stomach. Jazz? She had secretly hoped for gospel, but she didn't want to seem disappointed. She smiled and shrugged, even though inwardly she was trying to convince herself that jazz wasn't *that* bad.

"Hey, jazz is cool, you know," Rune said, nudging her playfully with his shoulder, sensing her disappointment. He was so casual, he wasn't even trying to be flirtatious, but Mita felt her heart skip a beat at his touch more than at his concern for her. *Great,* now she was going to have to try to focus on jazz instead of the way his broad shoulder felt brushing against her.

"Yeah, yeah," Mita replied, playing along. "I guess it's not too bad." She shot him what she hoped would come across as a teasing smile.

Rune's smile softened, and for a second, Mita felt like he wasn't just teasing her but genuinely enjoying their banter. It was small, but it was something; it was progress, *for them* or *to her* she didn't know.

After the meeting wrapped up, Rune walked her to her dorm, their conversation filled with the usual playful back-and-forths. He had that effect on her, making everything feel effortless, even their stupid banter.

When they reached the entrance to her dorm building, Mita paused. Her heart was still racing from the earlier interaction, and she suddenly had the urge to do something a little... out of character.

"Hey," she said, looking up at Rune. "Bend down for a sec."

He raised an eyebrow but obliged. She wasn't sure why, but the moment felt right. She reached up and tugged a small leaf out of his hair, something she hadn't noticed before she had asked him to bend toward her.

Rune, still bent down, looked at her with those striking blue-gray eyes, and she felt the familiar flutter in her chest, but this time with more verve. She didn't know what possessed her, but in that moment, she leaned in quickly and planted a soft kiss on his cheek.

Before she could stop herself, she pulled away, her heart racing, and dashed into the building before disappearing around a corner.

She leaned against the cold concrete wall of the building, hiding behind a random column.

What did I just do?

She peeked around the corner, her breath catching in her throat. Rune was still standing there, frozen in his bent position, eyes wide. After a long second, he straightened up, looking around in confusion. It was almost as if he were trying to process what had just happened. Then he turned, walking back toward the darkness of the campus. Mita couldn't help but watch him, her heart thumping. She waited, hidden, until she couldn't see him anymore, and only then did she allow herself to breathe.

She quickly ran up the stairs to her room, not in the mood to stand still in an elevator. Flinging the door open. She didn't even bother to turn on the lights; she just went to her room and collapsed onto her bed, burying her face in the pillow.

What did I just do?

Her mind raced. She could feel the intensity of the moment in every inch of her body. The kiss had been so impulsive. And yet… it felt so right. But now, everything was different. She couldn't just pretend it hadn't happened.

She kicked her legs in frustration, letting out a muffled scream into the pillow.

Why is everything so complicated?

Finally, after what felt like hours of internal chaos, Mita decided to pray. She needed guidance, clarity, anything.

"*God, what am I doing?*" she muttered, her voice breaking slightly. "*I know I'm supposed to focus on You, and I'm trying, but… this… that little kiss is messing with my mind. God is he the one? Please, just… guide me. And please, help me to stay focused. Help me not to lose myself in the things I don't need…*"

She spoke to God for what felt like an eternity, getting everything off her chest, treating it like a therapy session, because it was, at least to her. It was the only way she could make sense of everything happening in her life.

After she finished praying, Mita lay there for a while, staring up at the ceiling, trying to calm her racing thoughts.

Thank God it was the weekend. She needed all the time she could get to process everything that had just happened, plus she wouldn't wake up on time if she had class. And even though the semester was winding down, she had a feeling that this was just the beginning of something way more complicated than she was ready for.

But for now, all she could do was wait.

And pray.

Chapter 34: The Impromptu Sleepover

Mita woke up to the soft rays of sunlight streaming through the curtains of their dorm room. It was the weekend, thankfully. Her body felt heavy with all the week's stress, but today, she had the whole day ahead of her to relax. She stretched and rolled over to check her phone, only to find a message waiting for her in the group chat.

Her eyes squinted as she read the message from Amerei:

Amerei: *"We're overdue for a hangout. You guys up for an impromptu meet-up? It's Sunday, and I think we deserve to have fun."*

Mita grinned and sat up, stretching again before heading to the living room. She glanced over at Amerei, who was sprawled on the couch with her hair pulled up into the messiest bun, still half-asleep but clearly already in a good mood.

"Good morning, sleepyhead," Mita said with a playful smile.

Amerei groaned in response, a lazy but affectionate noise, before rolling her eyes dramatically. "Morning," she yawned. "I think I need another 12 hours of sleep. But hey, I'm down for whatever."

Mita laughed, then texted in the group chat to see if anyone else was up for the idea.

Mita: *"Hey girls, what do you think? Impromptu meet-up over here? We can hang, play games, and just chill for the day because* the person ***@Amerei*** *who suggested it is half dead atm."*

The replies came in fast:

Odessa: *"I'm in. I can't say no to free snacks and some girl time."*

Andromeda: *"You know I'm always down for a girls' day. I'll be over in 15 minutes."*

Mita leaned back on the couch beside Amerei, smiling to herself. There was something so simple, yet comforting, about the chaos they always ended up in when they hung out. She could already imagine how much fun it was going to be.

As promised, 15 minutes later, Odessa and Andromeda arrived at the door, each carrying a pillow, a blanket, and a bag. Mita blinked in confusion, taking in the sight of them standing there with all their supplies.

"Uh… what's all this?" Mita asked, looking back and forth between them. "Are you guys moving in or something?"

Andromeda grinned. "Girl, me and Odessa decided this meet-up needed to be a *sleepover*." She said. "Get ready for a full-on girls' day and night."

Mita stared at them, wide-eyed. "A *sleepover*?" she repeated slowly, trying to process the sudden turn of events.

"Yep," Odessa replied, her voice dripping with enthusiasm as she walked past Mita into the living room. "We're doing skincare, mani-pedis, board games, coloring… basically everything that makes us feel like we're 12 again."

Mita laughed, feeling the excitement bubble inside her. It had been such a long week, and she couldn't think of a better way to unwind.

"Well, I'm in," Mita said, grinning. "Not like I had a choice."

The girls spread out on the floor and couch, organizing their blankets and pillows in a chaotic but cozy setup. Andromeda turned on the TV to set the mood with some background music while Odessa went to grab snacks from her bag. Mita started setting up the skincare stuff on the coffee table, pulling out masks, lotions, and the little facial roller that Amerei had gotten for everyone the night prior, which made her wonder if her roommate knew this sleepover would happen.

"Alright, ladies," Odessa said, giving the group a serious look. "Let's start with some skincare. I brought face masks, and I know you two will want to fight me for the lavender one. Just don't."

Mita and Andromeda both laughed as they grabbed their own masks, putting them on in the same motion, and then they all slouched down on the floor, doing their best to relax in the masks that now made them all look a little ridiculous.

"This is... actually the best," Andromeda said, her voice muffled through the mask. "I can't believe we never did this earlier in the semester."

"I know, right?" Odessa chimed in, tossing a glance over at Mita. "You have to admit, we're all looking fly with these things on."

Mita snorted. "We look funny-looking, but pampered."

Once the masks were off and their skin was glowing (or at least, that's what they all pretended was happening), they moved on to the mani-pedi station that Odessa had set up. Each of them took turns giving each other foot rubs and painting their nails with the cutest shades. It wasn't a quiet moment, but no one had to think about homework, tests, or the crazy pace of the semester.

Then, after a few rounds of painting, it was time to kick things up a notch.

"Okay," Amerei said with a glint in her eyes, "now that we're all cute and pampered, who's up for board games?"

"YES," Odessa yelled. "But if you even *think* of suggesting Monopoly, I will *fight* you."

"I don't do Monopoly; those end friendships like UNO but worse," Mita said, shaking her head. "But I'm still down for some domino or Pictionary."

The game choices were made, and soon the room was filled with laughter, playful arguments, and some embarrassing drawings in the game of Pictionary. At one point, Odessa even tried to guess a stick figure as an abstract representation of a giraffe, which sent everyone into a fit of giggles.

As night fell, they gathered in Amerei's room, huddled together under the blankets.

"So," Andromeda began, raising an eyebrow, "what's the update on your *love* life, Amerei? We've been waiting *forever* for the details."

Amerei sighed, but her smile was soft and content. "That's what you always say," Amerei responded, causing a childish whine from Andromeda and Odessa. "Okay, okay. So, Merrick and I... What is there to say? Not much is happening, but things are going *great*. I'm really happy. We've been seeing each other intentionally more recently because of the whole stupidly packed semester; besides that, there's not much of an update."

"*Awwww*," Odessa cooed, crossing her arms over her chest, giving Amerei a teasing grin.

Mita smiled at Amerei, feeling genuinely happy for her. She loved seeing her friend having someone in her corner.

"I'm happy for you, babe," Mita said, nudging her shoulder. "You deserve all the good things."

"So what's the next update?" Odessa asked, looking right at Mita

Mita started, "So I might have an out-of-town trip with Rune, and I kind of kissed him last night ON THE CHEEKS, for your information, *Odessa*," she said, looking at Odessa, who was now grinning from ear to ear.

"So you got this trip coming up, and you finally kissed Mr. Loverboy. The tea is hot metaphorically and literally." Odessa squealed

Mita felt her cheeks flush. The memories from last night hit her all over again, and she didn't know if she was ready to dive into it.

But they were friends, and the anticipation on their faces was hilarious to her.

"I kinda planned it…" Mita said, holding her hands up in mock defense. "It was just a kiss on the cheek. Just a quick one, but still it feels like… *everything is gonna changed* after this."

They all stared at her, the excitement palpable in the room.

"Girl, what did *Rune* do?" Odessa pressed, her eyes gleaming. "Tell me he didn't just stand there, frozen, like, 'What do I do now?'" Odessa said, rolling her eyes

"Do you have cameras watching me?" Mita enquired, actually surprised by *how she guessed that accurately*

"Are you for real right now? That's what happened?" Andromeda said in boredom

"That's so cute," Amerei said, cooing.

Mita buried her face in her hands. "You're *not* helping."

"I bet you're dying to text him, huh?" Amerei teased, wiggling her eyebrows.

"I can't even think straight!" Mita groaned. "I just kissed him on the cheek and ran into the dorm like I was escaping a crime scene."

Andromeda clutched her chest, cackling. "That's so cute I can't stand it. I'm living for this. This is the kind of drama we need in our lives."

The night continued with laughter, more games, and karaoke. Each girl took turns belting out their favorite songs, and even though their voices weren't perfect, it didn't matter. They were all having a blast, kicking their feet up like little girls in the middle of the night. Thank the Lord the rooms were soundproof.

By the time they finally settled down to sleep, everyone was exhausted, but it was the kind of tired you felt after a day full of laughter, bonding, and joy.

Mita lay back, a smile on her face as she stared up at the ceiling.

She couldn't remember the last time she'd felt this at peace, surrounded by her friends, all of them just letting go of the pressures of school for one night.

She thought about Rune, and her heart fluttered at the memory of that kiss. It didn't feel like a big deal, but somehow, it *was,* and maybe it was the beginning of something new.

But for now, she was content just to be with her friends.

Chapter 35: A Day of Fun and Friendship

PLAYLIST- MIRACLE BY COLTON DIXION

The morning sun peeked through Ethan's window, casting a soft glow over his room. He stretched, feeling the weight of the weekend's end settling in. The hectic semester was winding down, but it didn't feel any less busy. But today? Today was different. Today was a day for fun, laughter, and memories.

Ethan stood in front of the mirror, adjusting his shirt one last time. His hair was freshly cut, shorter than usual, but he liked it. He'd gone for a clean look, a little more effort than usual, it would be a nice change. He had no idea why he was putting so much thought into it, but maybe it was because this time felt... special. It wasn't a date, at least, they both had made sure of that. No unspoken pressure between them. But he knew, deep down, that there was something about his friendship with Anika that felt different, like a spark that he couldn't quite ignore. He didn't want to lose that.

He grabbed his keys and headed out the door, heart beating a little faster than usual for the day ahead.

When he arrived at Anika's off-campus housing, he was greeted by the sight of her standing at the door, looking like she had just stepped out of his favourite imagination. Her outfit was simple but elegant: black jeans paired with a light green sweater that hugged her frame just enough to be flattering.

She always had this effortless vibe, like she could throw on anything and still look breathtaking.

"Wow," he muttered without thinking, his eyes widening as he open the car door for her before running around the car to open his door.

Anika smiled as he entered, clearly pleased by the compliment. "You clean up well," she said, her voice teasing.

Ethan smiled, trying not to blush. "Well, I figured it was a special day. I didn't want to show up in my usual professional *chic*."

Anika laughed, her eyes sparkling. "You look great, everyday" she said, bucking up. "Ready for our adventure?"

Ethan nodded, still a little flustered. "Yeah. I'm just happy we're doing this. I think we both needed the break."

As Ethan started the car, a comfortable silence settled between them. The road ahead was clear, the sky painted in shades of soft blue and yellow as the sun began to rise higher. Ethan glanced over at Anika and, for a brief moment, couldn't help but admire how natural it felt to be with her, before bowing his head in prayer making Anika do the same.

"Lord," he said softly, *"Please watch over us today, keep us safe, and help us make some great memories, in Jesus name Amen."*

Anika smiled at him, her voice quiet, saying her. 'Amen.'

The drive to the amusement park felt longer than usual, but when they finally arrived, it was like they were eight years old again, entering a world of candy-colored roller coasters, twinkling lights, and endless fun. Ethan could feel the excitement bubbling inside of him, his nerves melting away as they stepped out of the car.

"Tickets!" Anika exclaimed, her hand reaching for her purse grabbing them. "Let's make this count," she started as they made their way to the entrance.

"Yes ma'am!" Ethan shouted, matching her enthusiasm. "I'm ready to get on every ride here."

The merry-go-round was a calming start to the day, but things quickly picked up when they climbed onto the first roller coaster.

"I'm not sure I'm ready for this!" Anika shouted, holding onto the safety bar with one hand as the coaster clicked into place.

Ethan laughed, his adrenaline kicking in. "Too late for that now!"

The ride shot forward, and they both screamed as the coaster dipped and swirled, the wind in their faces. They laughed, their voices mixing together like a chorus of joy. When it finally ended, they were breathless, grinning from ear to ear.

"Okay, next!" Anika said, her eyes wide with excitement. "I'm not ready to stop."

They spent the rest of the day going from one roller coaster to the next, screaming at the top of their lungs, laughing so hard that their faces hurt. They didn't stop for hours. They went from one ride to the next, collecting photos and memories as they explored the park. After the bumper cars, where they both ended up *completely* drenched in the water rides, that's when they finally decided to take a break and grab some food.

Ethan took a big bite of his burger, glancing at Anika, who was laughing to herself.

"You know," he said between bites, "today's been amazing. I know I said this before, but we really needed this."

Anika looked at him, her smile softening. "Yeah. It really has. I think I forgot how much fun it could be to just *let go*, you know?"

Ethan nodded. "Yeah, life's been kinda heavy lately, huh?"

"Tell me about it," she said, rolling her eyes playfully. "But today was a load off, uggh. No deadlines, no pressure... just us having fun."

They sat for a while longer, letting the food settle in their stomachs, before heading to the indoor arcade. Ethan challenged Anika to a few rounds of air hockey, but, unsurprisingly, she *completely* beat him.

"Ha! I told you I was good," Anika said, high-fiving him after her victory.

Ethan feigned disappointment. "Okay, okay. I get it. You're the air hockey champion."

She grinned. "Don't worry, you'll get another chance... maybe."

174

Then it was time for the claw machine. They both stood behind a couple playing, watching as the claw descended toward a stuffed bear, but to no avail. The disappointed couple moved away and went somewhere else.

"Watch this," Ethan said confidently, dropping a coin into the machine. He maneuvered the claw with precision, and, *bam*, the claw picked up the bear, and it dropped neatly into the prize chute.

"Yes!" Ethan cheered, taking the bear and handing it to Anika. "For you."

Anika's eyes widened. "Ethan, that's so sweet. You're good at this."

He shrugged, smiling sheepishly. "What can I say? I've got skills."

Anika laughed. "You're definitely full of surprises today."

"I could say the same about you," he retorted slyly, bumping her shoulders with his.

They continued winning prizes for each other, laughing and sharing the little victories of the day. At one point, Anika won a cute stuffed animal for him, a small, fluffy fox,and Ethan's heart swelled a little bit.

"Thanks," he said, grinning. "I've got to step up my game next time," knowing that their time together was winding down

The sun began to dip lower in the sky, and they found themselves at the Ferris wheel, a perfect way to end the day. As they slowly ascended, Ethan took out his phone to capture another epic moment of the day, only to realize his phone storage was now filled with the events of today, and he would never complain.

The view from the top was breathtaking, but with his current situation, he was content to capture it with his eye and save it to *his* memory. The city lights twinkled in the distance, and for a moment, everything was still.

Anika was staring out at the view, and Ethan couldn't help but glance at her. There was something so calming about her presence, something that made everything else seem less important.

"So," he said softly, his voice quieter than usual, "this has been a pretty good day."

Anika turned to him, her eyes meeting his. "Yeah. The best. Thanks for planning this."

"You're welcome," Ethan said, his voice low. "I needed this, too." When the ride finally ended, they were both tired but happy.

Anika fell asleep almost immediately on the drive back. Her soft breathing filled the car, Ethan turned down the radio to not wake her, but her slow breaths were enough tranquility to keep him awake.

As he parked outside her house, he noticed she was still asleep, her head resting against the window. He didn't want to wake her, so he gently reclined her seat, pulled his jacket off, and draped it over her. Then, feeling a little too tired himself to drive back, he locked the doors, reclined his own seat, and allowed the warmth of the car to lull him into a light sleep with the intentions of waking up after 15 minutes to head back.

Ethan awoke, blinking against the sunlight that now poured through the windshield. He looked around, still groggy, and found himself still in the car. Anika, however, was already up on her phone.

"Good morning, sleepyhead," she said, a playful smile tugging at her lips.

Ethan chuckled softly, feeling the exhaustion still in his limbs. "Morning. How'd you sleep?" he blamed it on his restricted sleeping position in the car; he hadn't planned to sleep the entire night, but to get a bit of rest and then drive back to the dorm, and for Anika to have enough time to wake up on her own, but his brain had other plans.

He glanced around, noticing the blankets that had somehow appeared on him. "Wait..?"

"I woke up in the middle of the night and saw both of us sleeping, so I went in and brought us blankets," Anika said sincerely. "You didn't wake me, and I didn't want to wake you, so... I made sure you were comfy. And then I got a little comfortable myself."

Ethan smiled, his cheeks flushing just slightly. "You're too nice, you know that?"

Anika shrugged, feeling a little shy under his gaze. "It's no big deal."

"So, do you want to freshen up?" Anika asked, stretching. "I made breakfast. You can eat before you go."

Ethan nodded, feeling a little hesitant but grateful. "Sure. I could use a bathroom break."

As he stepped into her off-campus housing, he was struck by how *homey* everything felt. The place smelled like her, fresh, artistic, warm. The decor was thoughtful, the walls adorned with beautiful pictures of her travels and her performances. It was hard to believe this wasn't her actual house; she had clearly made it her own.

They ate breakfast together, chatting about everything and nothing, reminiscing about their childhoods, the highs and lows of their lives so far, and even going through the pictures they'd taken at the amusement park.

"Yesterday was perfect," Anika said, her eyes soft. "I'm glad we did this."

Ethan smiled, feeling a warmth spread in his chest. "Me too. I think it's the best day I've had at uni so far."

Later, after breakfast, Ethan left, his heart light. He couldn't wait to tell Aseal everything.

It had been an unforgettable day. And while Ethan wasn't ready to define whatever this was with Anika, he knew one thing for sure: whatever came next, he wanted to keep spending time with her.

There was no rush. Not yet.

Chapter 36: The Road to New Discoveries

※※※

PLAYLIST- MIRACLE BY COLTON DIXION

The day of the trip had arrived, and Mita couldn't help but feel a mix of excitement and nervousness. She'd spent the past few days prepping for the trip: making sure her suitcase was packed with just enough clothes (thanks to Amerei, who had lent her a few cute outfits), checking her phone for any last-minute updates, and nervously glancing at her reflection in the mirror this morning 10 times.

This trip felt significant, almost like a milestone. Sure, she was majoring in digital marketing, but music had always been something close to her heart ever since she joined the club. It was a chance to step outside the box, try something new, and see the world from a different angle. And as much as she was thrilled to experience that, the thought of seeing Rune again left her heart fluttering in a way she couldn't quite explain. After that kiss... well, everything was a little different.

As she rolled her small suitcase across campus toward the art building, her mind couldn't help but wander. She had spent Christmas visiting her mom, but this trip felt like her first real adventure in college, an opportunity to explore a passion that had always been a background noise in her life, quietly humming beneath everything else. The thought of it excited her, but the thought of Rune *and* the trip with him... well, there's gonna be a third person there, so it's not gonna be that bad. That added a bit of unpredictability and, at the same time, boosted her composure, though she wasn't quite sure how to navigate it all the same.

When she reached the music room, the buzz of activity and excited chatter filled the air. Students milled around, some already talking about the trip, some lost in their own little worlds, while others were just arriving, their energy radiating off them. The only thing that struck her was the absence of Rune and the girl in her group. She had spoken to the girl a few times before the trip's announcement, but that was it. She couldn't help but glance around once more , looking for signs of them to see if she had somehow overlooked them.

Minutes later, the door opened, and there he was. Rune strolled in with his signature relaxed confidence, a glimmer of playfulness in his eyes when he spotted Mita.

"Hey," he greeted her, flashing that familiar smirk that never failed to make her heart skip a beat. She felt a rush of warmth flood her chest, but she quickly forced a neutral expression.

"Hey," she replied, trying to sound casual.

The club leader cleared her throat, drawing their attention. "Alright, everyone, just a reminder: this trip is about learning and exploring music genres, but most importantly, having fun and building memories. I hope you all are ready to share your experiences and results when you return."

Mita nodded, trying to focus on the excitement of the trip and not the butterflies that seemed to have taken residence in her stomach every time Rune was around.

"Well," the leader continued, " OK, everyone, get into your groups of three, but Mita and Rune, your third member couldn't make it; she called me last night, so it'll just be the two of you. Are you both okay with that?"

The words hung in the air for a moment, and Mita glanced at Rune. Their eyes locked, and an unspoken conversation passed between them.

Just the two of us?

A small part of her felt relieved, it meant three days and three nights with him, no distractions, just the two of them. The other part... well, that part was a little unsure.

After a brief moment, Rune grinned and nodded, nudging her gently with his shoulder. "We're good with that. No worries."

Mita couldn't help but smile back. "Yeah, it's fine. Totally fine," she said, trying to sound more confident than she felt. Inside, she was already picturing how the trip would unfold.

As they made their way to Rune's car, Mita quickly shot a text in their group chat:

Guess what? It's just me and Rune on the trip! The replies were immediate, full of exclamation points and surprised emojis. Mita couldn't help but laugh. It felt a little surreal. Her mind was still reeling from the fact that she was about to spend the next few days alone with Rune, and something about the idea made her pulse race a little faster.

The car ride to their destination was an experience in itself…expensive, other than his car, of course. Mita had barely settled into her seat when she caught a whiff of the air. Something about it was different, rich, warm, and a little expensive. She glanced over at Rune, who had his sunglasses on, his hands casually gripping the steering wheel. His style, his presence… everything about him felt effortless but calculated. Like he belonged in a different world. Not that he was intimidating, quite the opposite. He was so easygoing, so *in the moment.* Still, there was an aura around him that made Mita think that he could probably make anything look good.

"So," Mita said after a few beats of silence, trying to push aside the strange mixture of nervousness and excitement boiling in her. "You always dress this well, or is this for the trip?"

Rune let out a soft laugh. "I just like to look good. Is that a problem?" he said, glancing at her for a moment, before setting them back on the road and then reaching across the console to adjust her blouse on her shoulder, his eyes still on the road, but the smirk on his lips suggested he knew what he was doing.

She smiled, playing along, reaching across to adjust his jacket. "No problem. Just wondering if I need to step up my game."

"Well, if you want, you can always borrow my jacket," Rune teased.

She rolled her eyes. "I'm good, thanks."

As the miles passed, the cities transitioned into the countryside, and Mita couldn't help but marvel at the changing scenery. The tall buildings of the city slowly faded into green hills and wide-open fields, dotted with small farmhouses and patches of trees. The air is fresher here, the wind a little cooler. She stuck her head out of the window, closing her eyes for a brief moment to let the rush of air wash over her face.

Rune chuckled when he noticed her antics. "You good there, Mita?"

She grinned, pulling her head back inside. "I feel like I'm in a movie, the wind, the fields... this is unreal."

"You want the full experience?" Rune asked, raising an eyebrow and glancing at her from the corner of his eye. "Try the sunroof. That's a little safer."

Before Mita could even respond, Rune was pressing a button on the dashboard, and the sunroof slid open smoothly, inviting the open sky above them.

"Okay, now *this* is perfect," Mita said, practically glowing with excitement. She popped her head through the sunroof, the wind ruffling her hair and the sun warming her skin. The freedom of the road, the endless fields, the feeling of being completely *away* from everything else. It was the most exhilarating thing she had felt in a long time.

Rune laughed at her enthusiasm, his voice rising above the wind in her ears. "You look like you're living your best life right now."

Mita looked down to see him, grinning ear to ear. "I *am*! You know, I think this is the best idea ever."

He gave her a look that almost seemed to say, *I knew it* but just shook his head. "It's nothing. Just wanted you to enjoy the ride."

As the miles passed, they sang along to a playlist Rune had put together for the trip, a mix of pop, jazz, and gospel songs. Mita was a little surprised by the range of music, but she loved how thoughtful Rune was about it. The gospel songs made her feel a sense of peace, while the pop and jazz tunes had them both laughing and belting out the lyrics, completely in sync.

The more time they spent on the road, the more the two of them seemed to fall into a rhythm. Their laughter echoed in the car, as did the way their voices harmonized on certain songs and the way they bounced off each other's energy.

"You're actually really good at this," Mita said, teasing him as they sang along to a particularly difficult line in a jazz song. "I thought you were just *faking* it."

Rune laughed, feigning offense. "You wound me. I'm a master of this, clearly."

Mita giggled, feeling a warmth spread in her chest once again because of this man before her. "Uh-huh, sure."

By the time they reached their destination, the sun was beginning to dip low on the horizon, painting the sky with rich hues of pink and orange. The car had become their own little world, a bubble of laughter and music. Mita couldn't remember the last time she had felt so carefree and filled with adrenaline.

As the trip stretched out ahead of them, she couldn't help but think that maybe this was more than just a musical exploration. Maybe it was a chance to learn something new about herself, too—something that she didn't even know she needed.

And with Rune by her side… well, things were definitely going to get interesting.

Chapter 37: Oui, Sí, Us

Mita's Pov

By the time we arrived at the hotel, I could feel the excitement building up inside me. The road trip had been incredible, and the anticipation for what was to come next had me buzzing. Rune and I checked in together, both of us getting rooms next to each other. As I settled into my room, it was just the two of us now for the next three days. I couldn't help but feel a small thrill at the thought. Three days. Three nights. Just me and Rune. I couldn't deny it: I was definitely more than a little excited.

We decided to spend the afternoon eating dinner and wandering around the city, enjoying the freedom that came with being away from campus and not worrying about assignments or schedules. We ended up having an early night, though, since Rune didn't want to go to the club yet. I couldn't blame him; it had been a long day of travel, and we both needed the rest.

The next morning, we had breakfast together at the hotel, then went sightseeing in the city. It was beautiful, everything felt new and fresh. The streets, the buildings, the people, they all had this unique idyllic quality. But even with all the sights around us, I couldn't shake the thought of what was waiting for us at the jazz club.

Finally, after a few hours of exploring, we made our way to the club. We were early, as Rune had suggested we be. It wasn't quite time for the real fun to begin, but he wanted me to get a feel for the place and see how the club prepared for the night ahead. When we arrived, there was barely anyone there except the manager and a few performers prepping for opening. He'd already been informed about our visit and greeted us warmly, welcoming us to the club. Rune's presence seemed to make the whole atmosphere a little more charged, like the place suddenly became more alive because he was there.

The manager took us on a tour of the club, explaining how everything ran. It was impressive, classy, but with a vibe that just screamed *jazz*. I had no idea what I was expecting, but this exceeded anything I had imagined. The dark wood floors, the low lighting, the vintage decor. And then the musicians, the regulars who performed here. They were incredible. I stood in awe as they showed me their instruments, and some even played for me, letting me hear the unique sounds that defined jazz. I'd always loved music, but this, this genre was something I had been sleeping on this entire time. Jazz was something different.

Then one of the musicians told me that *Rune's dad owns the club.* I thought he was joking, but when I actually observed how everyone was so familiar with him and how it was *I* who was being shown around and introduced to instruments while Rune was always just behind me, it didn't take long to figure out that Rune was more than just some regular student here. Of course, I thought to myself. Of course, he's a *nepo baby*. I mean, the school was an affluent one, so it's packed with rich kids, some spoiled, some not; some middle class and a few below the middle, so I was taken aback but not surprised. But honestly, it didn't bother me. He was still Rune. He wasn't acting like the boss's son at all. In fact, he was being more *Rune* than ever before, his usual chill demeanor never wavering.

Once the tour wrapped up, the manager led us upstairs to a VVIP lounge that overlooked the stage. It was quiet up here, but the view of the whole club made it feel like we were on top of the world. Rune and I sat down, each of us with a drink in hand. The sun was beginning to set, and the dim lights of the club were just starting to flicker on, setting the mood for the evening to come.

I took a sip of my drink, glancing over at Rune, still processing everything that had happened so far.

"So, why didn't you tell me your dad owns this place?" I asked, trying to keep my tone casual.

Rune, already looking me, gave me a half-smile and leaned back in his chair, crossing one leg over the other in a way that made him look effortlessly attractive. "Actually, I own the club. But I use my dad as a cover."

I blinked at him, stunned. "You *own* it?" I didn't know what to say to that.

"Yeah." Rune nodded, his gaze drifting off for a second as he seemed to think back. "When I was younger, I had a driver who was super into jazz. He always had it playing on the radio when he drove me to school, and I got obsessed with it. One day, I told my dad I wanted to open a club where I could listen to jazz whenever I wanted. He thought it was a crazy idea for a high schooler, but I kept pushing it."

I smiled at his story, imagining seeing Rune as a high schooler falling in love with jazz and asking his dad to open this club. "You were quite ambitious at a young age. I think that's a good trait."

Rune's smile softened as he met my gaze again. "Yeah, well, my dad wasn't convinced, but eventually, he agreed to help me out. And now here we are," he said, gesturing to our surroundings.

The silence between us stretched on for a few moments after that as we both took a sip of our drinks, but his eyes always found mine, and honestly, I wasn't sure what to say next. What else is there to say when the guy across from you turns your coherent thoughts into mush? It felt like everything had shifted since the kiss, at least for me. Rune was no longer just Rune, the chill guy I'd met at the treasure hunt event. He was... *someone else*, too. Someone with ambition, someone who had made his dreams come true. I wasn't sure what to think about all of it, but I could definitely respect him for it.

"Soooo," Rune's voice broke through my thoughts, low and teasing. He leaned forward, elbow on his knee, hands clasped, resting on his lips. His eyes locked with mine. "I don't even have your number, but you decided to kiss me, huh? I think we skipped a few steps."

Wow, let's address the elephant in the room, shall we

The question hung in the air for a moment, and I felt my heart skip a beat. I froze, trying to process what he'd just said. Then come up with a plan to disappear from existence itself.

"Well, umm... I'm sorry," I started to say, but he cut me off, dropping his hand from his face, before he got up and knelt before me. His eyes, leveled with mine, were soft but held a fierce dedication.

He neither touched me nor did he reach out to invite my touch; he remained there kneeling before me as though he was waiting for me.

"I didn't ask for an apology," he said, his voice smooth, his gaze piercing. I felt breathless as his words sank in.

I cleared my throat, shifting in my seat as I tried to pull myself together. *Because a girl is freaking out, where is oxygen when you need it!"*

Mmm... no, you didn't." I bit the inside of my cheek, trying my best not to squeak.

"Stop that, M". His gaze never wavered, and I felt my pulse race.

Then, before I could even react, Rune gently reached out, cupping my face with his hand, guiding me to look up at him. Using his thumb, he gently yet firmly pulled down on my jaw, freeing the tissue inside my cheek, allowing it to slip from between my teeth. His touch was soft but firm, sending a shiver down my spine. My breath caught in my throat as I realized just how close we were.

"I think I know what you're trying to say, but I want to hear *you* say it," Rune murmured, his voice low.

I pulled away from his grasp, my face flaming, trying to put together a coherent thought.

"I—" I cleared my throat, my heart hammering in my chest. "I don't know what you mean." I squeaked

Oh Mita, straggle me now, whattdu man, whattdu

Rune sighed, dropping his hand and sitting back in his chair, his eyes never leaving me.

"M," he called out, his tone soft but with that same teasing edge to it. "Can I have your number?"

186

The nickname he'd given me floated around in my head. *M.* I loved how it sounded coming from him.

My heart skipped again. I wasn't sure if I was ready for this, but something about him made it feel right.

Then, before I could stop myself, the words tumbled out of my mouth. "Can we just make this official?"

We both froze. Silence fell between us, thick and heavy, as we realized what had just been said.

hellllpppp, helllllp meeee, I could just-

If I leave now, maybe no harm can be done, and live happily ever APART

Rune's regard pinned in place that the thought running, ran out of my mind, his gaze felt so intense as though he was looking through me.

"Yes," he said, his voice firm, almost like a promise.

"Yes?" I repeated, confusion creeping into my voice. "Yes, what?"

Rune chuckled, a deep, rich sound that made my stomach flip. "Yes, let's make it official, *M.*"

I blinked. I couldn't believe what I was hearing. A stupid smile slowly spread across my face before I could stop it.

"Okay," I whispered, still processing the fact that we were now *official.* "Okay."

Rune leaned back in his seat, splaying his hand across the back of the couch. "lovely. Now, can I have your number? It's weird not having my girlfriend's number."

I snorted, feeling a little lightheaded. "Okay, okay, I'll give it to you," I said, pulling out my phone and getting up to sit beside him. We exchanged numbers with an ease that made everything feel as if we hadn't just had one of the most awkward and embarrassing confessions of the past hour, well, at least for me.

The afternoon drifted into evening, and the club began to fill up with performers as the energy in the air shifted with the night, nowhere near its peak.

But I couldn't shake the feeling that the real fun had already started. And

Rune… well, he was definitely going to be a big part of it.

Chapter 38: New Experiences

Night stretched onward, replicating a dark and velvety canvas punctuated by the electric pulse of music.

The performances were nothing short of epic, a crescendo that pulled more and more people upwards toward the lounge, their faces eager and expectant. They were keen on sidling up to the 'boss's son,' each looking for a moment of recognition with him.

The lounge filled steadily, a tide of bodies and voices. Rune had shifted his spot closer to Mita, curving his body protectively around her so that no unwanted attention would inch too near. Drinks appeared in their hands, like magic, and though Rune was the one they all spoke to, Mita felt like she had to be at least semi-present in some of the conversations, so she remained at his side, feeling somehow absent from everything.

It was as if she existed in a parallel world where words and meanings dissolved into a blur. Smiling faces and laughing voices swirled around her, and she found herself nodding and smiling back even when the clamor made no sense. Rune, perceptive as always, leaned in to repeat conversations to her, whispering translations of the social chatter so that she didn't feel left out in the conversations.

In the vast noise of the lounge, what broke through to her was the warmth of Rune's hand enclosing hers, his thumb rubbing in tender, reassuring circles. There was comfort in the way he anchored her to the moment. Mita marveled at how he noticed every small detail, how he managed to be present with her even while so many others vied for his attention.

The waiter appeared, poised to take another round of drink orders. She saw that she had run out, and quickly asked for another: a neon-bright, nonalcoholic electric lemonade. Rune ordered himself a blue lagoon and a tropical splash at the same time.

"You're ordering two drinks?" Mita asked, her curiosity piqued. Rune looked at her, half an apology in his smile.

"Y-yeah," he said. "You OK though? Enjoying yourself?"

"Yeah, yeah," she replied, her voice carrying the lightness she felt inside. While the drinks were on their way, Rune turned the conversation in the lounge deeper for her, bringing her into the discussion about music, letting the different musicians have input to educate Mita on how a piano's voice changed between jazz, pop, and R&B to better help with the presentation they had to give when they returned.

The waiter returned, placing two drinks down in front of them.

"Where is his second drink?" Mita asked, puzzled at his single glass.

"Oh no, it's a two-in-one drink," he explained. She just nodded, amused, as Rune launched into another detailed conversation with someone he was chatting with while Mita sipped her drink and enjoyed the random patterns Rune's thumb made against the back of her palm. She was happy; she was traveling. The guy she liked was now her boyfriend. School wasn't as bad as before, and her faith was growing in God. Life was good for Mita.

The next day, she woke up but was still half asleep. She got up to pee with the intention of returning to bed, as they were not planning on going out to the city again until the afternoon, so she would use the morning to sleep in. Last night was amazing but ran on longer than she could even remember. She came out of the bathroom. Curling under the covers, she longed to drift off to sleep, to pull herself back under its serenade, lulling her back to sweet slumber.

When something, or *someone,* shifted beside her, her heart jolted with a sudden, irrational fear. It must be a dream, she must be dreaming, she thought, squeezing her eyes shut as if, by force of will, she could bend reality. She clung to that thought, hoping she was not about to be murdered on this trip before she could even graduate from University. Whatever had moved was now creeping up over her. Under her cover, she closed her eyes so tightly. Her mind raced. Don't scream, she told herself. Don't scream, don't open your eyes, don't wake up

and find yourself dead? I think not, she thought.

She was fully awake now and desperate to find an explanation, any explanation that didn't end with her on the six o'clock news. The weight of it, solid and unmistakable, was pressing down on her chest. Through the pounding of panic,

she hoped it was a sleeping bag or a stray pillow gone rogue.

The longer she waited, the more real it became. Maybe it was a raccoon? Some small, furry creature that was less menacing in the light of day? She was almost too afraid to find out, to face the reality of what was actually happening. Steeling herself, she was about to scream. But then, she wasn't sure if she should even scream.

Mita's eyes opened to see Rune's face hovering above hers, his lips soft and eager as they pressed against hers. She noticed his bare chest and her own naked body beneath the covers.

What's going on? What am I even doing?

. . . .

Later that evening, they went back to the club and finished up their assignment, having some drinks to celebrate their last day, and came back to the hotel.

In the heat of the moment, Mita's senses were heightened as she and Rune finished their assignment; they gave in to their desires once again.

Rune's tastes were... peculiar. He wanted to be called things, wanted her to pretend to be someone she wasn't, and asked for things she wasn't sure were meant to be part of the act or part of something deeper, darker. But who was she to judge? What did she even know? The truth was, for all her bravado, for all the ways she'd tried to play it cool, she was out of her depth. Completely. She knew the outlines, the shapes, the whispered rumors traded between friends, but that was it.

This was her first time. No... her second. Or maybe third, if that one night counted that she doesn't seem to remember. She didn't even know anymore. The lines had blurred. Somewhere between his fingers on her skin and his voice asking her to be someone else, she realized she had no idea what she was doing, no idea who she was supposed to be. And yet, here she was, giving pieces of herself away like they didn't matter, like they wouldn't leave scars.

But they would.

They already had.

Chapter 39: the Consequences of my own actions

Rune's fingers traced idle, lazy lines along her back, each pass feather light, like he was trying to write her back into herself. The earlier tension in his touch had melted completely, replaced with something almost… tender. Protective.

Mita lay curled against him, her breathing steady now, her body still buzzing with leftover electricity, but her mind was anything but still.

He was quiet. Just holding her.

And maybe that's what made it worse.

Because now there was space. And in that space, thoughts bloomed: wild, messy, and unsettling.

She kept replaying it in her head: the way his voice had dropped when he told her what to do, the firm press of his hands, and how his eyes seemed to burn with something dangerous, something not quite soft. In the moment, she'd gone with it. She'd let herself go. She'd even liked it. More than she expected. But there had been a flicker of fear at first, something primal and sharp in him in his action in his eyes. It was there and then gone, smoothed over by the way he slowed down, giving her time to breathe, to nod, to adjust.

He saw her hesitation before she even said a word.

And that scared her in a different way.

How could someone be so rough, so *dominating*, and then moments later treat her like she was made of glass?

He shifted beside her, placing kissed her shoulder, his voice low against her skin. "You're okay, right?"

She nodded again, instinctively. But she felt it this time, the automatic response, the lie living just beneath the surface. She wanted to say yes and no. But something inside twisted the way her mind worked.

"I meant, M," Rune added gently, as if reading the knot in her chest, "are you *really* okay?"

Mita pulled in a slow breath. The kind you take when you're deciding whether to be brave or to stay quiet.

"I don't know," she admitted, her voice small. "It was a lot."

Rune was still. Not tense, just listening.

"I didn't hate it," she added quickly, maybe too quickly. "I don't want you to think that. I just... it was intense. You were intense."

He exhaled through his nose, brushing a kiss into her hair.

"I know," he said. "I should've asked more. I tried to go slow when I saw your face change, but I should've said something out loud."

Mita swallowed hard, the knot loosening, just slightly. "Why didn't you?"

"I didn't want to break it," he said simply. "The moment. And maybe part of me thought you'd tell me if you needed to stop. But that's not fair, is it? Putting that on you."

She blinked. The honesty in his voice caught her off guard.

"No one ever talked to me about this stuff, not in depth," she murmured. "What it's supposed to feel like. What's normal? What's too much?"

Rune shifted so he could look at her, propping himself on one elbow. His eyes were soft as the even in his gaze, he wanted to hold her with delicate tenderness.

"There isn't a normal," he said. "Just what you want. What you *need*. And if that didn't feel right... I want to know. I need to know."

The words settled between them, heavier than silence, but somehow safer.

She didn't have the right words yet. Not for everything she was feeling.

But this, this space, this moment, felt like a start.

She reached up and traced the curve of his jaw, letting her fingers linger at the edge of his mouth before tilting his head to place a delicate kiss on her fingertips.

"I don't know what I need yet," she whispered. "But... I want to figure it out."

Rune nodded. "Then we will, together."

And just like that, it wasn't about the sex anymore. It was about everything after.

Everything still coming.

The car ride back to campus felt surreal, like it was all happening too fast. The bright lights of the city faded behind them, replaced by the familiar, busy streets of the university. Rune didn't say much, his hand resting casually on the gearshift, his eyes focused on the road. Mita sat in the passenger seat, her mind racing with thoughts of their trip: of the laughter, the shared moments, the energy between them that had felt effortless, like they'd known each other far longer than just a few months.

When they arrived at her dorm, Rune pulled up to the curb and parked at the main entrance to the building.

The air between them was thick with unspoken words, an almost tangible tension that neither of them seemed ready to break. Rune turned to her, offering a soft smile, the kind that had become so familiar.

"You good, M?" he asked, his voice low, careful.

Mita nodded, her lips curving into a small, contented smile. "Yeah, I'm good."

She had meant it. The trip, the laughter, the moments they shared... It had felt like a dream, one that she didn't want to wake up from. But now, as the car sat in the dim glow of the streetlight, reality was slowly creeping back in.

"Thanks, Rune. For everything, the trip, the club...us," she said, her words sincere, her heart a little fuller than it had been before.

Rune looked at her for a long moment, his gaze intense, as if he could see all the unspoken things floating behind her eyes. Without saying a word, he reached over and gently touched her cheek, his thumb brushing over her skin in a soft, almost reverent way.

"Don't mention it. You mean a lot to me, M. As for us, you were the one who made the big step, so thank *you* for being bold."

The sincerity in his voice sent a wave of warmth through her, and for a moment, everything else seemed to disappear: the campus, the noise, even the busy streets in the distance. It was just the two of them, wrapped in a quiet, shared understanding.

"I'll see you later, right?" Rune asked, his voice soft, almost teasing.

"Yeah," Mita replied, a playful smile tugging at her lips. "Definitely."

She unbuckled her seat belt and opened the car door. Just as she stepped out, Rune's voice called out to her again.

"Mita," he said, his tone softer than usual. "I… I'm really glad you're in my life."

She looked back at him, her heart fluttering unexpectedly. "Me too, Rune. Me too."

With a small nod, she entered the building before watching him drive off, the sound of the engine fading into the night. Mita stood there for a moment, taking in the cool air, feeling the weight of everything she had experienced in the past few days.

As she made her way up the stairs to her dorm, she felt a flutter of excitement in her chest. She had never felt this way before: so alive, so full of possibilities. It was as if everything had fallen into place, even if she didn't fully understand it all yet.

When she entered her empty dorm, the silence greeted her, and for a brief moment, she felt the absence of Amerei's energy. But it didn't bother her for too long. She was content, at peace. She tossed her suitcase onto her bed and sat down on the edge, staring out the window at the campus below.

Everything had changed since she first arrived at university. The girl who had stepped onto this campus: shy, unsure, and hesitant, wasn't the same as the girl sitting here now. She'd grown in ways she hadn't expected, learned more about herself, about her desires, and about what she wanted from life.

Her phone buzzed, snapping her out of her thoughts. She picked it up, expecting a message from Amerei, but instead, it was a text from Rune.

Rune: "Hey, I know we just saw each other, but I just wanted to say... I had an amazing time with you. And I can't wait to see you again, M :)."

Mita's heart skipped a beat as she read the message. A warmth spread through her chest, and for the first time in a long while, she realized she wasn't afraid of where this was going. Maybe she didn't have all the answers, maybe the future was still uncertain, but for now, she was exactly where she needed to be.

She quickly typed a reply.

Mita: "Me too, Rune."

She put the phone down and leaned back on the bed, closing her eyes. As she drifted off to sleep, her thoughts were filled with the trip, with Rune, and with all the possibilities of what was yet to come.

And as sleep finally overtook her, she smiled, knowing that life, like her heart, was just beginning to unfold.

Chapter 40: Silence and Sound

Mita woke with a start.

Sunlight filtered softly through her dorm window, dust catching in the rays like suspended memories. At first, there was nothing, just warmth, the faint buzz of a new day, but then, all at once, it hit her.

Everything.

The club. The kisses. Rune's mouth against her skin. Her legs tangled with his. The look in his eyes. His voice low and commanding, calling her name. Not once. Not twice. But three times. Three times she'd let go. Given in.

Her breath caught.

That morning, after they made it official, she'd woken up in her bed, tangled up in sheets and sweat, both of them bare, clinging to each other like the night never ended. She didn't even remember the first time clearly, but their positions... the way she ached... it made too much sense.

"Oh God..." she whispered. "What the heck was I thinking?"

She slipped from her bed, dropped to her knees on the cold floor, and clasped her hands so tightly her knuckles paled.

"Lord, I'm sorry," she prayed, but her voice felt hollow. Like it was echoing back at her instead of rising up. *"Please forgive me."*

But something felt... off. Different. Distant.

She squeezed her eyes shut harder.

"I *know* You forgive me. I *know* grace covers all of it. But..."

But why didn't it feel like it?

A verse surfaced in her mind, uninvited: *"You honor me with your lips, but your heart is far from me."* Jesus, rebuking the religious leaders for their hypocrisy. For knowing what was right and choosing what was wrong.

Was she one of them?

Was she... a hypocrite?

A wave of nausea rose in her stomach.

"God, are You mad at me?" she asked out loud, her voice barely more than a breath. *"I know You don't punish us for the past once we repent. But this... this was just yesterday. And the day before is it considered a past? And, God, I didn't just fall. I **jumped**."*

The silence she felt wrapped around her like a void.

Maybe He needed time to cool off?

That thought alone made her chest cave in.

"Right...?" she whispered. *"You don't hate me, right?"*

Her heart thudded against her ribs like it was trying to get out. She kept praying, begging, even, but the words felt like they were hitting a brick wall. After what felt like hours, she sat back on her heels, numb.

"Maybe later," she mumbled. *"Maybe You'll talk to me when You're less angry..."*

....

She tried to move through the semester like normal. Went to class, smiled when she had to, but everything else, clubs, friends, Rune, she kept at arm's length. The mask of "Mita, the good Christian girl" stayed firmly in place. But inside? She was crumbling.

She skipped the Christian club meetings, not because she feared judgment from them, but judgment from herself. She couldn't stand the thought of walking into that room feeling this... filthy. She needed to be clean first. To be *Right with God again*. Then maybe she could show her face.

Weeks blurred.

She gave excuses in the group chat. "Busy semester." "Swamped with work." "So tired lately." Her roommate barely saw her. When she did, Mita pretended to sleep or stayed out until the lights were off.

She couldn't talk.

Not about this.

Not yet.

A full month passed before she set foot in the music building again. Rune had given the presentation, as she had come up with an excuse not to be present.

It was quiet in the hallway, just the soft hum of distant instruments. And then... she heard it. The low, aching cry of a viola, Rune's viola.

She stopped outside the club room, pressing her back to the wall, and slid down until she was seated on the floor. The music poured through the small crack in the door like a balm. For the first time in weeks, something inside her moved that wasn't guilt.

Tears welled up.

But they weren't tears of shame. They were relief. Peace. The smallest flicker of something,

~~emotions that weren't condemning.~~

Because condemnation was the only thing she felt this past month.

She covered her mouth, sobbing silently, letting the sound wash over her until she couldn't hold the stillness any longer.

When she had finally steadied her emotions and appearance, she pushed the door open quietly.

To her surprise, Rune was alone.

"Hey, you," he said, without missing a beat. "I had a feeling you'd still come."

Mita blinked. "Still come? What do you mean?"

He set his viola down gently. "Music club's canceled for the next couple weeks, some scheduling issues. So, it's just me tonight."

He walked over and wrapped his arms around her, pressing a kiss to her forehead. She stiffened, just a little, but let herself lean into him. It was the first hug she'd had in weeks.

"I've missed you," he murmured. "Between everything and exams coming up… I knew we probably wouldn't see each other again for a bit." He pulled back, his hands sliding to her shoulders. "You've almost made it through your first year. I'm proud of you."

She looked up at him, her lashes still damp.

"You were crying," he said softly.

"Oh," she stammered, caught a bit off guard by the directness in his tone. "I… was moved by your playing. It was beautiful."

Rune smiled. "Thank you. How long were you listening?"

"A while."

He reached for her hand, placing a kiss on it. "So if the club's canceled… what brought you here? You came to play by yourself?" she asked

"I had a feeling that you wouldn't see the message and come, and I would get to spend some alone time with you in our busy schedules." Rune's expression shifted, the playfulness fading into desire.

Mita's stomach dropped,

"Mita… what's wrong?" he said gently, noting the change in her demeanor.

She looked down, blinking fast, trying not to cry again.

"I don't know who I am anymore," she whispered. "I just don't want to be alone."

And for the first time in a month, she didn't feel entirely alone.

Rune stare was the kind that saw too much and said too little.

"I stayed back," he repeated softly, saying each word slowly as if he wanted her to digest each one, "because I *knew* you'd come."

Before she could respond, he took her hand in his and led her toward the piano tucked into the corner of the room.

"You've been learning fast," he said, pulling out the bench for her to sit. "But you still rush the transitions. Let's work on that."

She slid in beside him, letting the comfort of the familiar keys center her, appreciating that he was trying to change the atmosphere for her.

As her fingers moved through the notes, Rune watched her performance with a critically intense focus as a teacher would a student. When she faltered, he gently guided her hands, his fingers brushing hers over the right keys, correcting her form. He brought a level of connection to his teaching that went far beyond instructions. No pressure. No rush.

Just presence.

Then, she felt it, soft at first. The lightest press of his lips at the curve of her neck. Then another, lower this time. Slow, lingering. A third, just above her collarbone. She stilled, but he didn't stop.

He was kissing her like she was music, like every note mattered, making it clear that she mattered.

"Rune…" she whispered, not sure whether it was a protest or permission.

He turned her face toward him and kissed her—deeply, fully, like he was trying to pour every unspoken word into her mouth. She responded instinctively, leaning into it, into *him*, into the warmth she had longed for over the past cold, silent weeks. It felt good to be held. It felt real.

It felt like being wanted.

And for a moment, she let herself want it too.

But then,

She pulled away, breathless and heavy-chested, guilt slamming back into her like a wave against stone.

Rune blinked. "W–what's wrong, M? We've got the room. No one's coming."

She shook her head, unable to look him in the eye. "Rune, when we came back from the trip… did you feel bad? Like, on the inside. Like… something was off? Uncomfortable?"

She was trying to explain the unexplainable, the invisible weight pressing against her chest every time she tried to pray.

But he was silent, providing no help to aid her explanation.

"We had sex, Rune," she said finally, voice trembling. "That's a sin."

Rune stilled,

then sighed, almost like he'd been waiting for this moment.

"Yeah, I know," he said. "We did it outside of marriage…" He paused, causing Mita's gaze to crash into his, searching for something, something she couldn't explicitly understand for herself as yet.

"I didn't want to bring it up yet, but… I've thought about that. A lot." He sighed, running his hand through his hair.

Reaching for her, he took her hands in his, warm and steady.

"Mita... I want to marry you. I want *you* to be the mother of my kids. I didn't say it before because I didn't want to freak you out. But I meant what I said, I'm serious about us. Christians date to marry, right? That's what I'm doing. Did I not show you I'm committed to you?"

Her heart did something strange, clenched and bloomed all at once.

"Y–yeah," she said quietly, "you've shown me. I believe you."

He smiled into the kiss, softly this time, before standing.

"Okay, then. No more worrying for now. Let me grab us something to drink, yeah?"

She nodded, but she barely heard him.

Marry.

Kids.

Our **kids.**

The words spun around in her head like fireflies, pushing the fog of guilt aside, just for a second. The shame, the prayers that hit brick walls... all of it faded under the weight of *those* words.

When he came back, he handed her a vanilla milkshake, beaming down at her.

"To celebrate," he said.

They sat close on the bench again, legs brushing as she sipped slowly.

After their little milkshake break, she returned to the keys. They talked between notes, fingers dancing over ivory, laughing about their imaginary kids, who'd play piano and paint walls and probably be obsessed with cartoons.

It felt ridiculous.

And warm.

yet *safe*.

She laughed so hard at one of his comments about naming their daughter "Melody" that she nearly choked on her shake.

And just as her laughter quieted, Rune leaned in again, this time without hesitation, and kissed her.

Not rushed. Not desperate.

Just honest.

And in that kiss, for one long, silent moment, Mita wasn't a sinner or a saint or a hypocrite.

She was just *his*.

Interlude: Unspoken Prayers on the Keys

The music room was still, the overhead lights dimmed, and the piano behind Mita let out a soft sigh as she leaned against it, Rune's mouth still warm on hers.

She let him kiss her.

Not like last time—not with confusion clouding her thoughts or guilt nipping at her conscience. This time, she felt *present*. Every brush of his fingertips, every word whispered into her skin made her feel something she hadn't in weeks—*alive, loved, and most of all heard.*

Rune was gentle, but with purpose. That was his way. He liked to guide her—not control, but lead. His voice low, his hands steady, his body always watching hers for a sign. He leaned in again, lips grazing her ear.

"Say it how you did before..." he murmured, his breath a spark of fire igniting wherever it touched her.

Mita's cheeks flushed, but her body responded before her thoughts caught up. She said his name just the way he liked it—drawn out, soft, slightly breathless.

Rune groaned, pulling her tighter against him. "That's my girl."

He had his preferences. He liked it when she spoke. To look him in the eyes. To move at his pace. But he always gave her space to say no. He liked her obedience, but he loved her comfort more.

And tonight, Mita gave in willingly.

Because here, in this space between guilt and grace, she just wanted to feel.

Rune lifted her onto the edge of the piano, carefully, reverently—as if laying her across something sacred. His mouth trailed down her collarbone, his hands under her shirt, caressing with such focused attention it made her breath catch. He whispered what he wanted from her—specific, but never crude. The way he said it made it feel like art, not sin.

Mita followed his lead.

Her hands ran through his hair, her body arching into his as he traced a line down her side with his lips. Every kiss, every request, every whispered "good girl" untangled something tight and aching inside her.

She had been numb for too long.

Alone with her shame. Crushed beneath prayers that felt like echoes. And now, for the first time in weeks, she *felt* something.

Not just pleasure.

Not just desire.

But warmth. Connection. A heartbeat pressed against hers.

Rune's rhythm matched hers—steady, sure. When she shuddered against him, he held her tighter, anchoring her like he knew she needed it. He didn't let go until she whispered his name again, softer this time, like it was a secret prayer.

And when it was over, he didn't pull away.

He wrapped his arms around her and held her close, their skin still warm, her heartbeat still racing.

"Are you okay?" he asked, pressing a kiss to her temple.

She nodded into his shoulder. "Yeah. I think I am."

And maybe she wasn't okay in the long run.

But for now, wrapped in Rune's arms, she wasn't spiraling. She wasn't crying into silence or begging God to speak. She was breathing. She was held.

She was human.

Chapter 41: Confessions in the Quiet

Afterward, Rune held her.

They sat together, half-dressed, limbs tangled on the floor beside the piano bench, wrapped in the quiet hum of the empty club room. His fingers gently traced her spine, grounding her. His voice was low, whispering small affirmations like a rhythm only she could hear.

"You're so beautiful," he murmured against her shoulder. "And brave. I'm proud of you, M."

Mita didn't speak. She just nodded against his chest, letting herself believe,for a few more minutes, that she was safe here.

This time, the aftercare wasn't an afterthought. Rune kissed the crown of her head, stroked her hair, and helped her dress again with delicate hands. He wasn't the same person who had whispered those deep, commanding things into her ear just minutes ago. He was soft again. Gentle.

A protector.

Not a fire, but a blanket.

By the time they stepped outside, the sun had already dipped below the horizon, the sky a slow-burning blend of oranges and purples. Rune carried both empty milkshake cups, tossing them into the bin with a practiced flick, and reached for her hand without asking.

Mita let him.

He walked her back to the dorms without letting go of her hand once. He didn't ask why she was quiet. He didn't need to.

The warmth of his fingers in hers made her feel steady. Less alone.

Their conversation on the walk back was light, teasing, and full of little stolen smiles. The kiss they shared before parting was softer this time, shorter, but no less full than when he kissed her forehead; she fully relaxed in his affection. "Text me when you wake up," he reminded. "Even if it's late. Promise?" He asked,

"I promise," she responded, though her voice felt far away. The kiss lingered like a whisper against her lips and forehead long after he disappeared around the corner.

When she finally made it back to her room, she didn't turn on the lights. The stillness wrapped around her like a familiar friend.

And when she was finally alone—

It hit.

Like a wave to the chest, knocking the air out of her lungs.

She sat on the edge of her bed, shoulders slumped, vision blurry.

What have I done again?

It wasn't shame because of Rune. Not disgust. Not regret in the usual sense.

It was something deeper. A sadness that curled up in her chest like smoke and wouldn't leave.

What was worse was—

The act hadn't felt empty. It had felt... good. Too good. Like it patched the hole God was supposed to fill. And that terrified her.

She sat on the edge of her bed, dropped her bag, and opened her journal.

The pen hovered above the page.

What was there even to say?

She stared for a while, the silence pressing in on her chest, before finally beginning to flow on the paper through ink:

April 12th

I felt something tonight. Something other than guilt. Something like... peace. Like maybe I'm not completely lost.

Rune kissed me again. He held me like I was something worth holding. I laughed tonight. I smiled. I talked about the future like it belonged to me.

But God, I'm still scared.

Am I allowed to feel happy right now? Am I really happy?

Why do I keep having sex with Rune?

Am I allowed to dream about marrying him, even after what we did?

I know what the Bible says. I know what I was taught. But I also know what it felt like to be held. I know what it felt like when the music stopped and the silence didn't crush me. That was the first time in weeks I didn't feel like I was suffocating.

I don't want to lose You.

But I don't want to lose him either.

Is it possible to have both?

I'm trying, God. I really am.

But I still feel like I'm waiting for You to look at me again.

She closed the journal gently, her eyes stinging.

She stood up abruptly, dropping to her knees beside her bed.

"*God...*" she whispered, pressing her forehead to the mattress. "*Please...*"

But the words stuck.

Please forgive me.

Please don't hate me.

Please say something. **Anything.**

Silence.

The same silence that had followed her for weeks. The same silence that had driven her to this moment, this need to feel *something*. To be touched. Held. Loved.

Her tears spilled hot and fast, soaking the page below her.

She remembered that passage when Jesus rebuked the religious leaders once again. *You honor Me with your lips, but your hearts are far from Me.* The thought sliced through her <u>again.</u>

Is that me?

Am I one of them? A hypocrite who knows better and does it anyway?

She sobbed harder, words tumbling out between ragged breaths.

"I'm sorry, I'm sorry, I'm sorry..."

But her prayer felt like it was hitting a ceiling.

A month ago, she might've believed He forgave her on the spot.

Now?

Now it felt like He was silent because He *was* disappointed. Not gone. But turned away. Just a little.

Her heart clenched.

"Maybe later," she whispered into the sheets. *"Maybe when You're not so mad at me..."* she had been saying the same thing for the past month

She wiped her eyes with the back of her hand, climbed back into bed fully dressed, and curled into herself.

She didn't cry herself to sleep this time.

She just lay there, empty, eyes open in the dark, waiting for a voice that didn't come.

Chapter 42: Seen

It had been forty-two days since Mita last stepped foot into the Christian club meeting.

She counted.

Not because she wanted to go back. But because every day she didn't, the number grew louder in her head. Like a record of how far she'd drifted.

And yet, here she was, sitting outside the campus café, hoodie pulled tight, earbuds in but no music playing, pretending to study.

She hadn't even noticed Ethan until he pulled the chair across from her and sat down without asking.

"Hey," he said gently, his presence feeling like a breeze instead of a wave.

Mita blinked, startled. "Oh, Ethan. Hey."

She yanked her earbuds out and closed her textbook like she'd actually been reading.

He didn't say anything at first. Just sat there, arms crossed over the edge of the table, watching her in that quiet, calm way he always had. He wasn't intense. He wasn't dramatic.

That made it worse somehow.

"You've been gone a while," he said finally.

"Yeah. School's just been… insane." She forced a small laugh, eyes darting back to the book like it could save her.

Ethan nodded. "We all get busy. But… you're not *just* busy."

Her heart stuttered.

She felt the tears climb up her throat before she could stop them. She swallowed hard. Looked away.

"I'm fine," she lied.

He tilted his head, brows lifting softly. "Are you?"

That cracked something open.

Not wide. Just enough for air to leak in. Just enough for the ache to pulse through.

Mita shook her head, blinking hard. "I've messed up, Ethan. A lot. I've done things I can't even say out loud without... " Her words broke off, "...without hating myself," she lamented

Ethan didn't flinch. He didn't ask for details.

He just leaned in a little closer. "Okay. Then let me sit here with you in the mess."

Her lip trembled. She covered it with her hand, embarrassed at her display of emotions. Whether it was because she was in public or because she was in front of him, she didn't know.

"You're not going to lecture me?" she whispered.

"No." His voice was low and steady. "I just want you to know you're still *seen* and loved. Not by me, though I do care. But by Him, even now." He reassured, pointing to the sky.

She let out a shaky breath. "It doesn't feel like it. It feels like God's mad at me. Like I crossed a line, and now I can't go back."

Ethan's eyes softened. "Have you ever read the story of the prodigal son?"

She nodded, barely.

"Then you know he didn't find his way back by getting clean first. He came home dirty. And the Father ran to him."

Mita covered her face with both hands.

She didn't sob. Not this time.

But the tears came anyway, silent, steady, as Ethan sat across from her. He didn't try to fix her. Didn't throw Scripture like a weapon. Just waited.

Listened.

Stayed.

"I don't feel worthy," she finally said.

"You're not," he replied gently. "None of us _are_. That's why it's called grace."

She looked up then, eyes red, breath uneven. "I don't know how to start over."

"You don't need to," Ethan said, standing slowly. "You just need to turn around. He's already running toward you."

He placed a folded slip of paper in front of her on top of the book she was 'reading.'

It was about tonight's Christian club meeting.

A new series.

"When Grace Feels Far: Learning to Come Back Home."

He didn't ask her to promise anything. He didn't say "see you there."

He just smiled softly, nodded, and walked away.

And for the first time in weeks, Mita looked down at something about God and didn't feel condemned.

She felt seen.

Chapter 43 : The Return

PLAYLIST- FOUND ME JEREMIAH PALTAN FT AMANDA PEREZ
ODANE WHILBY

She almost didn't go.

Three times she got up to get ready.

Three times she sat back down.

Her heart was beating fast for no reason. Her fingers wouldn't stop twitching, and her eyes kept glancing at the clock like it might run out and save her from making the decision.

But then she remembered Ethan's voice:

"You just need to turn around. He's already running toward you."

So she stood up.

Slowly.

Pulled on a hoodie. Didn't bother with makeup. She wasn't trying to impress anyone. Pretending was the last thing on her mind.

She walked to the student union building as if her feet weighed a hundred pounds, but she was gonna get there, eventually.

Funny thing was, she didn't tell Rune. She didn't know how to put it into words for him. For some reason, she didn't want to, not yet. And she didn't know if she was selfish for not taking him along when they were both entangled in this mess or if it was something else.

The warm light from the windows of the room where she knew the club was held glowed against the late evening. Her stomach turned at nothing and everything all at once at the sight.

What if they all see right through me?

What if they smell the sin on my skin?

These thoughts she knew were nonsensical, but they still gnawed at her.

She pushed the door open anyway, also pushing away her thoughts.

The space was smaller than she remembered. Softer. Not filled with pressure, but gentle music and hushed conversation. There were no big declarations, no emotional theatrics. Nobody gasped at her sudden reappearance after such a long absence.

Just a circle of mismatched chairs, bean bags, blankets, and open Bibles, and a quiet sort of reverence that made her throat tighten.

Ethan saw her first.

He didn't wave or make a scene.

He just smiled.

Like he *knew* she'd come.

And somehow… that made her at ease.

She sat near the back. Not all the way, but not close to the middle either. Just enough to be present. Enough to let the words touch her without sinking in too deep.

The topic was what the flyer had said:

"When Grace Feels Far: Learning to Come Back Home."

Ruth began to read from the Book of Luke, chapter 15. The story Mita knew by heart.

"But while he was still a long way off, his father saw him and was filled with compassion. He ran to his son…"

Mita stared at the words printed in her Bible. The one she hadn't opened in weeks.

Her fingers trembled as she turned the page, devouring every word on it, reading ahead of the others.

and it was not just reading words, she felt it—

There were no fireworks. No booming voice.

Just a flicker.

A shift.

Like someone had cracked open a window in her soul, and a breeze swept in.

Her chest tightened. She didn't cry, but her eyes burned. Her lips parted like she might say something... anything. But no words came.

It was enough to *sit there*.

To not run.

To not hide.

And as the meeting progressed, Mita took a moment

to whisper silently into the ceiling,

"If You're still there... I want to come home."

No booming answer.

No miraculous sign.

But her heart beat lighter.

Just slightly.

A Lesson for the Wandering Heart

Mita stayed the entire session.

It wasn't her plan. She was going to leave after mid-way through the meeting, sneak out before anyone could talk to her. But Ruth, the club leader, stood up.

"Hey, so I did plan on sharing this tonight, but," Ruth said gently, "I wanted to share something that's been sitting heavy on my heart this week."

The room stilled in anticipation. People leaned in. No hype, no pressure. Just curiosity

"I know a lot of us are tired. I know some of you have been dealing with temptation, shame, maybe even questioning your faith entirely."

Mita's breath caught in her chest.

There is no way, God Mita thought

Ruth continued.

"I want to start in the book of **Ruth,** not just because I love the name," she smiled softly, "but because it shows us something about *commitment*. About what it means to choose *again*, even when everything around you feels lost."

She opened her Bible.

"But Ruth replied, 'Don't urge me to leave you or to turn back from you. Where you go I will go, and where you stay I will stay. Your people will be my people and your God my God.'" — Ruth 1:16

"When Ruth said this to Naomi, she wasn't just talking about loyalty to a person; she was making a *spiritual commitment*. She had every reason to walk away; her husband died, and both she and her mother-in-law were homeless, and Ruth hadn't had an easy life either before becoming a widow, but she chose God. She chose *again*. And Naomi didn't feel worthy enough to be a mother-in-law to Ruth; she wanted Ruth to live a better life without her burdening her, but Ruth said, 'No, I won't leave you'; maybe we are both of these women combined, at times. We are Naomi because we feel as though we are burdens, and we make everyone close to us carry our burdens, and we believe those lies and fall into various degrees of depression for numerous reasons, but sometimes we need to be Ruth and stand firm in our faith.

There are times when we are so caught up in our Naomi mindset, God steps in and becomes our Ruth.

That kind reminds me of two verses, Jeremiah 31:3 *"'I have loved you with an everlasting love; I have drawn you with unfailing kindness,'* and Deuteronomy 31:8 *'The LORD himself goes before you and will be with you; he will never leave you nor forsake you. Do not be afraid; do not be discouraged.'*[3]

Know that's what God needs some of us, as a matter of fact, that's what he wants all of us to know right now. Not perfection. Not performance. Just a moment to say: 'I'm coming with You, God. Even after I've walked away.'" Ruth explained, looking at the audience to see if they were following along,

---

[3] (A/N: Does anyone realize that the number locations of the chapters are literally almost the same? Look, they are both 31st chapters, and one is in verse 3 and the other in verse 8, and if you cut 8 in half, it would make two number 3s)

Mita looked down at her Bible, jaw tight, eyes stinging again. The message hit somewhere in her; she had thought she wasn't capable of sensation for the past month and more

Ruth flipped to another page.

"No temptation has overtaken you except what is common to mankind. And God is faithful; He will not let you be tempted beyond what you can bear. But when you are tempted, He will also provide a way out so that you can endure it. Therefore, my dear friends, flee from idolatry." — 1 Corinthians 10:13-14

"Let those who have the ears to hear and the mind to grasp this, understand what I am about to dish out," Ruth said, voice clear but gentle. "Temptation is not rare. It's *common*. But God doesn't leave us stranded in it. He always offers a way out, but we have to be willing to take it. Sometimes, like verse 14 says, we're not called to just stand there and be strong; we're called to *flee*. To walk or *run* from the things that keep pulling us away from God."

A few people murmured "Amen."

But Mita just gripped her knees tighter together.

"This doesn't mean you're weak if you've fallen into something. It means you're human. But it also means God believes you can still walk in freedom. Proverbs 24:16 confirms that the righteous do fall <u>more than once</u>, **but they get back up every time.**

And so should you,
Get up, guys!
don't stay down,
don't let the devil win!" she emphasized.

She turned to the next passage.

"A person is not a Jew who is one only outwardly, nor is circumcision merely outward and physical. No, a person is a Jew who is one inwardly; and circumcision is circumcision of the heart, by the Spirit, not by the written code." — Romans 2:28-29

"This is the one that really got me," Ruth laughed, placing her hand over her heart. "Because Paul is saying: It's not about what you *look* like. It's not about saying all the right things or acting holy on the outside, but what's on

217

the inside. God is after your *heart*. That is what matters. That's what He wants to transform. Not empty declarations."

She paused, letting it sink in.

"Some of us think we have to clean up before we come back to God. That we have to 'look saved' or 'act Christian enough' before we can sit at His table again. But His word says otherwise. It's not about *behavior modification*. It's about *heart transformation*. And that? That's what the Holy Spirit does, not us. Obedience is our Job, Reformation is his."

Ruth looked up from her Bible and scanned the room slowly.

"Maybe someone here feels like they've messed up too much. Maybe you've been carrying guilt that's left you numb or depressed, even distant. But I want you to know, I want all of you to remember that God doesn't love the version of you, you're trying to become. He loves *you*. Right now. As you are. He knew with who, when, how, and how many times you were going to fall and still chose you as his own, so take heart, whatever you do give in to, he already knew it would happen, so never let guilt tell you otherwise, get up, dust yourself off, and keep movin.'"

Mita broke.

Not loudly.

Just quietly, silently, the tears slipping down again as her heart cracked in places she didn't even know were still soft. That message, it wasn't general. It was *for her*. Every word. Every verse.

This wasn't about shame anymore.

It was about a *God, her God, who still wanted her*.

Even with the guilt.

Even with the dirt.

Even with her mess

She leaned into her kneea, eyes shut tight, and whispered:

"Thank You for still wanting me."

And for the first time in what felt like forever...

She felt Him whisper back.

More Than Good Enough

The room was quiet again, still from the weight of what Ruth had just spoken.

But she wasn't done yet.

She flipped her Bible once more, eyes steady, voice soft.

"I want to take us through Romans 3 and 4. Because this is where Paul really hits the heart of what it means to be saved, not by our works, but by *faith*."

She paused, letting the rustle of pages pass through the circle.

"Let's start in **Romans 3:10**."

"There is no one righteous, not even one."

She looked up, half-smiling.

"That's a tough one to accept, right? Because we try so hard to be 'good people.' But Paul isn't sugarcoating it; he's reminding us that **no one** is righteous on their own. Not me. Not you. Not even the kindest person you know."

She scanned the room again, making eye contact with each person.

"That includes those who grew up in church. Who knows the songs. Who reads their Bible every day. *None* of that saves us. Because we *all* fall short."

Then she moved down the page.

"For all have sinned and fall short of the glory of God." — Romans 3:23

Mita swallowed.

Her hand wrapped around her knees

"And this verse? We quote it a lot," Ruth continued. "But we forget what comes *after* it."

She read the next part, slower this time:

"And all are justified freely by His grace through the redemption that came by Christ Jesus." — Romans 3:24

"**Freely.** That word matters. God doesn't wait for us to earn it, because we can't. We're made right with Him, **justified** through Jesus. Not through fixing ourselves. Not through pretending. Not through guilt-trips."

Mita's lips parted slightly.

Something about that word, **justified,** echoed in her chest.

Ruth flipped the page.

"Now look at **Romans 4**. Paul uses Abraham as the example here. Let's go to verse 1."

"What then shall we say that Abraham, our forefather according to the flesh, discovered in this matter? If, in fact, Abraham was justified by works, he had something to boast about, but not before God."

Ruth looked up again.

"If Abraham, our faith giant, couldn't boast in his works, how can we?"

Then she went on:

"What does Scripture say? 'Abraham believed God, and it was credited to him as righteousness.'" — *Romans 4:3*

"Are you picking up what the Word of God is putting down?" Ruth asked, tapping the verse gently. "He *believed*. That's what made him righteous. Not perfection. Not performance. But *faith*."

She let that sink in the room before she went on.

"God didn't wait until Abraham had it all figured out. He *credited* him righteousness, like putting it into his account, just because Abraham believed. That's the kind of grace we've been invited into."

She kept reading, letting the Word speak for itself:

"Now to the one who works, wages are not credited as a gift but as an obligation. However, to the one who does not work but trusts God who justifies the ungodly, their faith is credited as righteousness." — *Romans 4:4-5*

"That's us," Ruth said, voice dipping low with passion. "The ones who stop trying to earn it and just…

trust that God has already given it to us.

That's the scandal of grace. God justifies the *ungodly*. That's not a license to sin. most definitely not, but it's a call to come home."

She leaned forward slightly, eyes sweeping the group.

"So if you've been caught in shame… if you've thought, *'God can't possibly still want me'*… then hear me when I say this:

You are the one He justifies.

Not because you're clean.

Not because you're worthy.

But because *you believed."*

Mita stared at the pages in her lap, tears once again welling for the nth time. She didn't think she had even stopped crying since she sat down because there was no shame in this.

But **hope**.

The Word of God didn't feel like a mirror showing her all her failures.

It felt like **a door**.

Still open.

Still waiting.

for **her**.

The Word That Brought Her Back (Romans 5–10)

Ruth set her Bible down on her lap for a second, her hand resting over the worn leather cover. She looked up slowly, her gaze sweeping across the circle.

"I don't know why," she said, her voice soft but certain, "but I really feel like the Holy Spirit's leading us to *stay right here,* to keep going. Through the rest of Romans, at least through chapter 10."

She glanced around, as if checking if anyone was in a rush to leave. No one moved. A few heads nodded.

"Okay," she whispered, a smile tugging at her lips. "Then let's go. Let's sit with this."

She opened back to **Romans 5**.

"Therefore, since we have been justified through faith, we have peace with God through our Lord Jesus Christ." — Romans 5:1

"Justified *through faith*. Peace with God. You guys, that's not some poetic line out of Shakespeare. That's a **status change**. You were once separated from Him. But now, because of Jesus, you have peace with God. That means there's no tension, no distance, no hostility anymore."

She looked around, eyes warm and glowing now. "Even if you feel far, He's made peace already. That's the gift. That's grace."

"But God demonstrates His own love for us in this: While we were still

sinners, Christ died for us." — Romans 5:8

Ruth paused.

"That's the heartbeat of the gospel. He didn't wait for you to clean up. He died *while you were still in the mess.*"

Mita exhaled shakily. That verse hit like a warm hug and a hammer in the back of her skull all at once.

Ruth flipped again.

"Now to **Romans 6**," she continued, voice steady and confident now, like she was walking into deeper waters with full trust in the leadership of God.

"Shall we go on sinning so that grace may increase? By no means! We are those who have died to sin; how can we live in it any longer?" — Romans 6:1-2

"This is where the shift happens," Ruth explained. "Grace isn't a free pass to stay in darkness, to keep doing what our flesh craves, what our impulses want. It's the power that brings us *out of all of that.* When you say yes to Jesus, you're not just forgiven, you're made new. The old you? The one caught up in guilt and confusion and brokenness? *That you died with Him on the cross,* **he** *carried.*"

She let that sink in before continuing.

"For we know that our old self was crucified with Him... so that we should no longer be slaves to sin." — Romans 6:6

"You're not a slave anymore," she said slowly. "You don't have to bow to sin like it owns you. Because it doesn't. Not anymore."

Then she turned to **Romans 7**, her voice softening.

"This chapter gets me every time. Because it's real."

"I do not understand what I do. For what I want to do I do not do, but what I hate I do." — Romans 7:15

She looked up, her expression tender.

"Anyone ever felt like that?"

Several heads nodded. Mita included.

"This is Paul, the same guy writing all this truth, saying,

'I. still. struggle.'

Following Jesus doesn't mean you don't battle sin. It means you don't have to battle *alone*. And you don't battle *as a slave*. You battle as a *free* person learning to walk in your freedom."

Then Ruth flipped the page, and her tone lifted, like light cracking through the sky, signaling dawn after a long night.

"Now for one of the most powerful chapters in the Bible."

She looked right at Mita, then said.

"Therefore, there is now no condemnation for those who are in Christ Jesus." — *Romans 8:1*

She said it slowly. As if speaking directly to the shame hiding in her soul.

"No. Condemnation."

She repeated it, louder this time.

"You are not condemned. Not because you haven't sinned. But because Jesus already bore the punishment. You are free. You are clean. You are loved."

"The mind governed by the flesh is death, but the mind governed by the Spirit is life and peace." — *Romans 8:6*

"Some of you feel like your mind has been stuck in fear, guilt, anxiety, shame. But the Spirit leads to life. And peace. That's your inheritance. That's your right as a Child of God."

She flipped further down.

For you did not receive a spirit of slavery to fall back into fear, but you received the Spirit of adoption, by whom we cry, 'Abba, Father.'" — *Romans 8:15*

"You're not an outsider anymore. You're family in The Kingdom of God, The kingdom of light."

Mita's chest trembled.

Her arms still wrapped around herself as she set her Bible on the seat beside her.

She was holding on to every word.

"Paul continues in chapter 9," Ruth said, "talking about how we are chosen, not based on works, but on God's mercy. And then in **chapter 10...**"

She paused, took a deep breath, and read it with the weight of freedom it carried :

"If you declare with your mouth, 'Jesus is Lord,' and believe in your heart that God raised Him from the dead, you will be saved." — Romans 10:9

"Everyone who calls on the name of the Lord will be saved." — Romans 10:13

"**Everyone.** Not the best. Definitely not the most religious. *Everyone.* If you're in here tonight and you've doubted whether He still wants you, this is your answer."

Ruth declared, ending the astonishing message of the night, closed her Bible, setting it down on her lap.

The room was quiet.

Not out of awkwardness.

But because the presence of God was *heavy,* not in a fearful way, but in a way that felt like being held.

"I don't know who that was for tonight," Ruth said softly. "But I know it wasn't random and that it was the spirit of God moving in the room for someone here tonight ."

Ruth smiled before saying one last thing:

"You are not too far gone. And the door is still open."

Mita didn't move.

But something deep inside had shifted.

This time, she didn't just feel *seen.*

She felt... **invited.**

Chapter 44: When God Met Her in the Quiet

❦

As the meeting ended, Mita quietly slipped her Bible into her bag and rose from her seat.

Ethan caught her eye as she moved toward the exit. He didn't stop her, just gave her a small nod. One of understanding. One of peace. Like he could sense that God was working, and that was enough. He didn't need to step in.

The night air was cool and still as she walked back to her dorm. Campus felt quiet, almost hushed, as if even the buildings were holding their breath.

When she got inside, the room was dark.

Her roommate wasn't home, likely out with her boyfriend again. Mita was grateful for the solitude. She went to her room, turned on her desk lamp, and sat at the edge of her bed for a moment, the soft light casting shadows across her journal.

She reached for it slowly.

Opened to a fresh page.

And began to write.

Journal Entry

"Tonight was... something I didn't know I needed. Ruth said things that felt like they were meant for me. Like the Bible wasn't just a holy book but a mirror I didn't even realize I was afraid to look into. Romans 3 through 10. Every chapter peeled away something that clouded my thoughts and sight. And for the first time

in weeks, maybe months. I didn't feel like I had to earn God's love. Or hide from it. I just had to receive it."

"I've been trying to make myself more holy, more worthy by staying away. But I was really just punishing myself, thinking He was mad at me when really, I was mad at myself. I treated God like He felt the same way I did about me. But His love isn't like mine. He doesn't give up. He doesn't guilt-trip. His love doesn't go cold."

Mita stopped writing.

She couldn't hold it in anymore.

She closed the journal, slid off the bed, and dropped to her knees.

The tears came fast, hot, accompanied by heavy sobs. No words at first. Just a river of emotion breaking free from the dam she'd been holding up for too long.

Then came the words.

Messy. Choked. Raw.

"Jesus... I'm so sorry..."

She cried harder.

"I thought You hated me. I thought I ruined it. I've been so lost, and I didn't want to lose You, but I thought I already had."

Her chest shook with every sob.

"I know now... You weren't gone. I was just blind. I was covering my own ears, thinking You were silent when You were still speaking. When You were still here."

She pressed her forehead to the floor.

"Thank You. Thank You for not letting go. Thank You for chasing me even when I was pretending to be fine."

Silence filled the room like warm oil over cracked skin.

And then… a whisper.

Not audible. But deep in her spirit. Like something spoken not *to* her ears—but *within* her soul.

"I need your heart."

Her breath caught.

She knew it wasn't her own thoughts. That this wasn't guilt, it wasn't shame. It was the Spirit of God, gentle yet firm.

God wasn't punishing her.

He was **inviting** her.

To intimacy.

To healing.

To a deeper season.

Alone.

With Him.

Mita sat up slowly, wiping her face. Her eyes were swollen. Her cheeks damp.

She whispered back through the ache in her chest.

"Lord... I know. I know. But... It's not gonna be easy. How do I even begin to give it fully? But I trust that you will teach me how."

She looked toward the small picture on her desk, Rune and her smiling at the jazz club, arms around each other, laughing.

"He's a great guy, and I really care about him," she whispered, her voice cracking. *"But if You're asking me to let go... even just for now... then I will. Just be with me. Please. Be near. In Jesus name I pray, amen."*

The moment felt sacred.

Heavy and light all at once.

And then...

Thunder rumbled outside.

Soft at first, then crescendoed.

Rain began to tap against the windows, slow, then suddenly heavy. A full-blown storm erupted, wild and beautiful.

It was as if **God Himself was weeping with her**. Not out of anger. But out of love. Sharing the weight of what obedience looked like.

Her phone lit up on the desk.

She reached for it absentmindedly, expecting a group text or notification.

Instead, it was her daily Bible verse alert, late, for some reason.

But right on time.

Hebrews 4:14–16

"Therefore, since we have a great high priest who has ascended into heaven, Jesus the Son of God, let us hold firmly to the faith we profess.

For we do not have a high priest who is unable to empathize with our weaknesses,

but we have one who has been tempted in every way, just as we are, yet he did not sin.

Let us then approach God's throne of grace with confidence,

so that we may receive mercy and find grace to help us in our time of need."

Mita broke again, but this time with joy.

Tears slipped down silently as she hugged her pillow to her chest.

She wasn't dirty.

She wasn't forgotten.

She wasn't disqualified.

She was His.

Even in her weakness.

Even in the letting go.

Even in the rain.

Chapter 45: A Whisper in the Quiet

A few days before the rain fell and Mita whispered her surrender, Ethan sat across from Anika at a small café near campus. The warm hum of music blended with the soft clinking of mugs and casual conversations in the background. Outside, the early evening sky glowed a soft peach.

They laughed over inside jokes. Swapped stories about childhood mishaps. Talked about how weirdly addictive Christian memes were. It was just so easy with her. Effortless.

But under the ease... There was a spark ready to be ignited.

He felt it.

The way she was looking at him made his chest feel tight, in a way that made it hard not to feel something back.

They walked the long way back through campus afterward, the breeze brushing past like a soft reminder that this moment wouldn't last forever.

When they reached her car, parked on campus near her previous class, Anika smiled, the corner of her lip quirking up slightly.

"Same time next week?" she asked.

Ethan nodded, trying to keep the warmth in his chest from showing too clearly. "Definitely."

And with that, she opened her car door and drove off.

Back at the dorm, his roommate was already knocked out, headphones in, blanket half-off the bed like usual.

Ethan moved quietly, set down his keys and backpack, and slid into his room, closing the door with a soft click.

He didn't open his Bible yet. Not his journal either.

He just sat at the edge of the bed, head bowed, in reverence.

And spoke.

"God..."

He exhaled slowly.

"You know how I feel about her."

He swallowed hard.

"I've tried to be cautious. Tried to guard my heart. You know I've even tried pulling away... but it's not like I can ignore it. She's not like anyone else I've known."

He shifted, leaning his elbows on his knees, looking at the floor.

"She doesn't have it all figured out yet... but neither do I."

He chuckled dryly. *"You know that more than anyone."*

Then he got serious again.

"But I see something in her. She's different than when I met her. She's leaning in. She's asking about You more. Initiating prayer, asking about Scripture... It's not a front. I can tell."

He grew quiet for a moment.

Then whispered,

"So... is it time? Can I pursue her? Or do I need to wait?"

He closed his eyes tightly, tears almost stinging, not from sadness, but from **desire**. The desire to do this *right*. To not move ahead of God's timing.

"To be honest," he continued, *"I'm not sure I'm the man I want to be yet. I still feel like I'm under construction. I want to be a husband one day, but I want to be Your son first. I want to lead with honor. I want to protect, not just physically, but spiritually too."*

He looked up toward the ceiling, knowing his words were reaching heaven.

"But God, I also don't want to miss something You're trying to give. I pray this in Jesus name, amen."

Silence followed.

Still.

Then a sense of peace filled the room. Not a loud answer. Not a booming voice. But that same, familiar **stillness** he'd come to recognize.

A whisper of presence.

Chapter 46: The Right Kind of Pain

A few days later, Ethan had just wrapped up Bible study in his room when he felt a strange pull.

Nothing loud. Just... a nudge.

Go to the coffee shop.

He didn't argue. Didn't even fully understand *why he had to go.* But he wasn't going to argue with an all-knowing God. He closed his Bible, threw on a hoodie, and grabbed his keys.

Within minutes, he was there, door chimes jingling softly behind him as he entered the cafe, the smell of espresso wrapping around him like a blanket.

That's when he saw her.

Mita.

Sitting alone by the window.

Hood pulled over her head. A book was open in front of her, but she looked too far away to actually be studying. Her fingers rested on the spine like she meant to be studying... but her eyes said otherwise.

Empty.

Hollow.

Not in appearance, though, she still looked like herself, quite so, but the

light in her eyes had dimmed to a flicker.

Fragile.

Ethan swallowed hard. His chest tightened, not in anxiety, but compassion. Grief. Love.

He walked over, sat down across from her without saying a word at first.

When she looked up, he offered a gentle smile.

"Hey," he said softly.

Mita tried to smile back, but it barely reached her lips.

"Oh, hey, Ethan."

He didn't push. But they had talked; he asked questions, and she gave answers. He encouraged her before handing her the flyer, nonverbally inviting her to the club meeting that day.

That evening, the room filled with warmth and quiet laughter as familiar faces trickled into the club. Ethan was seated a few rows ahead of Mita, but he kept glancing back now and then.

She was there.

Really there.

And when Ruth began teaching, her voice full of fire and tenderness, Ethan noticed something shift.

Mita started crying.

Not a soft tear. Not a casual sniffle.

Full-on breaking.

Shoulders trembling. Eyes shut tight. Like the Word of God had finally cracked the wall that guilt had built around her heart.

Ethan blinked quickly, fighting back his own tears. He hadn't known how bad it was for her. How far she'd fallen into herself.

But he was so, **so glad** she was here now, being mended.

When the meeting wrapped up, Mita quickly gathered her things and slipped out the door.

But Ethan didn't chase her.

He knew.

She wasn't running away anymore.

She was running **toward** something.

Toward **God**.

PLAYLIST ALTERS OVER STAGES BY JOSIAH QUEEN

As he packed up his own things, his phone buzzed. A message from **Anika**:

"Hey, I don't feel like going home yet. Want to hang for a bit?"

He paused.

Then typed back.

"Sure. Meet you outside in 10."

They met under the soft glow of campus streetlights, walking side-by-side with no real destination.

The conversation flowed easily as usual. Light jokes. Some teasing. Then a deeper pause when Ethan started sharing what he'd learned from Bible club that night, how grace doesn't just meet us at the altar but walks with us back into the world.

Anika listened. Really listened.

And as they reached the parking lot and stood beside her car, she turned to him, her gaze cast up to his, and was a little more serious now, with a slight touch of nervousness made obvious in her smile.

"Ethan…" she said slowly.

He turned to face her, heart beginning to race. He caught the subtle stiffening of her shoulders, a silent sign that everything in that moment had changed.

She looked down for a second before gazing up at him once more.

"Do you like me?"

His breath caught,

"Because I think you do," she paused, taking in a breath, " And I want to make this" she gestured between them, " I want it to be real." Anika declared.

Her voice was sure, but beneath the confidence was something vulnerable.

Raw. Brave.

And Ethan…

He wanted to say yes.

God, he wanted to say yes.

But his spirit wouldn't let him.

So he did the only thing he could.

He broke both their hearts.

"No… Anika. I want to. But… I can't."

His voice stayed steady. Barely.

He saw the way her face dropped, the way she swallowed hard and blinked quickly.

"Oh. Oh, I—I totally get it. So… I'ma go now."

She smiled that sad, forced smile. Gave him a quick, awkward wave. Then got in her car and drove off.

Ethan stood there, hands in his pockets, staring after her taillights until they disappeared.

The ache in his chest was so sharp, so piercing.

But beneath it… was peace.

Painful peace.

Chapter 47: Obedience With Tears

Ethan stood still for a long time in the empty parking lot after Anika drove off, the glow of her taillights swallowed by the night. The air was warm, but his skin was cold. The streetlamp above him flickered once, twice, then steadied, its pale light catching the shimmer in his eyes.

And then he was reminded of ...

MISSING

(This part will be revealed in Anika's Book)

Chapter 48: When the Song Becomes the Prayer

The next morning, **Mita** woke up with a different kind of stillness in her chest.

Not peace exactly... but the weight was lighter.

She sat up in bed, sunlight filtering through the curtains, and took such a deep breath as if she hadn't in weeks. Her fingers hovered over her phone screen for a long time before finally sending the message she'd written in her notes the night before.

Mita: *"I think we need some time apart. Cliché, but no, we **are** the issue. I need to fix my part in the issue by fixing me. Please understand and respect my decision."*

She stared at the screen.

Read it again.

And hit **send**.

Almost immediately, her phone buzzed.

Rune: *"I understand. I'm here when you need me."*

Her shoulders dropped. That went... far easier and better than expected.

She got dressed, grabbed her bag, and headed to the **music building**.

It was exam day for the music department, and her exams didn't start until tomorrow. That meant the **club room** would be empty. Quiet. Safe. Aka

No Rune.

The perfect place to breathe.

She stepped inside the familiar room, her fingers grazing the piano's glossy edge. She sat down gently, the bench creaking beneath her as she let her fingers fall into place.

She started playing softly, the melodies Rune had taught her. A few chord progressions. Some lyrics she half-remembered.

Her voice followed the keys, tentative but warm.

It was the first time she'd sung in weeks.

And it felt... good.

Freeing.

Like she was returning to herself.

Then **a knock**.

She turned, startled, to see someone in the doorway.

Ethan.

Her eyes widened. "Oh—hey."

He smiled and stepped inside. "Hey yourself... So *this* is the famous music club room."

She chuckled, brushing her hair behind her ear. "Yeah. What are you doing here?"

He walked in, hands in his pockets. "Was out for a run, like I usually do around this time. Sometimes I pass the building, but I've never been in this room." He looked around, taking in the surroundings, then back at her. "I heard someone singing and playing... followed the sound. Didn't expect to find you."

She looked down at the keys, then back at him.

"Do you maybe want to sit with me? Are you busy?"

Ethan shook his head. "No. I can sit with you; please continue." He replied, taking a seat next to her on the bench

Mita nodded, her fingers touching the ivory again. This time, a song rose in her heart, one she needed.

"Don't Stop Praying" by Matthew West.

She played the opening melody slowly, hesitantly. Then her voice came through.

"Don't stop praying...

Don't call Jesus' name; keep on pounding on heaven's door. Let your knee wear out the floor..."

The words echoed in the room like a chorus from Heaven.

Suddenly, to her surprise, Ethan joined in. His voice wasn't perfect, but it was full of **truth**. Strong. Broken. Alive.

And the two of them, Mita and Ethan, sang their hearts out.

They sang from different wounds but found the same healing.

They cried.

They poured their exhaustion and sorrow into every word, every chord, until the end of the song fell into silence.

And in that silence... **tears fell freely**.

Mita turned to Ethan, her voice caught in her throat.

Without saying a word, they leaned in and hugged each other, shoulders shaking, breaths shallow, understanding one another without words.

Just **human beings**, held by one another and by **God**.

Eventually, they calmed down, and they sat down on the floor, backs against the piano, and began to talk. Honestly.

No mask. No filters.

Mita shared everything.

Rune. The guilt. The confusion. Her messy prayers. The feeling that God had gone silent, only to realize she had been comparing His love to her own limitations.

Ethan listened with his whole heart.

Then he shared his story. Anika. What happened, and how was he faced with the decision he disliked but knew was necessary.

They sat there for a long time, together.

Not fixing each other.

Just being **with** each other.

Two souls stripped bare by life and refined by **grace**.

And in that little music room, they didn't just find comfort.

They found the sacred middle space where suffering and faith *meet, and* **God shows up**.

Chapter 49: Summer in the Waiting

PLAYLIST- *I NEED YOU MORE JOSIAH QUEEN FT HENRIK*

The first week of summer break felt like a long exhale.

After the emotional whirlwind of finals, quiet goodbyes, and late-night journaling sessions with God, **Ethan** found himself back in his childhood home, surrounded by floor-to-ceiling windows overlooking the landscape of his parents' house, the scent of his mom's cinnamon rolls, and the occasional sound of his younger cousins battling it out in Mario Kart downstairs.

But something was different this summer.

He wasn't just *resting*.

He was **waiting**, actively, expectantly, like a man on the edge of something sacred.

"When God made His promise to Abraham, since there was no one greater for Him to swear by, He swore by Himself... And so after waiting patiently, Abraham received what was promised."

—Hebrews 6:13–15

That verse became the banner over his summer.

A quiet whisper in the back of his mind when he woke up. A bold declaration on sticky notes he left all over his room, taped to his mirror, on the cover of his Bible, and even one on the fridge his mom kept smiling at.

Ethan wasn't just *living*.

He was *leaning into God*.

…………………

Every morning started the same: jogs through the forest on his parents' land down to their private beach with his headphones in, no music, just prayer.

He prayed about *everything*. His heart. His future. His purpose. Anika.

Even though they had agreed to give each other space emotionally, their friendship hadn't died. In fact, they had slowly started talking again, texts at first, then the occasional call.

It was *awkward* at first. Their old rhythm stuttered like a scratched record. But God had a way of smoothing things out.

So when **Anika texted**, saying she'd be visiting family nearby and wondered if they could meet, Ethan hesitated for a second and then said **yes**.

He didn't know what to expect.

But what followed… was nothing short of **beautiful**.

……………

Anika arrived with her overnight bag, three devotionals, and way too much candy.

Ethan met her at the door with a bottle of water and a nervous smile. Her driver had dropped her off at his house.

"Still prefer Skittles over M&Ms?" he asked.

She grinned up at him. "Some things never change."

And just like that… it was easy again.

They spent the days laughing with his little cousins, biking down old trails on the land he used to take in high school, and sitting in the backyard under a string of fairy lights, talking about God, purpose, and what healing looked like when you weren't rushing it.

They prayed together.

They studied the Word side by side.

They even made worship playlists and had worship karaoke nights with

242

his siblings.

One evening, after everyone had gone to bed, they lounged on the seats of the rooftop balcony, stars blinking overhead, the warm summer breeze brushing past them.

Anika whispered, "I'm learning not to be afraid of being alone with God anymore."

Ethan smiled. "I'm learning to stop rushing what He's still building."

They looked at each other, not with romance, not with pressure, but with the **peace** of two people being rebuilt by the same Father.

They weren't dating.

They didn't need tension.

They were growing **together**, but also **separately**.

And that was enough.

....

Summer didn't look like mountaintop moments every day.

Sometimes it looked like dodgeball tournaments with his church's youth group.

Sometimes it looked like water balloon fights that ended in chaotic, breathless laughter.

Sometimes it looked like quiet mornings, sipping orange juice and reading Romans on the roof while the sun painted gold across the land.

But you know what was always there? Jesus.

In the joy.

In the awkwardness.

In the waiting.

And as August approached, Ethan wrote one final note in his journal before heading back to campus:

"I don't know what's next. I still love her. I still want her. But I want God more. So I'll wait, not with bitterness but with joy. Because if Abraham could wait decades... I can wait one season. Even if that season stretches longer than I expect."

Chapter 50: The Answer Was the Storm

PLAYLIST- *NOTHING ELSE FORREST FRANK FT THOMAS RHETT*

Summer had always smelled like mango trees and sea breeze in her childhood town, but this year, it carried something deeper. A softness. A stillness. A **calm** after the storm.

Mita had come home for the break not just to rest but to **rebuild**.

She stepped off the bus that dropped her at the corner of her old street, suitcase in one hand, journal in the other. As she rounded the block, she saw them, **her neighborhood brothers,** the same funny and loving bunch.

"**MITAAA!**" Ruach yelled, already dropping his basketball.

She grinned, arms flung wide open.

They piled onto her in a tackle-hug, the kind that made your ribs ache but your heart even more so.

And standing on the porch, just behind the screen door, was **her mom**.

And, finally, **her dad**, home.

Not on a business call. Not off on a trip. But here.

Present.

That first night back, Mita lay curled up on her childhood bed, staring at the fairy lights she never took down, remembering a prayer she whispered half-asleep back in January.

"God, I want to be more patient. I want to grow closer to You."

At the time, she had no idea what she was truly asking.

Now she did.

She learned the hard way that God doesn't **give** patience.

He **builds** it.

Brick by brick.

Through delays. Through heartbreak. Through moments that twist your insides and force you to either run away… or run **to Him**.

He doesn't hand you a deeper relationship with Him on a silver platter.

He lets you walk through fires that strip away distractions, idols, comfort, and sometimes, people you love.

He **shakes you** until all you're clinging to is **Him**.

And only then do you realize… **that's enough.**

She had broken up with **Rune**.

Not because he was terrible. But because her heart had already been claimed by someone else. **Jesus.**

Her **first love**.

And she finally understood that no relationship would ever truly thrive unless it was **anchored** in Him.

It hurt to leave.

But obedience usually does.

Her **brothers**, when they found out, didn't tease her as she feared. Instead, they clapped her on the back and said things like:

"You made the right call."

"I always had something better for you." Joshua said

"So… you're really serious about Him, huh?" Ruach said

And her reply?

"More serious than I've ever been about anything in my life."

That summer became something holy.

…………………………………

She spent her mornings journaling and reading by the windowsill with her mom.

Afternoons were filled with her helping her dad fix the old fences while they talked about real things: faith, fear, and forgiveness. He wasn't just **dad** anymore; he was her **brother in Christ,** too.

Evenings were filled with laughter, card games, and Bible studies on the porch with her neighborhood brothers, who, to her surprise, had all grown more intentional in their walks with God, too.

She wasn't just rebuilding herself.

She was rebuilding her **community**.

One night, while watching the stars from the backyard hammock, Mita whispered aloud:

"Lord... I asked for patience. You sent me pain.

I asked for closeness. You sent me storms.

I asked for love... and You showed me how much You loved me by taking everything else away. hurt me, but hurt to be separated from."

She smiled.

And **meant it**.

"You didn't give me what I thought I wanted...

You gave me what You knew I *needed,* **You.**"

Her phone buzzed once with a message from Ethan:

Ethan: *"Just finished praying for you. Hope summer's been a blessing."*

She smiled, heart full.

Mita: *"It has. It really has, and I pray it's the same for you."*

Epilogue

Final Chapter: Wrecked and Washed

The sun melted into the horizon behind the campus chapel, painting everything in gold.

Golden hour had a way of making even broken things beautiful. Sidewalk cracks looked like art. Empty benches glowed. The prayer garden shimmered with a quiet holiness.

It felt fitting, really, how the year was ending in the same place where it began.

Mita sat beneath the old oak tree just beside the chapel path, her journal open, Bible resting in her lap, turned to Romans 8. The pages fluttered slightly in the breeze.

Not too far away, Ethan and Anika were seated side by side on the stone bench by the fountain. They were laughing, low and unforced, as they shared a devotional and warm cups of coffee. They weren't rushing toward titles or relationships. They were just rooted. Present. Growing into something deeper than romance.

Rune hadn't been around.

Not much.

But a message had come through a few days ago. Simple. Quiet.

"I'm learning to follow Jesus for real. Thank you for not pretending. You helped

me see the difference."

That was it. It was enough.

Mita closed her eyes and breathed in slowly. The kind of breath that feels like exhaling and surrendering all at once. A small smile touched her lips.

This wasn't closure.

It wasn't a happily-ever-after either.

It was something better.

It was a becoming.

Because the Gospel doesn't wrap up neatly when the tears stop, or the relationship ends, or the shame fades.

It doesn't climax at the apology or conclusion.

The Gospel begins when you're wrecked—

and still wanted.

When you realize you can't fix yourself, and Jesus never asked you to.

It begins when grace becomes more than a word.

When you see it's a Person.

And that Person stepped into your ruin, not to condemned, but to save.

Not with pointed fingers, but with pierced hands.

"But God demonstrates His own love for us in this: While we were still sinners, Christ died for us."

—Romans 5:8

He had never left her.

Not when she sobbed on the dorm floor, ashamed and desperate for forgiveness.

Not when she sat in the music room trying to worship with a fractured heart.

Not even when she shut Him out.

He stayed.

Patient. Gentle. Waiting like a Father who knows His child will return eventually.

And when she did… He didn't flinch.

She lowered her pen to the page and began to write.

I thought I had to be clean to come back.

But You never asked for perfection, just my heart.

You broke me to rebuild me.

Stripped me to clothe me in righteousness.

Let the storm rage... to bring me back to shore.

I know it now.

Your love never changed.

Not when I fell.

Not when I ran.

Not even when I forgot who I was.

She looked up, her gaze locked onto the cross on the chapel wall, glowing in the last light of the day.

For the first time in a long time, Mita didn't feel like a hypocrite trying to earn her place.

She felt like a daughter.

Washed.

Wrecked.

Redeemed.

Not because her story was neat.

But because her God was faithful.

And He was still writing.

Afterword

Samantha Shreves is a faith-driven storyteller committed to writing stories that reflect the raw, unfiltered reality of the Christian walk. With a voice rooted in grace and boldness, she writes about the narrow path not as a perfect journey but as a daily act of surrender, struggle, and perseverance.

Her debut novel, *Journey of the Heart: Wrecked and Washed*, was born out of a desire to break the illusion that Christians have it all together. Through her emotionally honest characters and spiritually rich plots, Samantha explores the tension between temptation and truth, the beauty of redemption, and the unshakable love of Christ.

When she's not writing, Samantha is reflecting, praying, and encouraging others to rise again when they fall; reminding every reader that **your soul was a worthy cause for the cross**, and every day is a new chance to walk in grace.

Worship Journal

September 14

God,

I don't even know where to start today. I've been so confused. I thought I knew what it meant to follow You, but I feel so far from where I thought I'd be. I've been trying to fill my life with distractions: relationships, school, everything but You. I thought Rune was what I needed, but I've been ignoring You in the process.

I asked for patience, Lord, but I didn't expect it to come in the form of breaking me down. I didn't expect the painful lessons, the guilt, or the confusion. But here I am, broken and stripped bare, and I can't deny that You've been here all along, waiting.

I'm sorry. For the times I've run from You, for the times I've ignored Your call. But today, I'm choosing to turn back to You. I want to be washed clean by Your Blood. I want to build my life on You, not on the things of this world.

Please, guide me as I walk this path. Teach me to trust You, even when I don't understand. Show me how to love You the way You love me. I need You, God.

In Jesus' name,

Author's Message

I wanted to write a book series that was realistic, highlighting that the Christian walk is not just about telling people about God, being modest, dressing up for church, and looking like we have it all together, because we don't. Every day is a blessing, but some days are a challenge. Some days are a test.

I wanted to highlight that even on the narrow path, we still stumble. We still sometimes look over at the broad path to destruction because: some of us miss it, some of us get distracted, and sometimes there are pathways the enemy creates ahead of us, shortcuts, to lead us right back to that broad path to destruction.

I wanted people to know: we are still human. We still want things. We still struggle. We may not want to go back to our old life, but we are reminded by the enemy about it. He doesn't remind us of how lonely or confused we were when the hype calmed down; no, he reminds us of how excited we were when the hype of sin was at its peak.

But we know better.

Sometimes we fall, but the Bible says, *get back up.* Don't stay where you are. Keep pushing. Keep moving.

One thing, the most important thing, is that we have Jesus. Sin may call out to us, but keep moving. Even if we look back at it, like Lot's wife looked back, **thank God we don't become a pillar of salt,** we have another chance to get it right.

Free will is not an opportunity to sin. It's an opportunity to become righteous.

As we, as children of God, deny ourselves and pick up our cross daily, I want people to know: **that cross is not light.** But it is not more than we can bear, because God doesn't give us more than we can bear.

To my brothers and sisters in Christ: don't stop. Keep going. Because Jesus Christ didn't die for the *best* version of you. If we were the best version of ourselves, the cross wouldn't be necessary. No, He died for **you now**. The worst version of you. And He knew when, where, and how many times you would sin **before and after** you accepted Him.

You

your soul

was a worthy cause for His death.

Don't forget that.

To anyone who's ever felt too far gone, too messy, or too tired:

He's not done with you.

He's just getting started.

And you, beloved, are not alone.

Key point to remember

- God's faithfulness through storms
- Sin, guilt, and the illusion of being "too far gone" are lies from the devil.
- The ache of waiting and surrendering relationships a part of obedience and that act of obedience is rewarded
- Young adulthood, identity, shame, and spiritual growth are areas where the tactics of the enemy are abused so often against the children of the kingdom of God to delay, distract, manipulate, and negatively influence us to believe lies.
- The Gospel—not as a fix to feel good now and fall again later, but a foundation to start transformation.

📖 Author Judgement & Reflection

Samantha writes not to impress, but to awaken. She doesn't sugarcoat the Christian life or wrap it in clichés. Instead, she pulls back the curtain and exposes the grit beneath the grace. Through *Journey of the Heart: Wrecked and Washed*, Samantha proves that faith-filled storytelling doesn't have to be clean-cut to be Christ-centered.

As a writer, she is bold. Not because she seeks controversy, but because she's unafraid to show the whole journey: the slips, the wandering eyes, the temptation to turn back, and the fight to stay grounded. Samantha's characters reflect real people walking the narrow path, eyes occasionally glancing toward the broad one, hearts breaking and healing in rhythm with God's mercy.

Her storytelling is honest and reflective, designed to convict, comfort, and remind readers that Jesus did not die for a polished version of us, but for the broken, bruised, and still-beloved version of us on any given day.

Samantha doesn't write to entertain. She writes to equip, to remind the weary believer that the cross may be heavy, but it's not without purpose. Her stories offer hope without denial of hardship, grace without gloss, and Christ without compromise.

Acknowledgment

First, I would like to share that I had the honor of working with the Creator of this world, Jesus Christ, on this book and throughout this series. We collaborated closely on the plot and storyline, and I am grateful to continue that collaboration in the books to come.

Next, I want to thank my family for their unwavering support throughout this journey. You counseled and mentored me when my emotions were all over the place as a new author with no literary background, learning everything later than expected. You stood by me, helping and encouraging me every step of the way.

I also want to thank my amazing friend Micky. She provided a path for me during a time when the Lord was bringing a major transformation in my life leading up to this book. I am also deeply grateful to her mom, Aunty Nat, for being such a wonderful mother figure. You are kind, rare, and truly a blessing to have met. I have said it before, but I am so grateful for you. You have impacted my life and my heart in a deep and lasting way, and I will always treasure you.

To her younger daughter, Zan, your funny and witty personality brought so much light into my life. Your energy was truly appreciated. All the best to you, track star. I am so thankful I was blessed to meet all of you.

I also want to thank my other friends who have supported me over the years, offering encouragement and proving themselves to be true friends.

Last but not least, cousin Novalee Dxion for stepping in and helping me with the final draft editing, encouraging me, and demolishing my imposter syndrome in the process. I will forever be grateful.

Lastly, I want to take a moment to acknowledge myself for choosing to obey God when I did, despite everything.

Journey of the heart: The way we break, The way we heal

INTRO: Amerei

Amerei never meant to stand out. But somehow, without trying, she became part of something unforgettable.

Her first year at university was a whirlwind of awkward hellos, midnight snacks, and unexpected friendships. She came in quietly, more of an observer than a participant, but life had other plans.

She ended up rooming with Mita, who wore sarcasm like armor and had more layers than a psychology textbook. Somehow, they clicked. Then came Odessa, sharp-tongued, stunning, and wildly confident. Andromeda, all precision and ambition, could probably organize the stars if given the time. They weren't supposed to work as a friend group. But they did.

It wasn't all perfect. The semester turned upside down when Reed, one of their first friends, got caught in a freak accident that left everyone shaken. Amerei stayed close, helping where she could. Quiet support, that was her thing. She didn't speak loudly, but when she was there, you felt it.

And somewhere between the chaos and coffee-fueled cramming sessions, she met Merrick Hughes.

Tall, composed, way too good-looking for someone who knew how to fix a spreadsheet and charm an entire student council room. He wasn't just smart; he was calm, steady, and kind. The kind of person who didn't just notice people… he remembered them.

He noticed her.

He remembered *her*.

And maybe that was the most unexpected thing of all.

260

Amerei didn't plan to fall for someone. But then again, she hadn't planned for most of the things that made her first year unforgettable.

www.ingramcontent.com/pod-product-compliance
Lightning Source LLC
Chambersburg PA
CBHW030247030726
47493CB00023B/877